"You want me in your bed, but not in your life."

Brody swore. "That's a low blow. Don't play games with me, Victoria. I'm an expert at it. I survived three years in prison mostly by my wits. And don't think I'm going to be moved by your implication that I'm using you. You understood my position before we ever got involved, and I'm not going to defend it now."

He stood with his back to her, his voice cold and biting. "If marriage is what you want, then you never should have gotten involved with me. I told you that. You said you'd accept me on my terms, and I believed you. I don't know why you'd want to be married to me, but if you thought you could change my mind, you're badly mistaken."

Dear Reader,

Welcome to Silhouette **Special Edition** . . . welcome to romance. Each month, Silhouette **Special Edition** publishes six novels with you in mind—stories of love and life, tales that you can identify with—romance with that little "something special" added in.

We've got a celebration going here this month! We're introducing a brand-new cover design for Silhouette **Special Edition.** We hope you like our new look, as well as our six wonderful books this month. We're pleased to present you with Nora Roberts's exciting new series— THE DONOVAN LEGACY. *Captivated* is the first tale, and it's full of magical love galore! The next books, *Entranced* and *Charmed,* will be heading your way in October and November. Don't miss these enchanting tales!

And rounding out this month are books from other exciting authors: Judi Edwards, Marie Ferrarella, Billie Green, Phyllis Halldorson and Betsy Johnson.

In each Silhouette **Special Edition** novel, we're dedicated to bringing you the romances that you dream about— stories that will delight as well as bring a tear to the eye. And that's what Silhouette **Special Edition** is all about— special books by special authors for special readers!

I hope you enjoy this book and all of the stories to come.

Sincerely,

Tara Gavin
Senior Editor
Silhouette Books

PHYLLIS HALLDORSON

LUSCIOUS LADY

SPECIAL EDITION

Published by Silhouette Books New York

America's Publisher of Contemporary Romance

SILHOUETTE BOOKS
300 East 42nd St., New York, N.Y. 10017

LUSCIOUS LADY

ISBN: 0-373-09764-6

First Silhouette Books printing September 1992

All the characters in this book have no existence outside the imagination of the author and have no relation whatsoever to anyone bearing the same name or names. They are not even distantly inspired by any individual known or unknown to the author, and all incidents are pure invention.

®: Trademark used under license and registered in the United States Patent and Trademark Office and in other countries.

Printed in the U.S.A.

Books by Phyllis Halldorson

Silhouette Romance

Temporary Bride #31
To Start Again #79
Mountain Melody #247
If Ever I Loved You #282
Design for Two Hearts #367
Forgotten Love #395
An Honest Lover #456
To Choose a Wife #515
Return to Raindance #566
Raindance Autumn #584
Ageless Passion,
  Timeless Love #653
Dream Again of Love #689
Only the Nanny
  Knows for Sure #760
Lady Diamond #791

Silhouette Special Edition

My Heart's Undoing #290
The Showgirl and the Professor #368
Cross My Heart #430
Ask Not of Me, Love #510
All We Know of Heaven #621
You Could Love Me #734
Luscious Lady #764

Silhouette Books

Silhouette Christmas Stories 1991
"A Memorable Noel"

PHYLLIS HALLDORSON

At age sixteen, Phyllis Halldorson met her real-life Prince Charming. She married him a year later and they settled down to raise a family. A compulsive reader, Phyllis dreamed of someday finding the time to write stories of her own. That time came when her two youngest children reached adolescence. When she was introduced to romance novels, she knew she had found her long-delayed vocation. After all, how could she write anything else after living all those years with her very own Silhouette hero?

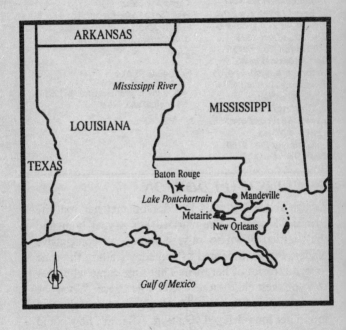

Chapter One

After searching for several minutes, Victoria finally found an empty space in the crowded parking lot assigned to workers in the maintenance directorate of the New Orleans Army Depot. As she stepped out of her red Toyota Camry, a hasty glance at her watch told her she was ten minutes late for work, and her stomach clenched.

Not that she didn't have a legitimate excuse. She did. She'd been running a little early as usual when she'd gone out to the garage and found that one of her tires was flat. Since she'd never changed one before, it had taken her forever. She'd even called in and been given an excused emergency absence, so it wasn't a penalty she was concerned about. It was Jimmy Lee, Buddy and Chester, the three good old boys who worked with her as repairers in the Electronic Test Equipment and Repair Department, and made her life miserable with whistles, catcalls and double entendres.

She strode briskly across the lot toward the maintenance building. Since transferring here from the army depot in California two months before, she'd learned that the only way to deflect her tormentors was to get there early and be already seated at her bench before they arrived. They usually came in just under the wire and didn't have time to amuse themselves by seeking her out, but anytime she walked in after they'd started work they were loud and long in their so-called "good-natured" teasing.

The problem was that cursed gait of hers. She had an undulating sway that had something to do with the way her hips were jointed, and there was nothing she could do about it. Coupled with her enticing bust line and cinched waist, it apparently brought out the animal lust in men, and too many of them reverted to behaving like rutting beasts.

She stopped just before reaching her area and took a deep breath, then continued on toward her workstation.

A sharp wolf whistle rang through the shop. "Hey, hey, hey, look who finally showed up." It was Buddy, a strapping blond teenager who was already a committed chauvinist.

"Well, hello, gorgeous." Jimmy Lee's tone was low and sexy as his brown eyes traveled down her tailored green blouse and brown fitted skirt, along her calves and ankles then back up again, undressing her all the way.

Victoria cringed inwardly but continued on, her head high and her steps steady, giving no indication that she heard them, other than the blush of embarrassment that she couldn't control.

"Have to give up them strenuous nights if you can't get out of bed in time to come to work, doll." That was Chester, the oldest who had long black hair and was the raunchiest of the trio.

Victoria's workbench was at the back of the area, and it seemed to take forever to walk the distance down the aisle with twenty pairs of male eyes watching. There were only two other women in the shop, both middle-aged, matronly and disapproving—not of the men who were bedeviling her, but of her, for attracting all that male attention.

She finally reached her destination and sat down, then looked toward the front, from which she'd just come, to see how the foreman, Walter Fields, was taking all this. Walter was fiftyish, medium height and weight, with receding sandy hair and faded blue eyes behind dark-framed glasses.

As Victoria had expected, he was shuffling papers on his desk and ignoring the whole shameful scene. Damn him, he was almost as bad as the others, assigning her "women's" chores that had nothing to do with her job description, making sexist comments and giving tacit approval to the other men's actions by allowing it.

In the two months she'd been here, she'd complained to him three times, twice verbally and once in a formal letter. He'd told her she was overreacting, that it was all in fun, and, except for telling them to get back to work if it went on too long, he had taken no action to stop it.

Well, Victoria was through trying to settle this amicably. She'd only let it go on this long because she hoped that once the novelty of a new woman in the shop wore off, the idiots would settle down and find some other way to amuse themselves.

Now she was going to take her complaint to Brody Monroe, Mr. Fields's supervisor and Branch Chief of Metrology.

During the ten o'clock break she hurried upstairs to the shops office, introduced herself to the secretary, Donna, and told her that she wanted to see Mr. Monroe.

"He's in a meeting right now," Donna said. "I can leave him a note to call you when he's free."

Victoria's heart sank. "You mean on the foreman's phone?"

The only way to contact workers on the telephone was through the shop foreman, which in her case was Mr. Fields.

"Yes. He'll want to talk to you before he sets up an appointment to see you."

Victoria frowned. "But this isn't a matter I want to discuss in public with Mr. Fields and anyone else listening."

Now it was Donna's turn to frown. "I'm sorry, but the usual procedure for a person wanting to talk to a division chief is to ask his or her immediate supervisor—in your case, Mr. Fields—to arrange the appointment. Since you're new here and probably didn't know that, I'm sure Mr. Monroe will be willing to contact you personally, but in any event it has to go through Mr. Fields so he has a record of why you're not at work during the time of the interview."

In order to avoid as much unpleasantness as possible, Victoria had hoped to talk to Brody Monroe before Walter Fields found out that was what she planned to do. How was a worker supposed to register a valid complaint against a supervisor if she had to go through that supervisor to do it? It wasn't fair; it would put her in an even more difficult position, and she was in no mood to knuckle under.

"In that case I guess I'd better lodge a complaint with the union and ask them to handle the matter for me," she said, abandoning her submissive tone for a more forceful one.

The secretary hesitated. Victoria was new at the New Orleans Army Depot, but she'd worked at the Sacramento Army Depot for more than three years before it was slated to be closed and she'd transferred here. She knew that, whenever possible, management preferred to settle problems without involving the union.

Donna looked startled. "If this is a confidential matter, why don't you let me talk to Mr. Monroe, and then I'll get back to you? Maybe we can work something out."

Victoria nodded, thanked her and went back to work.

It was shortly after lunch when Walter Fields came to her bench. "Telephone for you, sweetie," he said. "The secretary up in shops office. When you're finished talking, run over to the cafeteria and get me a ham sandwich." He reached into his pocket and handed her a five-dollar bill. "Lettuce, tomato and plenty of mustard. I had to go into town and missed lunch."

He turned and went back to his desk followed by a steaming Victoria. Running personal errands for him was definitely not one of her duties, and he never asked the men to do it, only the women.

"Victoria, this is Donna," said the voice at the other end of the telephone line. "Mr. Monroe will see you, but he wants to talk to you first. Don't worry, he'll only ask questions that can be answered yes or no. Hold on just a second."

Victoria was both relieved and apprehensive. Relieved because Mr. Monroe had agreed to her terms of confidentiality, but apprehensive because she'd never gone over a supervisor's head before. She hadn't had much of a problem with sexual harassment at the places she'd worked in California, but then she'd never had co-workers like Buddy, Jimmy Lee and Chester. What she couldn't understand was why the foreman let them get away with it.

"This is Brody Monroe," said a baritone voice in her ear, startling her out of her reverie. "I understand you want to talk to me?"

Victoria had seen Brody around, but this was the first time she'd ever spoken to him. He sounded just the way he looked. The strong, take charge, no-nonsense type. He was older—late thirties at least—and there was even a sprinkling of gray in his dark hair. He wasn't classically handsome, but had the same rugged good looks as some male actors.

She cleared her throat before she attempted to speak. "Yes, I do."

"Does it involve a problem with Walter Fields?"

He was being abrupt, and she was afraid he was angry.

"Yes, partly."

"Is he there now?"

She glanced at the shop foreman sitting behind his desk just an arm's length away from her and listening to every word.

"Yes."

"All right, hand him the phone and tell him Donna wants to talk to him. I'll put her on so he won't know you've been talking to me. She'll say you're wanted up here. You won't have to tell him why."

"Thank you," she said into the phone, then handed it to Walter. "Donna wants to talk to you," she told him as instructed.

Walter listened and grunted for a few seconds, then put down the instrument and looked at Victoria. "You're wanted up in the shops' office. What in hell's going on?"

She shrugged, then laid on his desk the five-dollar bill she had in her hand. "I'm not sure, but you'll have to get your own sandwich," she said, and walked away.

Brody Monroe hung up, thanked the secretary and strode into his small office.

Victoria Chambers. There'd been no need for Donna to fill him in on who Victoria Chambers was. She was the new kid in Test Equipment and Repair with the abundant bust and the sexy walk.

What was her problem? And why had she bypassed Walter and come to him? He was always available to talk to any of the workers in the ten shops under his supervision, but he expected them to go through the usual channels to get to him. It was an orderly process designed to catch difficulties at the lower levels before they got blown all out of proportion.

She'd better have a good reason, because if she was just seeking to bring herself to the attention of a top-line supervisor, and that wasn't an unusual ploy, he was going to discipline her. Everyone who worked here for more than a short time knew by now that the only way promotions were earned in his department was through hard work and dedication to the job.

A voice from the open doorway caught his attention. "Mr. Monroe, Victoria Chambers is here."

He looked up and saw the two women standing there. "Thank you, Donna," he said by way of dismissing the secretary. "Come in, Ms. Chambers. Please, sit down."

Vicky quickly put up a hand. "Call me Victoria, please."

He nodded and motioned to the chair in front of the desk, then sat down after she was seated.

Brody had never been this close to her before, and now he could see that it wasn't just her walk that made her so sexy. There was also her rich, dark auburn hair that fell to her shoulders and was tied back with a scarf in the same color green as her wide, deep-set eyes. High cheekbones accentuated her almost oval face that squared slightly at the jaw, her creamy complexion was soft and blemish free, and her lips were full and moist.

An involuntary stirring of desire shocked him. He mentally shook himself and wished to God that she worked in someone else's department! His body might be eager for a woman, but the rest of him wasn't. He had no intention of getting romantically involved with anybody, and definitely not someone who worked in his shops.

Victoria clasped her hands in her lap to keep them from trembling, and hoped the knot in her stomach wouldn't become a nuisance. She was still angry, but the adrenaline that had put her in a fighting mood earlier had stopped flowing and left her tense and uncertain.

She'd only seen Mr. Monroe from a distance, and she wasn't prepared for the sadness that looked out of his expressive brown eyes. It wasn't exactly pain, but it could well be the memory of pain, and she felt a tug of compassion.

What could have hurt a man like him so badly that the agony settled in and grew older with him? He seemed to have everything: good looks that were accentuated rather than negated by the deep lines around his mouth and eyes, a full head of thick dark brown hair with just enough gray to look distinguished, a build that included muscles even his sport coat and slacks couldn't hide, and a well-paying job with plenty of power and prestige.

She'd heard that he was a widower. Was the loss of his wife still that raw?

"What can I do for you?" he asked brusquely, bringing her back to the problem at hand. "I understand you were told the correct procedure for making an appointment with me but insisted on bypassing it. I hope you have a good reason for requesting special treatment."

That started her adrenaline flowing again. "I wasn't asking for *special* treatment," she informed him, "just a little consideration. I've put up with enough garbage without giving Mr. Fields something more to hassle me about."

His eyes widened with surprise. "Walter Fields is hassling you?"

Obviously he wasn't just going to take her word for it. "To an extent, yes. Actually, it's three other men in the shop who are the most blatant about it, but Mr. Fields refuses to put a stop to it."

He stared at her as if she were speaking a different language. "Does he knew what's going on? You're supposed to take these things to your immediate supervisor first. Have you complained to him about it?''

''Of course he knows what's going on,'' she said bitterly. ''He's part of it, and I've complained three different times, the last time in writing. He says they're just teasing, and I'm being a poor sport.''

Brody shook his head, as if trying to make sense out of what he was hearing, then leaned back and sighed. ''Perhaps you'd better start at the beginning and tell me what's happening.''

She clenched her fists and forged ahead. ''I seem to have the unfortunate capacity for inciting the...umm...primal instincts in three men in the shop, and they treat me like a sexy plaything instead of an intelligent woman. I've done nothing to provoke it, and I don't have to meekly submit to such harassment.''

Brody frowned. ''Can you be a little more specific? Exactly what are these men doing?''

She shrugged. ''You know. Wolf whistles, catcalls, leering looks, suggestive remarks, off-color jokes.''

''Are you saying this has been going on openly in one of my shops?'' Brody sounded shocked.

She was certain that he still didn't believe it, and she nodded vigorously. ''Ever since I came here. The Test Equipment and Repair shop is predominantly men, but only three of them are causing the problem, and Mr. Fields isn't much better. He doesn't get vulgar, but he calls me 'sweetie' and 'honey' and has me run personal errands for him that are not part of my job.''

She looked away and continued. ''Also, he's...he's too free with his hands. He's always touching me.''

''Walter?'' This time, Brody's tone was incredulous.

''Yes, Walter,'' she snapped. ''Why do I get the idea you think Walter Fields is a candidate for sainthood?''

Brody glared at her. ''Maybe because in the five years I've been here I've never had even one complaint about

him. Not one. He's a hardworking, conscientious foreman who goes out of his way to help the people who work
for him."

Victoria's adrenaline was flowing just fine now. She
stood up and leaned over the desk where she could look
Brody squarely in the eyes. "He also gets his jollies out of
listening to other men make sexy remarks to me," she
raged.

Without warning, Brody also stood and banged the
palm of his hand on the desk, startling Victoria so that she
fell back into her chair. "If that's an accusation, you damn
well better be able to prove it," he yelled.

Before Victoria could pull herself together and make an
equally furious reply, the door opened and Mr. Lindberg,
the shop's division chief, strode in. "What's going on in
here?" he asked, then looked from Brody to Victoria and
back to Brody again.

Brody straightened and ran his hand through his hair.
He looked both ashamed and chagrined. "Sorry, I'm
afraid we got a little loud. It won't happen again."

The other man looked at Victoria. "Ma'am? You all
right?"

She was as embarrassed as Brody. "Yes," she assured
him. "I'm fine. Really. There's nothing wrong."

Lindberg looked at Brody again, and Victoria caught the
warning in his glance before he left, shutting the door behind him.

For a moment there was an uneasy silence as Victoria
slumped in the chair and Brody stared in shock at the
closed door. She'd gotten off to a great start. She'd not
only made Brody mad at her, but she'd gotten him in
trouble with his boss.

Finally she regained enough composure to straighten up,
and he turned his gaze on her. It was filled with remorse.

"My God, Victoria, I'm sorry," he said, his voice gravelly. "I didn't mean to frighten you. I don't know what got into me."

He sat down with a thump, as if his legs wouldn't hold him any longer.

"I'm sorry, too," she said softly. "I shouldn't have said what I did about your friend. I can't read his mind and know what motivates him, but he has refused to take my complaints seriously."

"Walter *is* a friend," Brody said. "He was unusually helpful and supportive when I first came here, but that's no excuse for losing my temper. He's also under my supervision, and if you have a problem with him it's my job to listen to you calmly and then investigate it. It's just that he has a wife and three grown daughters who are employed. I can't believe that he'd abuse a female employee unless—"

He stopped abruptly, and Victoria felt sick. She knew what he'd been going to say; she'd heard variations on the same theme all her adult life.

Her eyes narrowed. "Unless what?"

He looked away. "Unless he was encouraged," he finished, then continued quickly as Victoria gasped. "I'm not saying you do it deliberately, but you are...uh... very pretty. Possibly if you would dress a little more sedately—"

She felt the familiar hot rage that boiled through her every time those words were thrown at her, but she made a massive effort to control it.

"Oh, so it's all my fault." She was surprised at how calm she sounded. "Perhaps you could tell me what you find wrong with the way I dress."

She stood and walked to the side of the desk so he could see her full length from where he sat. "Is my skirt too short?"

He looked decidedly uncomfortable. "No, not at all. It's a becoming length."

"Maybe it's too tight," she said as she pulled at the side seam. The skirt was loose on her.

He was turning red. "No, it's not too tight," he said shortly. "Now look, I—"

"Surely you don't find the blouse too snug." She fingered the generous amount of material in the silky garment.

He jumped out of his chair and raked his hand through his hair. "Victoria, if you'll just—"

Victoria was warming to her subject. "Could it be the neckline? I've always found Peter Pan collars to be modest—"

"Dammit, will you just keep quiet for a minute and let me get a word in edgewise?" he grated.

"But how am I going to know what it is you object to about my clothing if you won't tell me?" she asked reasonably. "Really, Mr. Monroe, I'm trying to cooperate—"

"You're enjoying this," he said flatly.

"You're darn right I am." She looked him straight in the eye. "I'm not going to be blamed because some men can't or won't control their male urges. I'd truly expected better of you."

She turned and walked out, but remembered to shut the door quietly and thank the secretary with a smile as she left.

Brody slumped back in his seat and closed his eyes. The first thing on his agenda was to mend his fences with his boss, Edwin Lindberg, and the sooner the better, before Ed came to him and asked for an explanation.

He got up and stopped at Donna's desk in the outer office. "Is Ed busy?" he asked.

"He's on the phone, but you can go on in," she said.

Brody knocked lightly on the closed door, then opened it and stuck his head in the office. Ed looked up from his desk and motioned Brody to come in and sit down. Brody took the seat in front of the desk and waited for the man to finish his conversation.

Brody felt decidedly uneasy. He'd never been called on the carpet before, and, although technically he was just reporting an incident to his supervisor, he'd also caused a disturbance and would be held accountable for it.

Ed Lindberg was a nice guy and a first-rate supervisor. A longtime employee of the depot, he'd worked his way up through the ranks to his present position, and he was well liked and respected. He hadn't chewed Brody out in front of Victoria, but he'd let Brody know with a look that he was expecting an accounting of the incident ASAP.

Ed concluded his conversation and hung up the phone, then looked at Brody. "Thanks for reporting in so promptly," he said, his tone pleasant but firm. "Is there a problem I should know about?"

Brody ran his hand over his face. "Yeah, I'm afraid so. Victoria Chambers is charging Walter Fields and three other men in his shop with sexual harassment."

Ed looked as shocked as Brody had felt. "Walter Fields?"

Brody shrugged. "My reaction exactly. I wouldn't put it past some of the men in his shop, but I can't believe that Walter..." He let the sentence hang unfinished. "She claims that he's feeling her up."

"Oh, hell," Ed said with a groan. "I knew that woman was going to cause trouble."

Those had been Brody's sentiments exactly, but somehow Ed's way of expressing it struck a nerve. "It's hardly fair to blame her until we've checked it out. After all, she's the victim."

Ed grimaced. "Sorry, I didn't mean it that way, but even without meaning to, women who look like Victoria

Chambers can stir up all kinds of problems on the job. Why was she hired into a mostly all-male shop?''

"She transferred in from the same area at the Sacramento Army Depot,'' Brody explained. "She has a sharp mind and is a good worker. This is the first I've heard about her being harassed.''

Ed settled back in his comfortable executive chair. "Tell me exactly what she said to you. Sexual harassment is a blazing hot issue. If it's really happening we've got to put a stop to it pronto, or we'll have both the state and the federal governments screaming for our hides.''

Brody recounted everything Victoria had told him, and when he finished there was a pregnant silence.

It was Ed who finally broke it. "Do you believe her?''

Brody shook his head. "I don't know. She's one sexy lady, and she's intelligent. I don't know whether that works for or against her. She's smart enough to initiate something like this, but too smart to think she would gain much by it unless she thrives on attention. If it were anybody but Walt that she's accusing...''

Ed nodded. "I know. Walt's record is spotless, but he wouldn't be the first middle-aged family man who let his hormones rule his good sense where a woman is concerned.''

"Yeah, I guess so,'' Brody admitted reluctantly. "I'll go up to Civilian Personnel and see what I can find out from her 201 file, then I'll have a talk with Walter. Maybe it's just a misunderstanding that can be cleared up quickly.''

Yeah, sure it is. And maybe pigs can fly!

"Fine,'' Ed said. "And, Brody, I'd like to be kept posted.''

Brody stood. "You bet,'' he said, then left and headed for the personnel office with a feeling of dread.

Chapter Two

At eleven o'clock the following morning, Brody was sitting at his desk reviewing the previous day's production records when Walter Fields appeared in the open doorway. "You wanted to see me, Brody?" he asked.

"Hello, Walter," Brody said, without his usual smile. "Come on in and sit down."

It seemed to him that Walter looked somewhat anxious, but he couldn't trust his own judgment. He hated what he was about to do. He'd been up most of the night, going over and over in his mind the right way to proceed.

Not that dealing with accusations against a foreman under him was anything new—he'd done it several times before. But Walter was not only a friend but a hell of a nice guy. Brody was inclined to think that Victoria Chambers was exaggerating, but he couldn't just go on that assumption. He was duty-bound to make sure, and that meant confronting Walt.

He pushed aside the papers he'd been working on. There was no easy way to do this, so he just waded in. "A woman in your shop has lodged a complaint against you and three of your workers—for sexual harassment."

Walter blanched, then smiled uncertainly. "You're kidding, right?"

"I don't kid about such things," Brody snapped. "Can you tell me what this is all about?"

"How in hell can I tell you what it's about when I don't know?" Walter demanded. "Who's the woman?"

"Victoria Chambers. She says she's being harassed and you're not doing anything to stop it."

Walter grunted. "Yeah, well, it figures. That babe is nothing but trouble. I should file charges against her. She waltzes in every morning with that shimmy she calls a walk, and dresses in those tight clothes that leave nothing to the imagination, then complains if some of the guys whistle. Hell, Brody, if she's going to wiggle her bait she has to expect to have takers."

"No, Walt, she doesn't have to expect that," Brody said. "This is a workshop, not a singles' bar, and there's nothing suggestive about the clothes she wears. Besides, if those men were doing their jobs, they wouldn't have time to notice how she walks or what she's wearing."

Walter rolled his eyes. "Oh, come on, Brody, give me a break. Have you ever seen this woman?"

Brody hadn't expected this reaction from Walt, and he was not only surprised but disturbed. "Of course I've seen her. I've also gone over her personnel records. In all the time she's been employed at government installations, her work performance is consistently excellent. There's no indication that she's ever been a 'troublemaker.'"

Walter snickered. "Then she's been sleeping with her foremen to keep them happy so they won't report her."

Brody's stomach muscles knotted with anger, and he took a deep breath to keep his voice steady. "That remark was uncalled for, and just this once I'm going to pretend I didn't hear it. Now I want this thing stopped, right now. Ms. Chambers says she's complained to you three times, once in writing, and you've refused to do anything about it. Is that true?''

Walter's gray eyes narrowed. "Dammit, Brody, she's making a big thing out of a little good-natured horsing around. Hell, she should feel complimented. The guys are just reacting to her sexy performance. Does she expect them not to notice?''

Brody got a grip on his temper. "Yes, she does, and so do I. She also says that you've been coming on to her—''

Walter jumped out of his chair and glared at Brody. "That's a damn lie!'' he thundered. "I don't have to sit here and listen to that bull.''

Brody stood and met him eye-to-eye. "Yes you do, Walt,'' he said calmly, "unless you want to request a formal hearing by Civilian Personnel so you can respond to the charge, in which case it could go into your permanent record. So far, this is just between you and me. I'm willing to give you one more chance to handle it, but I'm warning you, this thing can get really messy. If you don't put a stop to it right now she'll go over my head and take it to the Equal Employment officer. I don't need to tell you that could mean a black mark on your record as a supervisor. Am I getting through to you?''

Brody could see the rage in Walter's expression. "Oh, yeah, boss, you're gettin' through to me loud and clear. That little tart builds fires and I'm the one who gets charged with arson.''

Brody opened his mouth to protest, but Walter held up his hand. "Okay, I know, it's part of my job, but I don't have to like it.''

He turned and slammed out of the office.

"Nobody promised you a rose garden, pal,'' Brody murmured to the empty room as he sat back down.

* * *

Victoria arrived at work the day after she'd talked to Brody in plenty of time to be seated at her bench before Buddy, Jimmy Lee and Chester arrived. But they came just as the bell rang, so she had no way of knowing whether her complaint had done any good. Also Walter Fields didn't show up that morning, and his assistant, Sid Oswald, who had never given her any trouble, was in charge.

She didn't know whether she was relieved or disappointed. If there was going to be any unpleasantness, she was anxious to get it over with, but the thought of it set her teeth on edge. She'd never registered a complaint against a supervisor before, and she doubted that Walter would accept it graciously and change his ways.

She was right. He was back at his desk when she returned from lunch, but he was talking to a couple of the men and didn't notice her when she walked past. Her reprieve was short-lived when a few minutes later he came back to her bench. "I'd like to talk to you for a few minutes, Vicky," he said pleasantly, and loud enough for everyone around her to hear. "Would you come up to my desk when you've finished what you're doing?"

She was puzzled by his demeanor. If he'd been told of her complaint she would expect him to be angry, but what else could he want to talk to her about?

"Yes, of course," she said. "Will five minutes be okay?"

He smiled, nodded and went back to his desk, but she noticed that the smile didn't reach his cold gray eyes.

When she walked down the aisle a few minutes later, a loud raucous whistle split the air, and to her amazement, Walter stood up and glared. "There'll be no more of that in this shop," he bellowed. "If it happens again I'll take disciplinary action."

He motioned her to a chair by his desk. When they were both seated, his expression changed from welcoming to kindly concern, and for a moment she was caught off guard. Was he actually going to admit he'd been treating her badly and apologize?

He lowered his voice, and his first words exploded that myth. "If you think you're going to cozy up to Brody Monroe by lodging nuisance complaints about me, young lady, you'd better think again," he said coldly. "Brody's a friend of mine, and he's also immune to sexy broads like you who try to turn him on by rubbing up to him on the pretext of being mistreated by the big bad foreman."

Victoria was too astounded to react as his taunting voice continued. "He and I had a good laugh over your performance the other day, but I'm warning you, girl, you'd better clean up your act. You start any trouble around here and you'll never work at a government installation again. I promise you that. We can't be bothered with cheap little tramps who climb up the ladder to success on their backs."

For the first time in her life Victoria was speechless. Too enraged to form words in her mind, she just stared helplessly as he plastered a big grin on his face and raised his voice so everyone close by could hear him. "Glad we got that straightened out, Vicky," he said jovially. "I'm sorry about the misunderstanding. After this, you just come to me anytime something's bothering you and I'll take care of it."

Even through the red haze of her rage, Victoria knew that the best thing she could do right now was to keep her mouth shut and get out of there until she'd cooled off a little and could think straight.

Without a word she got up and marched out of the shop. She kept going until she came to the ladies' lounge, where she collapsed, shaking, on the worn brown sofa.

It took her a long time to pull herself together and start thinking again. When she did, she realized that she'd been royally outmaneuvered. That bastard! By speaking softly and keeping a pleasant expression on his face, he'd made everyone believe that he'd apologized to her and smoothed everything over.

She was sure her outrage had been mirrored in her expression, but he'd placed her chair so that she had her back to the shop. Only he could see it.

Her first thought was to go immediately to the personnel representative and tell Mrs. Ramsey how Walter had talked to her, but by the time she'd calmed down enough to act, she realized that it would just be her word against the foreman's. Everyone in the area would back up his claim that all he'd done was apologize because he'd apparently unintentionally offended her in the past.

The most painful jolt of all, though, was the fact that Brody had ridiculed her instead of taking her seriously. She guessed she should have expected it, but she'd heard that he was one of the best-liked and most effective supervisors in the department, and she'd assumed that he'd at least be fair and look into it. He'd talked to Walter Fields as he'd promised, but he'd only been going through the motions. Between the two of them she'd never had a chance.

When she was sure her legs were no longer trembling, she got up and splashed cold water on her face, then repaired her makeup and combed her hair. She wasn't going to let Walter see how badly he'd upset her.

Thank goodness today was Friday and she'd have the weekend to decide what course of action to take. But one thing she knew for sure: she wasn't going to meekly submit to the treatment she was receiving. Come Monday, she'd be prepared to take some kind of action, and when she did, the whole damn army depot was going to be aware of what had been going on.

By Sunday night, Victoria knew what she had to do, and she sat down to compose her thoughts. Calmly, she wrote out a formal complaint in which she documented every grievance, reported on her meeting with Brody Monroe, and gave, as thoroughly as she could remember, a word-by-word account of her last conversation with Walter Fields.

She was painfully aware that she had no way of proving what Walter had said to her, but by putting it in writing she would force an investigation. Even if it came down to just her word against his and she lost, his record would never again be spotless. It would embarrass him and raise doubts that might help some other woman in the future if he didn't change his ways.

She added a cover letter to Ruth Ramsey, the Civilian Personnel representative, addressed it to her and mailed it at the nearest branch post office on her way to work. Now she could only bide her time and wait to see what she'd stirred up.

Brody spent all Wednesday morning escorting a group of high-ranking army brass through the facility, then had lunch with them at the Officers Club, so it was nearly two o'clock before he got back to his office. As he walked past Donna's desk, she called to him. "Brody, Ed wants to see you the minute you come in."

Brody frowned. "Trouble?"

She shrugged. "He didn't say, but he's checked several times to see if you were back yet."

Brody changed direction and headed for the division chief's office. Now what? Ed wouldn't be that impatient unless it was important. Damn, it seemed that lately he'd no sooner handled one problem than another one popped up.

Ed's door was open, and Brody strode in. "Donna said you wanted to see me," he said as his immediate supervisor looked up from behind his desk.

"Yes, I do." Ed motioned to the chair across from him. "Sit down. Any problems with the tour?"

Brody shook his head. "No more than usual. Do you want a report now?"

"No, we'll get to that later." Ed picked up a file folder and handed it to Brody. "Here, read this. It just came down from Ruth Ramsey this morning."

Brody took the folder and noticed that it was marked *Chambers, Victoria*. He muttered an oath. "I thought this had been taken care of."

"Yeah, so did I," Ed said, "but obviously Ms. Chambers doesn't think so. Go ahead and read it."

Brody opened the file and read the cover letter. A feeling of dread pervaded Brody. What had happened to cause Victoria to go over his head after he'd assured her he'd handle her complaint?

He laid the letter down and picked up the other document. It consisted of several, single-spaced typed pages, and the further he read the more irritated he became. When he got to her latest charge, her version of what Walter had said to her, he was steaming mad.

"I don't believe this," he said angrily, as he slammed the folder and papers down on the desk. "Either Walter's gone off the deep end, or Victoria is lying. I sure didn't laugh with him over her complaint. In fact, I came down on him hard. Maybe too hard, but I didn't like his attitude."

Ed straightened. "You didn't mention an attitude problem to me."

His tone told Brody that omission had been a mistake and he'd better rectify it.

Brody rubbed his hand over his face. He'd had a grueling day so far, and it was certain to get worse. He was tired, and in no mood to suffer fools gladly. Especially not ones who worked in his shops.

"I know," he acknowledged. "I let him know he'd better change it, so I saw no reason to report it to you. I'm still not sure that he said these things. She admits that she doesn't have any proof. It wouldn't be the first time a worker has filed false charges against a supervisor.''

''Well, we're damn well going to find out what's going on,'' Ed said. ''Civilian Personnel has given this top priority. They're mad as hell that it's gone this far, and they're not going to put up with any delaying tactics from anyone. Not Walter, not you and, unfortunately, not me. I don't appreciate being dragged into this, and if you don't want to apply pressure to Walter, I will.''

Brody knew Ed had good reason to be upset. A problem with a worker in the shops had to be pretty badly mishandled before it got to Ed's level. It should have been straightened out by Walter, but when it wasn't, it sure shouldn't have gotten past Brody. Still, Brody felt he'd done everything that was required of him, and he resented Ed's pulling rank on him.

When he left Ed a few minutes later, he asked Donna to call down and tell Walter Fields he wanted to see him immediately, then went into his own office and waited.

Damn it to hell, what was going on in Walter's shop? He'd known the man well for five years. He'd been a helpful friend to him when he'd first come here. He'd had meals in the Fieldses' home, they sometimes went fishing together after work in the little creek outside of town in the summer and he knew and liked Walt's wife, Hester, and his three daughters, the eldest of whom worked here at the depot in another division.

He'd even gone on a weekend camping trip in the Great Smoky Mountains with Walt and Hester once, and he'd swear that they had a good solid marriage. Hester was a strong husky woman, not really pretty, but not homely, either, and they seemed to get along well together.

She was a meat cutter and worked in one of the supermarkets. Not an occupation usually sought out by women, but if they were strong enough to lift the heavy sides of meat and wield the necessary cutting tools there was no reason why they shouldn't. Hester was good at it, and she always saw that Brody got the best cuts when he shopped in her department.

If Victoria's accusations were true, why would Walt put his job, and possibly his marriage, on the line? He wasn't the brightest guy in the world, but he was far from stupid. His education had stopped with high school, but he'd been a first-rate journeyman in instrument repair before being promoted to foreman of the shop almost six years ago.

He probably wouldn't go much higher without more schooling, but he could sure be demoted if he was abusing a woman in his shop.

Brody was startled out of his musing when the object of his speculation walked through the open doorway, looking harried. "What's up?" he asked breathlessly. "Donna said to drop everything and get my butt up here."

Brody couldn't help but chuckle as he stood up. "I doubt that she put it in just those words," he said.

Walt grinned. "Well, maybe not, but she has a way of getting the message across."

Brody's fleeting amusement was gone. "Yes, well, shut the door and then come over and sit down. We have to talk."

He thought he saw a flash of fear in Walt's eyes before he turned away and closed the door.

They both sat down, Brody behind the desk and Walter across from him, and Brody picked up the file from Civilian Personnel. "This has been brought to Ed's attention," he said, referring to the shops' division chief. "I want you to read it carefully. Take all the time you need, because you have a lot of explaining to do."

He handed the folder to Walt, and Walt's gaze immediately went to the name on the label. His face paled. "You mean now?"

"Yes," Brody said, and pushed his chair back. "I have some mail to go over with Donna. I'll be in the outer office. Come and get me when you're ready to discuss it."

He stood, picked up a stack of letters and walked out of the office, feeling as sick as Walt looked.

Less than ten minutes later, Walter stalked out to the secretary's desk, looking stunned and carrying the sheaf of papers in one hand. "This is a pile of garbage." He shook the report at Brody, but his tone lacked the conviction of honest outrage.

Brody stood up. "All right, we'll go into the office and discuss it," he said, and led the way.

When they were again seated in the privacy of the small room, Brody picked up the papers that Walt had tossed on the desk and straightened them. It gave him something to do with his hands while he searched for the easiest way to start his interrogation.

"Am I to understand that you deny Ms. Chambers's allegations?" he finally asked.

"Damn right," Walter snapped. "We went over all this before, and I told you then that she was just making trouble."

"Did you put a stop to the harassment?"

"Hell, yes I did, although I still wouldn't consider a few whistles as harassment," Walter blustered. "If anyone in the shop is still doing anything to upset her delicate sensibilities they're not doing it in front of me."

Brody mentally winced. Walter still had a bad attitude problem, and he wasn't opening up to tell his side of the story. He was simply answering Brody's questions, and doing so as briefly as possible.

Was he just teed off by the accusations, or did he have something to hide?

"Victoria says you called her to your desk and talked to her. Is that true?"

Walter's pale face colored to a red flush that started at his neck and spread upward, and he hugged his arms across his chest. "Yeah. That's what you wanted me to do, wasn't it?"

"I wanted you to assure her that you'd protect her from unwanted attention from the men in the shop," Brody reminded him. "Did you?"

Walter's gaze shifted slightly so he wasn't looking Brody directly in the eye. "You told me to, didn't you?" His tone was defensive. "I always follow your orders."

That was no answer, and they both knew it. For the first time in his career, Brody wished he could walk away from an unpleasant situation and let someone else handle it.

Instead, he straightened his shoulders and glared at the man. "I'm not going to play games with you, Walter," he said, his tone harsh. "You've read what Victoria says about that talk. That's a serious charge. Now I want to hear your version, and I don't intend to drag it out of you question by question."

He settled back and made a conscious effort to relax, or at least *look* relaxed. From the way Walt was acting, Brody was almost certain that at least most of what Victoria had accused him of was true.

Now it was up to Brody to get Walt to admit that he'd mishandled the situation, but he'd clam up and continue to deny everything if Brody lost his temper.

Walter slumped, and his hands fell open onto the arms of the chair. For several minutes he said nothing. Brody waited patiently, and when Walter finally spoke it was completely off the subject. "Hester won't sleep with me anymore." His voice was low, almost a whisper, and his gaze shifted to the wall behind Brody.

Brody blinked, but quickly masked his surprise. Walt hadn't mentioned that he and his wife were having problems.

"I'm sorry to hear that," he said softly. "Would you like to tell me about it?"

One of Brody's duties as a supervisor was to counsel his workers with job-related difficulties, but most of the time their personal problems and work problems were too closely entwined to separate so he'd had a lot of experience with both kinds.

Walter shrugged. "What's to tell? She never did care much for sex, but she was usually willing to accommodate me. I'd have liked it to be mutual, but we got along good in every other way so I figured what the hell, few people get everything they want."

He hesitated, and Brody gently prompted him with a question. "So what happened?"

Walter shook his head. "Who knows about women? She began refusing me more and more after she started..." He paused and seemed embarrassed. "You know, the change. She'd complain of a headache or cramps or any number of other things, but it wasn't until after our first grandchild was born last year that she announced that now we were grandparents and we were too old for that kind of carrying on, as she put it."

His voice was getting stronger, and Brody could see the agitation building in him as he straightened in his chair.

"Hell, Brody, I'm only fifty-four. I'm not over the hill by a long shot, and she has no right to make me suffer just because she's frigid." His hands clenched. "I ... I finally got tired of her turning away from me all the time, and ... well ... I insisted."

Brody's jaws clenched, and he swallowed down the instinctive protest that clawed to be spoken.

My God, Walter, you didn't rape her, did you?

He knew that would end the conversation and he'd never get any more information out of the man. Instead he phrased it differently. "Did you hurt her?"

"Of course not," Walter said indignantly, "but she moved into another bedroom and now she won't even let me in bed with her. It's been six damn months—and I'm climbin' the walls."

He balanced his elbows on his knees and put his head in his hands.

Brody knew an explosive situation when one was presented to him, and he wasn't even going to attempt to give advice. He was the last person to try to patch up a troubled marriage.

"Look, pal, I'm sorry. You and Hester are two of my favorite people, but I'm not qualified to help you in this. You need professional counseling...."

Walter raised his head and looked at Brody. "No way," he protested. "I couldn't talk about this to a stranger, and Hester won't admit there's a problem. She thinks I'm a dirty old man to even want sex."

Brody had studied human sexuality in college, and he regularly attended government-sponsored seminars on personnel management that covered all phases of counseling. He knew this situation wasn't unusual. A lot of couples discovered after they were married that they had incompatible sex drives, one high and one low. Some of them eventually divorced, but a lot of them worked out a compromise as Walt and Hester had for so long.

It would be a shame if this couple split up after nearly thirty years because they were both too stubborn to seek help.

There was one thing Brody could do and that was to lay it on the line to Walter. It might shock him into seeing a professional.

"I'm going to tell you something, Walt," Brody said in a businesslike tone to the man who had once more dropped his head in his hands. "The situation between you and Hester is affecting your job performance, and this is in my area of expertise. You can't come to work and take your rage against your wife out on the people who work for you.''

Again Walter raised his head, and this time he straightened up. "I'm not!" he thundered.

"Oh, yes, you are." Brody said. "You're taking it out on Victoria. She's young and sexy and she turns you on, and that makes you all the more frustrated.''

A rosy blush stained Walter's leathery cheeks. "That woman would turn any man on who still had a heartbeat, and don't tell me you don't throb when she gets near.''

"I might if I worked with her every day like you do," Brody admitted, "but I'd find a way to control it. And that's what you'd better do, fast.''

There was no longer any doubt in Brody's mind that everything Victoria had accused Walter of was true. He sympathized with Walt, who was going through a bad time, but that didn't give him any right to behave like a jerk at work.

Brody also felt a sharp thrust of anger at the thought of this middle-aged married man lusting after Victoria. He was even more appalled to realize that he'd feel the same way about any other man who wanted to touch her, hold her, kiss her....

Good Lord, was it possible that he was jealous because he wanted her for himself?

He immediately rejected the idea and returned his attention to Walter. "I don't have to tell you that this is a serious situation, both at work and at home. You've got to find a way to resolve your relationship with Hester or it's going to get worse. It's gone so far now that I have no choice but to give you a letter of reprimand and put a copy in your 201 file. That's a permanent blot on your record, Walt. If you get another one it could lead to dismissal.''

Walter slumped back and closed his eyes. "I know," he said tonelessly.

An idea occurred to Brody. "Look, why don't you let me make an appointment for you to talk to the army chaplain who has an office here at the depot? He's also available to civilians."

Walt opened his eyes. "I told you, I—"

"I know," Brody interrupted. "You're embarrassed to discuss your sex life with a stranger, but I know this guy. I've sent people to him before, with good results. If you don't like him he'll refer you to a private counselor, but you've got to start somewhere."

Walter thought about it. "Hester won't go."

"Then go alone," Brody said. "I think she'll agree to it once she realizes that you're serious."

"I guess I don't have a choice, do I?" Walter said, and stood up. "Get me in as soon as possible, will you, and if it's okay with you I'd like to take the rest of the afternoon off."

Brody stood, too. "That's a good idea. Take the rest of the week if you want, I'll arrange it for you. Things will be better once you start getting some help."

Walter left, and Brody picked up the telephone to ring the chaplain's office. He'd done all he could do for Walt, but now came the really hard part. He had to talk to Victoria and try to undo the damage.

Chapter Three

Victoria was both excited and anxious that Wednesday afternoon as she drove home from work. Walter Fields had left the shop shortly after lunch and hadn't come back, but just before quitting time the work leader told her that Brody Monroe had made an appointment to talk to her at two o'clock the next afternoon.

Did that mean Civilian Personnel was taking action on her complaint? She hoped so, but regretted the unpleasantness still to come.

Victoria had always been the peace-loving type, and usually tried to soothe things over rather than fire them up. She'd learned over the years to insist on her rights when they were being tampered with, but it never got easier.

She especially didn't want to fight with Brody. It still hurt that he would treat her legitimate complaint so lightly, but she couldn't shake the attraction for him that held her enthralled even though the respect she'd felt was diminished.

She slowed down as she traveled the quiet, tree-lined street that led to her small, five-room house in a neighborhood of similar homes in the Lake Ponchartrain area. After turning into the driveway, she shut off the car's motor and sat there for a moment, surveying her little domain.

The pride of ownership was still strong, and she felt a thrill every time she looked at the property that was now hers. Well, hers and the bank's. The house, which sat on a good-sized lot of green lawn and shade trees, had been completely renovated before it had been put up for sale with new blue-gray vinyl siding on the outside and sparkling clean paint on the inside.

It still seemed odd to have a whole house to herself. For the past four years she'd lived in tiny apartments, but real estate in Louisiana was considerably cheaper than in California. Her monthly mortgage payments for the house, which included two bedrooms and good-sized front and backyards, were only slightly more than the rent on her small apartment in Sacramento. Of course she had to pay the gardener who came once a week, but it was worth it.

The following morning, as she dressed for work, she had her appointment with Brody in mind. Walter must have had a talk with Buddy, Jimmy Lee and Chester, because since that one incident when he'd reprimanded them in front of everyone in the shop, they'd conspicuously ignored her. She felt safe in dressing up.

She chose a gold cotton dress with a wide belt and a flared skirt that swirled to midcalf. With it she wore matching flat pumps and patterned stockings. It wasn't an outfit she usually wore to work, but today she wanted Brody to see that her taste in fashion was as classy as that of any of his women friends.

Walter didn't show up that morning, and the work leader said something had come up and he'd taken emergency leave for the rest of the week. The tension in Victoria grew. Did Walter's absence have anything to do with her complaint?

She didn't like the foreman, and she hated the way he'd been treating her, but she also hated the thought that she might have gotten him into real trouble. Especially if it put his career in jeopardy.

Or was she the one in trouble? Was Brody going to call her on the carpet because she'd dared to complain about a supervisor? She was the interloper here. Everyone else in the shop except Buddy, who was just out of high school, had been here for years.

If they all banded together against her, she'd be labeled an agitator, and even though she was a permanent employee and couldn't easily be fired, they could make her life miserable.

Suddenly her hand slipped, and she dropped her pliers on the printed circuit board of the oscilloscope she was repairing and broke it. Oh, damn! Now she'd have to go to the parts bin and get a new one.

She'd better keep her mind on what she was doing before she caused some serious damage.

The morning dragged by, and her tension built. The lunch break finally came and then it was almost two o'clock. She arranged her unfinished work neatly on her bench, notified the work leader that she was leaving to keep her appointment with Mr. Monroe and then headed for the stairway to the mezzanine.

Donna wasn't at her desk, so Victoria went straight to Brody's office. He stood when she appeared in the doorway, and again she was aware of the magnetism that drew her gaze to his broad shoulders, slender waist and flat belly that were covered but not camouflaged by the blue tweed sport coat he wore with navy blue slacks.

He wasn't very tall, an inch or two under six feet she'd guess, and he had an average build, maybe a little on the slim side, but he was all male and drop-dead sexy. Even now, when she was afraid of what he might be going to say to her, she still had a nagging urge to reach out and brush the lock of dark hair off his forehead.

"Come in, Victoria," he said, and although he didn't smile, he didn't look angry, either.

She felt a sharp jab of disappointment when Brody hardly looked at her. His expression was neutral as he motioned her to the chair across from him.

When they were both seated, he opened a folder that was lying on his desk. "It's been brought to my attention that you still feel that you're being subjected to harassment in the shop...."

"I don't feel that I am, Mr. Monroe. I know that I am. I documented it all in my complaint."

Brody nodded. "I've read it, and I'm sorry that you think I didn't follow through with the investigation I promised you."

He sounded as if he really was sorry that she thought badly of him, and she instinctively qualified her statement. "I don't know whether you did or not. I only know what Mr. Fields told me, and because of that, I saw no alternative but to take it up with the Civilian Personnel representative."

He nodded. "Yes, I understand that, but believe me, I did not laugh at your complaint, nor did I authorize him to threaten you. Actually, I told him to put a stop to any unprofessional behavior that was going on, and to do it immediately."

Maybe she was a fool to believe him, but she had a strong need to do so. "Oh, he did that as far as Buddy, Jimmy Lee and Chester were concerned," she told him, "but then he threatened me with dismissal for exercising my lawful rights, and I won't stand still for that."

Brody's compelling glance met hers. "There's no reason why you should. I'm only sorry you didn't come to see me again, but I can understand why you didn't."

He tore his gaze from hers, then continued, "I've talked to Walter, and you have a right to know that I'm initiating disciplinary action against him. As you're no doubt aware, this is serious because it will be a negative factor in future performance appraisals and promotions."

The initial thrill of triumph that swept Victoria was quickly dulled with apprehension. "Yes, and I'm sorry it had to come to that," she said, "but it will also give him more reason to get back at me."

Brody looked startled. "That's not likely," he said, but she detected a hint of uncertainty in his tone. "Walter's intelligent enough to know that would be grounds for dismissal, but you have brought up a good point. It's bound to be uncomfortable for you working with these people."

He paused for a moment. "We have a few openings in other departments. Would you like to transfer—"

"No way," she interrupted angrily. "I'm not the guilty party, and I shouldn't be punished by being sent away. If anyone's moved it will have to be Buddy, Jimmy Lee and Chester."

She could hear the strident tones in her voice, but she had a right to be enraged.

Brody sighed. "Victoria, I'm only trying to protect you. I can give orders to the men in your shop that you're not to be harassed, but I can't be there all the time to see that they're carried out. Neither can Walter. I know these men you've complained about, and I can't guarantee that they won't make working with them miserable for you."

She frowned. "I . . . I don't know what you mean," she said, but she was afraid she did.

"There are any number of ways to harass a person without doing it publicly," Brody explained. "They could sabotage your work, make rude personal remarks to you when no one is around to hear them, start nasty rumors about your morals. The possibilities are endless. I'm not saying any of the people in your shop would do this, but the potential is there, and there'd be no way to prove who's behind it."

Victoria's short-lived victory turned to ashes. The fact that she was a woman made her a second-class employee, and no matter which of the alternatives she chose, she was the one who would suffer.

"It's not fair," she said, and heard the quaver in her tone as she blinked back sudden tears.

Brody's composure slipped, and she saw compassion and regret in his expression. "Of course it's not fair," he agreed softly, "but I can't change human nature. 'The wheels of justice grind exceedingly slow.' It's an adage because it's true. I can't promise you justice, but I can make things more pleasant for you if you'll let me."

The concern in his voice was her undoing, and she lost her battle with the tears as two of them spilled over and trickled down her cheeks. "But I...I can't just cop out now and meekly let you move me out of the area." The tears were flowing freely, and she gulped back a sob. "Then the men who've been hassling me would win. It's time to put a stop to men treating women like sex objects in the workplace. It still happens far too often. What they've been doing is illegal, and someone has to take a stand against it."

The sob won out, and Brody handed her a tissue from the box on his desk. Her crying seemed to unsettle him, and she hadn't intended that. She had no use for women who used tears to bring a man to heel, and she dried her eyes and took a deep breath in an effort to bring her emotions under control.

"Are you all right?" he asked anxiously. "We can continue this later.... Damn, I didn't mean to make you cry...."

For some reason she couldn't bear the thought of him feeling guilty. "No, please, it's not your fault," she hastened to assure him. "I've been under a lot of stress lately, and . . . well, I guess I'm just behaving like a woman."

"That's understandable," he said tenderly. "You are a woman. A beautiful and intelligent woman, and you have no reason to apologize for it."

She opened her mouth to tell him that hadn't been her intention, but he hurried on. "But try to recognize that the men in your shop are male, and for as long as there have been human beings, males have been the dominant sex. It's been bred into them, both by design and tradition, and it's going to take more than a few years to reprogram them."

Victoria's tears were replaced by determination. "I have no problem with men being the dominant gender. They're bigger and stronger, and when I marry I want a man who will take care of me. But—" she paused for effect "—I also want to take care of him. It should be a mutual caring."

Brody relaxed somewhat and even allowed himself a tiny smile. "You're a woman after my own heart. That's what I'd like in a marriage, too, and I'm sure it's possible for both of us, but in the workplace . . ."

His voice trailed off as though he was giving a lot of thought to what he wanted to say.

He began again. "In the workplace the average man isn't going to give up his advantage without a fight. I'm sure if the genders were reversed, women would react the same way, but it's going to take at least another generation before males accept the new, more passive role they're expected to play in the social order. Meanwhile, females are going to have a certain amount of outrageous behavior to put up with."

Victoria bristled. "Are you saying we should just accept it and wait twenty-five years for our daughters to reap the benefits of the new improved male?"

Brody's expression hardened. "No, that's not what I'm saying, and you know it. Don't insult my intelligence, Vicky. You know exactly what I mean, but you want massive changes made immediately. It just doesn't work that way. We have laws that protect the guilty as well as the innocent, and we still have to prove a case against the accused."

Victoria felt thoroughly chastised, but realized that she deserved it. He was right; she had been challenging him without fully realizing it.

She pushed a long strand of hair off her cheek. "I apologize," she said huskily. "I didn't mean to make light of your logic. It's very good. You should have studied law."

He smiled at that. "I'm afraid I don't have the temperament for it. I'm just as impatient as you are when I know I'm right. You and I clash head-on when we have opposing views, but if we ever teamed up to fight for something we both wanted badly we'd be dynamite."

That idea appealed to her greatly, and she smiled back. "You know, I'll bet we would at that. Look, may I have until tomorrow to think about a transfer?"

"Sure. Take all the time you need. Meanwhile I'll check into the openings in the other shops and let you know what's available. Why don't we get together again on—" he flipped through his daily calendar "—Tuesday of next week?" He chuckled. "That should give me time to put together an offer you can't resist."

She chuckled with him as she stood up. "Don't be too sure," she teased. "I can be pretty hardheaded at times."

He stood, too. "I'd noticed," he murmured, but he smiled when he said it. "Goodbye, Vicky, I'll be in touch."

Oh, yes, please do, she thought as she turned and left.

Brody watched her walk away from him until she started down the stairs and he could no longer see her, then he sat down and breathed a sigh, but he wasn't sure whether it was of relief or regret that she was gone. He felt as though he'd been put through the proverbial wringer.

That young woman was undeniably sexy, but there was a lot more to her than that. She looked like a cross between a seductress and a saint. Her wide, full mouth that begged to be kissed was at variance with the sweetness of her smile, and her erotic walk belied the childlike innocence that looked out of her sparkling eyes.

How was a man to know whether she was angel or witch?

Not that it made any difference to him. He had too much good sense to get involved with her on a personal level. He had a gut feeling that if he did, it could never be anything less than a lifetime commitment on his part, and for him a second marriage was unthinkable.

He flinched. The very thought of a relationship with Victoria made him sweat. Her appealing vulnerability tugged at his heart. As she'd lost the battle to hold back the tears, it had taken all the control he could muster not to take her in his arms and hold her, comfort her, offer her anything if she'd just stop crying and let him kiss away the hurt.

He groaned and muttered an oath. This nonsense had to stop. It was bad enough to be physically attracted to Victoria, but that was a natural reaction and only meant he needed a woman. On the other hand, wanting to take care of her, and worse, wanting her to hold and soothe him, was veering into a much more dangerous situation. One that could tie him in knots and bring back all the demons he'd wrestled with for so long.

No way! He wasn't going to take the chance of walking into that nightmare again.

Walter Fields was back in the shop when Victoria arrived at work on Monday. Although they managed to avoid making eye contact and they ignored each other, the tension between them was oppressive. She felt guilty for getting him in trouble even though he'd brought it on himself, and she couldn't really blame him for being resentful.

The situation with Buddy, Jimmy Lee and Chester was even more upsetting. They weren't just resentful, they were furious, and although they didn't say or do anything to her openly, they never missed a chance to give her a dirty look, a leering glance, or whisper an obscene comment when they got close enough.

Brody had been right. There was no way she could work in this shop any longer. The harassment by the three good old boys had simply gone underground. Much as she hated to back down, she decided that tomorrow, when she was to talk to Brody again, she'd agree to a transfer.

Victoria was surprised when the workday ended without Brody making an appointment for her. He'd said they'd talk on Tuesday.

She was even more surprised when she answered the phone at home that evening and heard his voice at the other end. "Vicky, this is Brody Monroe. I know I promised to get back to you tomorrow, but my schedule has changed and I'm going to be away from the depot all week."

Her elation at receiving a call from him at home turned to disappointment. "Oh, I'm sorry," she said, before she remembered that he wasn't apologizing, just rescheduling.

"That…that is, there's no hurry," she finished lamely.

"I liked it better when you said you were sorry." His tone was low and husky, and made her whole body tingle. "I'm sorry, too, and I do have the information about openings in other departments. I was wondering… That is, I hope you won't think I'm coming on to you, but would you consider having dinner with me tomorrow evening? Strictly business, of course. I'm afraid it's the only time I'll have available until next week."

The man was a master at fine-tuning her emotions from highs to lows. She'd hoped that he was asking for a date, which, of course, was stupid of her. One of the things she'd learned about Brody Monroe was that he didn't fool around with any of the women under his supervision.

She knew he was single, widowed, and gossip had it that he occasionally dated one of the secretaries in Personnel, but otherwise his private life was just that—private.

Oh, well, she'd take what he was willing to give and try not to hope for more.

"I . . . I'd be happy to have dinner with you," she stammered, "but it's not necessary—"

"It's necessary for me," he said, once more slipping into that low husky tone, although he probably only meant that he wanted to finish up his business with her and get her off his conscience. "Will seven-thirty be all right?"

"Seven-thirty's fine," she assured him. "I'll be ready."

By seven o'clock on Tuesday evening, Victoria had taken a shower, shampooed and styled her hair, applied her makeup and now stood in the closet and surveyed her wardrobe, unsure of what to wear. Her blue suit was very businesslike, actually too much so for evening wear. On the other hand, the outfits she wore to work were too casual.

If she'd asked Brody where they were going it would have helped.

New Orleans was a city of restaurants. French, seafood, Creole, Cajun, Greek, Italian, fast-food, barbecue, even dinner cruises on the Mississippi. They ranged in ambiance from places where patrons ordered at windows and stood up to eat, to the top of the dome at the Hyatt Regency, New Orleans's revolving restaurant and lounge, offering a breathtaking view of the Crescent City.

Finally she chose a soft challis print dress in pewter-blue-and-gray tones. It had a lace shawl collar, long full sleeves with cuffs at the wrists and a knee-length swirling skirt. She'd bought it in Sacramento just before she left and had worn it only a time or two. The pumps in a matching blue had been a lucky find, and the medium heel was informal. The ensemble should be correct for almost any occasion.

On the stroke of seven-thirty the doorbell rang, and she opened the door to find Brody looking smashing in an olive suit. She didn't even try to hide the wide smile of welcome that lit her face as she unlocked the screen for him. "You're right on time, Mr. Monroe. Please, come in."

His answering smile was as bright as her own. "Can't we be a little less formal?" he asked, as she led him into the living room. "My name is Brody."

"I'd like that, Brody," she said happily. "Can I fix you a drink?"

He glanced at his watch. "I wish we had time, but I made reservations at Granny's Parlor for eight o'clock and it's out on the old River Road."

"Then we'd better get started," she said.

With true Southern courtesy Brody helped her into his Oldsmobile Cutlass. It was too dark to tell whether it was black or navy, but the leather upholstery was cream, as was the carpet. When he got in and started the motor, they were surrounded with classical music from the FM stereo.

Victoria leaned back in the contoured seat and sighed. "I love your taste in cars and music," she said. "My dream is to own a red Ferrari with a CD player and four speakers."

Brody chuckled. "Dream on, child," he said gently. "You can't accomplish big things unless you dream big dreams."

She turned her head to look at him. "Do you dream big dreams?" Her voice was whispery.

She thought his shoulders slumped just a little. "Not anymore." His tone had a hard edge. "I just concentrate on getting through one day at a time."

He sounded so sad that before she could stop herself she put her hand on his arm. "Brody? Is something wrong?"

Immediately she was contrite. She had no business prying into his personal problems, but before she could snatch her hand away, he reached over and put his hand on top of it, holding it against him. "I'm sorry," he said, and glanced down at her. "I didn't mean to sound so down. I only meant that as you grow older you learn to compromise and be more realistic in your dreams."

She had to remind herself not to caress his arm with her fingers. Instead, she grinned. "Yes, Papa." Her tone was deliberately sassy.

He grinned back. "Don't be a smart aleck," he teased. "It's been a long time since I was your age."

Her eyes widened. "How old do you think I am?"

He put his hand on the steering wheel, and she dropped hers into her lap. "You're twenty-four, you have an A.A. degree from Sacramento City College and you were employed at the Sacramento Army Depot for nearly four years."

This time her eyes widened involuntarily.

"It's all in your personnel file at work," he told her. "You must have known that I'd have to check your records as well as the records of the men you were accusing."

Victoria felt somehow let down. "Oh, yes, of course you would. I guess since I knew I had nothing to hide I just didn't think about it." She paused as a thought occurred to her. "Now you have me at a disadvantage because I don't know anything about you except that you seem like a very nice man."

He turned to her again, but it was too dark to see his expression. "Does that mean you've forgiven me for fumbling the ball the first time you appealed to me for help?" He sounded as if it really mattered to him.

"Yes," she said. "Once I cooled down and talked to you again, I could see how it was possible that you didn't know what was going on."

"Thank you for that," he said. "As for knowing me better, I'm thirty-eight, graduated from State University of New York at Albany, and have been at the New Orleans Army Depot for five years."

She wanted to know so much more about him. Where he was born. What he was like as a boy. How his wife had died. If he had children. The questions tumbled over one another in her mind, but she didn't feel free to voice them. He'd revealed his statistics only in the three areas that he'd learned about hers—age, education and work experience, and if he'd wanted her to know more he'd have told her.

Some time later they were being seated at the restaurant by the hostess wearing a long brown-and-gold-striped gown over rustling petticoats. All the attendants wore old Southern-style costumes.

In spite of its down-home name, Granny's Parlor was an upscale restaurant in a converted old plantation house. It featured authentic home cooking served at round tables set with white linen cloths and sparkling china, crystal and silverware.

Victoria was impressed. There were numerous rooms on the ground floor, all furnished with period pieces in addition to the tables and chairs, and in the center of the house a sweeping staircase disappeared into the second floor.

"This has got to be the most magnificent restaurant in the whole country," she said to Brody as she opened the huge menu. "Do they serve upstairs, too?"

It was easy to see that he was familiar with the place. He took it all in stride.

"Yes, but those are the private banquet rooms," he explained. "This house was one of the local showplaces from the Civil War era that had become too expensive to keep up. The local historical society put it up for sale with the provision that the seller adhere to the society's restrictions. It was bought by a restaurateur in Baton Rouge and restored to its original splendor. The kitchens in these old mansions are detached from the main house because of the heat they generated, and, although it was necessary to modernize the one here, they kept the original brick ovens."

The cocktail waitress appeared and asked if they'd like to order drinks. Victoria ordered white wine, and Brody asked for club soda with a twist. Victoria was surprised. She'd never before dated a man who preferred nonalcoholic drinks, and she self-consciously switched her order to the same as his.

"That's not necessary, Vicky," Brody protested. "Order anything you like. I wish I could join you, but alcohol makes me sick so I stick to soft drinks."

"But I really prefer the club soda," she said, and the cocktail waitress left.

He started to protest again, but Victoria stopped him. "Really, Brody, I don't even care for the taste of liquor, but I learned to order light amounts of it because it always makes my dates uncomfortable if I don't drink with them."

Brody frowned. "There's nothing wrong with being a teetotaler. If your dates are uncomfortable, that's their problem. Don't let anyone shame you into drinking liquor."

"You're right," she agreed. "I should take a firm stand. It's just that, well, I know you won't believe this after the trouble I've caused you, but I'll do almost anything to avoid upsetting people or creating a scene."

His gaze searched her face, then a grin replaced his frown. "Do you expect me to believe that my snarling little tiger is really a pussycat after all?"

His grin was infectious, and she returned it. "Now you've learned my secret. I only bite when I'm sufficiently provoked."

Chapter Four

After their drinks arrived and they'd given the dining room waitress their dinner order, Brody reached into his inside breast pocket and brought out a small notebook. "I hate to intrude on this special time with a business discussion," he said regretfully, "but I'd like to get it out of the way so we can enjoy the rest of the evening without having it hanging over us."

For a little while Victoria had forgotten that this wasn't a date but a business meeting, and the reality was jolting. She had to work to keep her smile in place.

"Of course," she answered brightly. "After all, that's why we're here."

She thought he looked a little crestfallen by her ready agreement, but she couldn't be sure.

"Have you given any more thought to accepting a transfer?" he asked.

She took a sip of her club soda. "Yes, I have, and I've decided that you're right. There hasn't been any outward unpleasantness in the shop, but there's a lot of tension."

Brody looked up. "Anything I should know?" he asked sharply.

"No," she assured him. "Nothing I want to complain about. Walter and I speak only when necessary, but that's as much my fault as his. I'm afraid we'll never be comfortable with each other, and as for the other three... Well, let's just say I can't work in that atmosphere."

"I'm sorry," Brody said, "but I think you'll be happier in another division." He opened his notebook. "There's a position in Electro-Optics that I'm sure you could fill with very little training."

"Electro-Optics," she mused. "Isn't that where they repair night-vision equipment?"

He nodded, and she continued. "I've always found that subject fascinating. Imagine looking through goggles in the darkest part of the night and being able to see your target as clear as day. That must be invaluable to the fighting forces."

He seemed pleased by her enthusiasm. "It is, and it's also a boon to civilian law enforcement. The FBI, border patrol, narcotics agents and game wardens all use it, and we do the maintenance on most of their equipment at the depot, too."

Victoria felt a prickle of excitement. "Oh, Brody, it sounds really interesting. If the pay and grade are the same I'd like to transfer over there. Can you arrange it?"

He smiled and looked relieved. "No problem. The pay and the grade are the same, and there's probably a slightly better chance for advancement. I've already talked to the division supervisor, and he's willing to accept you. I don't think the men there will give you any trouble...."

Victoria didn't hear the rest of the sentence. She was too busy wrestling with a fact she'd overlooked until Brody mentioned the other supervisor.

Electro-Optics was a different division, and she would no longer be working under Brody. She wouldn't even be working close to him because it was clear at the other end of the block-long building.

Was that why he was so anxious to transfer her there? Did he think of her as a troublemaker to be pawned off on another supervisor as quickly as possible?

"Vicky, what's the matter?" The anxiety in Brody's voice snapped her attention back to what he was saying. "Did I say something to upset you?"

She wasn't going to let her suspicious mind ruin what would probably be the only evening she'd ever spend with him. Shaking off her moodiness, she decided to tell him the truth. "No, of course you didn't. It's just . . . well . . . I suddenly realized I wouldn't be working for you anymore, and I . . . I'll miss working under you."

She saw his surprised expression and forged ahead before she lost her nerve. "I'm truly sorry that I didn't talk to you again before I went over your head and got you in trouble with Mr. Lindberg. I didn't mean for that to happen, but I don't blame you for not wanting me in one of your shops. I should have thought before I acted. It's just that I was so mad at Walter. . . ."

Brody frowned. "Do you think I want to transfer you because I don't want to work with you?"

There was a strangled tone to his voice, and real anxiety in his golden brown eyes.

"Not just that," she said, finding it important to reassure him. "But it must be a factor."

"The thought never entered my mind," he said gruffly. "In fact, if you must know, I'm going to miss you, too. I don't like the idea of losing you, but there aren't any openings in any of my shops that are as good as the one

I'm offering you. Dammit, Victoria, tell me what it is you want, and I'll do my best to arrange it for you."

She wondered what he'd say if she told him that what she really wanted was the chance to get to know him better on a strictly personal basis.

But, of course, that wasn't what he was asking. He'd told her clearly that this was to be a business dinner, and she knew it was important for her own peace of mind to remember that.

"If you could magically grant me one wish it would be that none of this unpleasantness had happened," she told him, "but since it did, I'm satisfied with the position you've offered. I can only hope that my next supervisor is as understanding as you've been."

"Perhaps if our female employees would tell us what they consider sexual harassment we could deal with it more effectively," Brody suggested. "How is a man to know when he's crossed the line between friendliness, or even romantic interest, and harassment?"

Victoria felt a stab of impatience. "I should think that would be obvious," she said coolly.

"Well, of course, the crude talk and advances are," he admitted, "but how about the smaller matters? Compliments, joking or light touching? The usual things men do or say when they want to know a woman better. Are they always off-limits in the workplace?"

Victoria paused a moment to think about the question. "They are unless the man and woman know each other well away from work. After all, the workplace is what the name implies—a place to work. Not a place to pick up women. If a guy is attracted to one of the women he works with, he should contact her at home, or somewhere socially, and he should never persist if she says she's not interested."

The conversation was cut off when the waitress arrived with their dinner.

Granny's Parlor proved to be a gastronomical delight. Victoria's fried chicken was almost as good as the farm-style delicacy her grandmother used to fix, and it included thick cream gravy, fresh string beans and biscuits with honey. Brody's prime rib came with baked potato, fresh peas and French bread made on the premises and still warm. The meals started with seafood gumbo and a tossed spinach salad, and concluded with rich pecan pie, a New Orleans specialty.

Victoria was quite sure she wouldn't be able to eat again for days, and said so as she sipped her coffee.

Brody looked pleased. "I feel the same way," he said, and patted his stomach. "I love this Louisiana style of cooking even though it's loaded with cholesterol, sugar and calories."

Victoria saw an opening and took it. "You're not a native of New Orleans, then? I'd noticed that you don't talk with an accent."

"No, I was born and raised in a small town in upstate New York. Are you a native Californian?"

"Oh, yes," she said. "I lived in Sacramento all my life until a little over two months ago when I transferred out here."

"Do you like it here?" he asked.

She had to ponder that for a moment. "I think so," she finally said, "but I have to admit that I'm homesick. I miss my family and my friends, but I've been so busy settling into both my job and my house that I haven't had time to get to know the area and the people here."

He smiled and sipped his coffee. "Tell me about your family. Do you have brothers and sisters?"

She was happy that he was interested in her background. "I have an older brother and two younger sisters. Dad works for the State Department of Motor Vehicles, and Mom was a full-time mother until my youngest sister started high school. Then she went back to school and trained to be a legal secretary. Now she works for a law firm and loves it.''

"Sounds like you had a happy, well-adjusted childhood." There was a wistful note in his voice that made her wonder about his own background.

"I did," she admitted. "Oh, we had our problems— everyone does—but nothing serious. My most pressing difficulty was having to share a bedroom with my two sisters while our brother had one all to himself." She laughed. "I thought I was really put upon, but now I have two bedrooms and no one to share them with. It gets lonely at times. I guess we should be careful what we wish for."

Brody's gaze met hers. "Yes, that's true," he agreed, and his voice sounded hollow. "Too often we don't appreciate the blessings we have until they're irretrievably lost."

He looked away then, and she understood that he would say no more on the subject, but the pain in his eyes and his voice told her that he spoke from experience.

She had to force herself to sit quietly and not reach out to take his hand in hers.

They sat in a companionable silence for several minutes, and Victoria listened to the dreamy music being played on the piano in the bar where there was a dance floor. She swayed gently to the rhythm, and Brody must have noticed because he smiled. "Would you consider it improper if I asked you to dance?" His voice was low and inviting.

Had he known how badly she'd wanted him to ask? No, he couldn't have. She wasn't that transparent. "Not if we consider the rest of the evening as purely social."

"I'd like that very much," he said, as he stood and helped her up.

The bar, or lounge as it was called, was in what must have been the original ballroom. It was furnished with comfortable sofas and chairs placed around three sides of the room, and a massive bar had been built along the fourth. Behind it in the place of honor on the wall was a large oil painting of an opulent reclining nude in a massive carved gilded frame.

Brody seemed embarrassed as they both spotted it at the same time. "Sorry," he said. "I'd forgotten that was there. I hope you're not offended."

She sighed, and wondered if he'd ever truly understand her. "Brody, no apology is necessary. The picture is a beautifully executed work of art, in the Goya style I think. How can I make you understand that I'm not a flaming activist for the women's movement. I've never burned my bra, or marched in a protest march, or been insulted when a man opened a door for me, and I don't think paintings of nude women, or men for that matter, are demeaning. All I ask is to be treated with respect, but, as you've noticed, I'll put up one hell of a fight if I don't get it."

He chuckled and led her to the center of the room, then put his arm around her. "That fact has been called to my attention," he assured her, and began moving to the beat of the music.

It was a fast piece, and Victoria was delighted to find that Brody was an excellent dancer. They dipped and twirled and two-stepped along with several other couples. Then, after only a few seconds of silence, the haunting strains of a familiar waltz floated above the murmur of voices, and Brody pulled her close.

They fit together as if their bodies had been made for each other. Her breasts against his chest, her stomach against his hard, flat belly, and her thighs moving against his.

His arm held her around her waist, and his hand rested on the rise of her buttocks where it rose and fell with her movements. He was doing nothing that wasn't perfectly acceptable. His hand never strayed, he didn't attempt to push her groin into his, and though her cheek rested against the smoothness of his, he made no suggestive comments, but she'd never been held in such an erotic embrace before in her life.

The seductive music flowed around and through them, and her heart pounded as they melded together in the semidarkness. She knew he felt it, too. He couldn't hide his involuntary reaction to her closeness, but neither did he attempt to make her more aware of it.

With a tiny moan she put both arms around his neck, and he put his other arm around her waist. The faint fragrance of his shaving lotion was musky and expensive, and she buried her face against his neck.

"Victoria," he whispered raggedly. "Oh, God, Vicky." She felt the tremor that knifed through him, and realized that she, too, was trembling as he turned his head and bit gently on her earlobe.

Just moments later they were jolted out of their trance by a change in the music. The pianist switched tempo as abruptly as before, and the invigorating lilt of a polka rang through the room.

At first they just stood there holding each other while the dancers swirled around them; then they finally managed to pull themselves together and join in.

They stayed for another hour after that, but by unspoken mutual consent they sat out the slow dances while they sipped cooling Perrier with a twist of lime.

It was almost midnight when Brody pulled into Victoria's driveway and stopped the car. Victoria had had a marvelous time. The brief episode on the dance floor had shaken them both, but they'd regained their composure during the prancing pace of the polka and neither of them had mentioned it afterward.

On the drive home, though, it was there between them again, the thick sensual tension that could neither be ignored nor admitted. Victoria's emotions were in a state of confusion. Was she nervous because she was uncertain? Or uncertain because she was nervous?

Would Brody kiss her good-night? Oh, how she hoped he would! Should she invite him in? If she did, would he assume she wanted to make love? If so, would she be able to refuse? Would she even want to refuse?

He got out and came around to open the door for her, then took her arm as they walked up the short sidewalk that led to her porch. She'd left her outside light on, and her hand shook as she found her key in her purse and gave it to Brody.

He unlocked the door and pushed it open into the lighted entryway that led directly to the living room, then turned to look at her. There was an awkward silence as they just stood there, neither of them looking directly at the other.

Please let him kiss me good-night, Victoria prayed silently.

Help me summon the strength it's going to take not to kiss her, Brody petitioned.

"Brody..."

"Vicky..."

They spoke at the same time, canceling out each other's words.

Brody smiled and gestured toward her. "Ladies first."

She swallowed and tried again. "I had a wonderful time. The dinner was delicious, and I loved the dancing. I know it was only supposed to be a business dinner, but—"

Oh, Brody, please kiss me. Just one little kiss.

"There was never any chance of its being just a business dinner," he interrupted, "and I think we both knew it."

Dammit, Victoria, don't look at me like that. I can't stand much more.

"Yes," she agreed, or was it a surrender? "Would... would you like to come in for... for coffee?"

He reached out and cupped her cheek with his palm. "I'd like that far too much," he said huskily. "I'm no more immune to your charms than any other man, Vicky, and I'm too old and too battle-scarred to play with fire."

He brushed his thumb across her mouth, and it was almost as electrifying as a kiss. "Thank you for giving me a memorable evening," he murmured, and then he was gone, leaving her standing in the open doorway long after he'd backed the car into the street and driven out of sight.

Victoria didn't see Brody again before she transferred. She found out through the shops' grapevine that he was attending a week-long seminar in Baton Rouge, but he'd kept his promise to arrange for her reassignment. The following week she reported to Paul Osmond, foreman of the Electro-Optics shop, where she was immediately accepted and made to feel one of the team.

It took only a short training period for her to learn the new equipment and how to repair it, and the difference in attitude between the two shops was unbelievable. Here, the balance between male and female was almost equal. There were several women her age, but no one was subjected to the harassment she'd endured in Walter's shop.

All that first week she kept hoping Brody would seek her out to ask how she liked her new position, but if he ever came down to that end of the building she didn't see him.

That weekend she stayed close to the phone in case he called. They'd had such a good time the night he took her out, and the sexual tension between them had been so charged, that she'd thought surely he'd keep in touch. Especially since she no longer worked under him.

She'd been wrong. He neither sought her out at work nor called her at home. After the second week of hoping, she had to face the fact that he'd meant exactly what he'd said. He'd had business to discuss with her so he'd taken her to dinner since he wasn't available during the day, but he truly had no desire to "play with fire."

Why did he think of her as fire that would burn him instead of warmth that would be companionable and loving?

Was it the fourteen-year difference in their ages? That shouldn't be a problem. At twenty-four she was no teenager. She had a good education, marketable skills and had been living on her own and supporting herself for four years. Surely that meant she was grown up.

And at thirty-eight Brody wasn't old. He wasn't even middle-aged, but he was mature, and that appealed to her. She'd never been seriously attracted to boys her own age during high school, and although she'd had a lover in college, the relationship had been based more on infatuation than on love. The affair burned brightly for a while, then died painlessly of gradual neglect.

During these two weeks Victoria made friends with the other people in the shop and developed a more active social life. She was invited by co-worker Troy Sullivan, a real Adonis, who looked like a candidate for the cover of *GQ*, to join one of the depot's bowling teams. In his midtwenties, he had curly blond hair, blue eyes and a smile that kept most of the other women in the shop vying for his attention.

Victoria accepted his invitation and went with him to her first game. She'd belonged to a team in Sacramento, and while she'd never dazzled the others with her skill, her score averaged a respectable 140.

Brody obviously wasn't interested in her, and she was determined not to sit around and brood over him. The best way to prevent that was to date other men, and Troy seemed to be a nice guy. Maybe in time she would stop longing for the sound of Brody's voice, the touch of his hand and the crooked little smile that had gone straight to her heart and nestled there.

* * *

On Thursday of the third week, Victoria and Brody ran
into each other in the cafeteria.

She'd overslept that morning and hadn't had time to fix
a lunch, so she was standing in line at the eatery when
Brody came up behind her. "Hello, Vicky," he said in that
low, unhurried tone that always made her feel that he was
concentrating all his attention on her.

She'd watched for him for so long, and now that he was
here, her tongue seemed to cleave to the top of her mouth
and her brain closed down. He was wearing a dark gray
herringbone sport coat with navy slacks and a maroon tie,
and that endearing smile that looked more sad than happy.

She knew her expression must mirror the joy she felt at
seeing him again. She could feel the glow that seemed to
radiate out of her and split her mouth with a wide smile.

"Brody, how nice to see you," she said, when she finally got her tongue unlocked.

He didn't answer, just continued to look at her with a
longing that turned her insides to mush. Was it a longing
for her, or for the food that was so temptingly displayed in
the counter in front of them?

*Get real, Victoria. The poor guy's probably hungry. If
he'd been longing for you he could have come to you anytime.*

As if by mutual consent, they wrested their gazes apart
and picked up their trays and silverware. She continued to
silently scold herself for coming unglued just because he
got stuck in line behind her, and was only vaguely aware
of what she chose for lunch.

When she came to the cashier she paid her tab, then
stepped out into the crowded room. The tables were all
filled.

As she stood there holding her tray and scanning the
crowd, Brody came up beside her. "The people at the table over by the coffeemakers are getting ready to leave,"

he said. "Let's get over there before somebody else beats us to it."

He intended to eat lunch with her! She grasped her tray and happily followed him across the room.

A few minutes later, after they'd settled down to eat, Brody again caught her gaze with his. "Paul Osmond tells me you've learned your new duties quickly and are a fast and accurate worker. How do you like the job?" He sounded as if her answer was important to him. "Are you having any problems?"

So he *had* inquired about her! She felt a huge sense of relief to know that he'd cared enough about her well-being to check with her supervisor. Maybe he wasn't indifferent to her after all.

"I'm glad Mr. Osmond is pleased with my work," she said with a smile. "And there's been no harassment. I'm learning all about the night-vision equipment and how it operates, and everyone is so friendly. There's no comparison between the shop I'm in now and the other one...."

She stopped when she saw him wince, then cursed herself for being a sentence too late. The other shop was Brody's, and she hadn't meant to rub it in.

"Oh, Brody, I'm sorry." Her words tumbled over themselves as she rushed to make him understand. "I didn't mean—"

He reached over and touched her hand where it lay on the table, and her mind went blank.

"It's all right," he said softly. "You needn't spare my feelings. I should have been aware of what was going on—"

"No!" She'd raised her voice, then lowered it as she continued. "No, you're not to blame. You trusted Walter to do his job and he let you down, but it's all worked out for the best. At Electro-Optics I'm treated like one of the guys."

A little bark of laughter escaped Brody, and he removed his hand as his exaggerated teasing gaze roamed over her. "That, I'll never believe."

She laughed with him. "Okay, maybe not exactly like one of the guys, but I've been invited to join the bowling team."

One of his eyebrows raised. "Oh. All women, or mixed?"

She felt the warm flush of guilt, as if he'd caught her cheating on him. "Umm...mixed," she admitted, and took a quick drink of water to wet her dry throat.

Almost immediately his expression changed to one devoid of emotion. "Are the men behaving themselves?" His tone was cool and businesslike.

"Yes, but, Brody, it's not—"

"No explanation is necessary, Vicky," he informed her. "Your personal life is none of my business. My only concern is to make sure you're no longer being harassed on the job."

Now it was her turn to wince. He sure didn't beat around the bush. There was no way he could have made his disinterest in her any plainer than that.

During the rest of the meal they carried on a stilted conversation about impersonal work-related subjects, and when it was over, Brody pushed his chair back and stood. "If you'll excuse me, I have to get back to work," he said. "It was nice talking to you, Victoria. See you around."

He turned and walked off.

She was both sorrowful and annoyed. Darn it, why did he suddenly go all cold and impersonal? For that matter, why had she felt guilty about dating another man? Brody obviously wasn't going to ask her out again, so he couldn't be jealous.

Or could he?

No, she wasn't going to get on that merry-go-round again. From now on she was going to put him out of her mind and forget about him.

Yeah sure, Victoria. Good idea, but how do you plan to get that imaginative mind of yours to cooperate?

The next day, Troy, whose workbench was next to Victoria's, asked her to go to a depot-sponsored party with him. One of the top-line supervisors in the division was retiring, and a party in his honor was being held the following Friday at the Officers Club.

Victoria quickly accepted, and told herself how lucky she was that Troy had asked her, since he could have his pick of any woman in the shop. She was going to have a wonderful time and not give Brody Monroe another thought.

On the evening of the party she rushed home from work, showered, and shampooed and styled her auburn hair into a loose and stylish chignon.

Since it was unlikely that her three tormentors from Brody's shop would be there to embarrass her with their juvenile behavior, she chose a dressy gown that was one of her favorites. A red body-skimming silk chemise that accentuated the dark red highlights in her hair. It featured a wide scalloped neckline, short sleeves with scalloped edges and a hem above the knee. Simple and elegant.

With it she wore matching high-heeled pumps and long, dangling earrings.

The invitation for the party had read cocktails at seven, dinner and program at eight-thirty and dancing from ten until two. Since neither of them had wanted to spend a lot of time in the bar, Troy arranged to pick Victoria up at seven-thirty.

He arrived on time, wearing a dark blue suit that fit as though it had been tailor-made. She couldn't help staring as he walked into the entry.

"Troy," she said, only half teasing. "You're the most drop-dead gorgeous man I ever met. How come you're not in New York modeling?"

He grinned and winked at her, obviously pleased by the compliment. "And you're the most drop-dead gorgeous woman I ever met," he teased. "So how come you're not modeling in Los Angeles?"

They both laughed. "I guess we'll just have to settle for knocking their eyes out in New Orleans," she said, as she picked up her black satin evening wrap and let him drape it around her. "Shall we start with the Officers Club?"

The party was in full swing in the lounge when they got there, and was already spilling over into the banquet room where couples were choosing dinner partners and reserving tables. Troy knew everybody, and they were invited to join several groups. They chose to sit with one from their own shop, and a Reserved sign was put on the table so they could all circulate until dinner was announced.

Troy and Victoria returned to the lounge and ordered drinks. A whiskey and soda for him, and she asked for her usual glass of white wine, which she intended to make last all evening.

When they were served, she picked up her drink and turned to leave and make room at the bar for somebody else, when she bumped into the man standing behind her. Wine sloshed over the rim of her glass, and he put his arm around her waist to steady her.

In a blink she recognized his familiar scent, and the firm muscular body she was being clutched against. She didn't even have to focus her eyes to know that it was Brody who held her in such a protective embrace and sent her blood racing through her veins.

Her one hand tightened around the stem of the glass to keep from dropping it, and her other hand caressed his shoulder as his lips brushed her cheek in the dimness of the crowded room.

Chapter Five

Brody pulled Victoria even closer and for a moment they just stood there in what had started out as an accidental embrace, but instantly became much, much more. Victoria hoped that to the casual observer it would appear that he was simply giving her a chance to regain her balance, but in reality, his mouth trailing tiny kisses across her cheek played havoc with both her balance and her sensitive nerve ends.

"Ah, Vicky," he murmured into her ear. "I think you must have been sent to me as a penance to test the limits of my self-control."

While she was still reeling from the implication of his words, he released her and stepped back to look at her, then raised his voice. "Victoria, I hardly recognized you," he said jovially for everyone to hear. "You look all grown-up." He nodded toward the woman standing next to him. "Have you met Illa Vaughn? She works in Personnel."

Victoria took a second look at the lady. So this was the woman she'd heard he sometimes dated. To her dismay, Illa was close to forty and had stylish blond looks.

Victoria smiled brightly at the other woman. "No, I haven't," she said. "I'm Victoria Chambers, and I used to work in one of Mr. Monroe's shops."

She looked at Brody again. "And I've been all grown-up for a long time now," she told him.

His gaze roamed over her face. "I know," he said, too softly for anyone else to hear.

Troy, who had been paying for their drinks and hadn't been aware of what was going on behind him, turned around just then and spotted Brody. "Hey, Brody," he yelled happily. "It's been a while, man. Where you been keeping yourself?"

He slapped Brody on the shoulder, and Brody punched him lightly. "Working, as usual. Everything okay with you?"

Troy nodded, suddenly serious. "Everything's fine," he said, and Victoria had the strange feeling that he was speaking in a code that both men understood.

It surprised Victoria that Brody and Troy were such close friends. They had worked in different divisions, and there was at least ten years' difference in their ages.

Aside from that, they appeared to have little in common. Troy acted like a college kid with his breezy, devil-may-care attitude that made him fun and extremely popular, but it was in direct contrast to Brody's quiet, withdrawn, almost brooding demeanor that made him seem older than he was.

Troy noticed Illa and smiled again. "Illa, you're looking great. Have you met Vicky?" He put his arm around Victoria's waist and beamed.

Brody frowned as Illa answered, "Brody just introduced us." She looked at Victoria. "Didn't you recently transfer into Electro-Optics?"

Victoria wondered how much the other woman knew about the reason for that transfer. "Yes, I did."

"That was my lucky day," Troy said happily. "She works with me now."

Victoria didn't appreciate Troy's show of possessiveness. He was giving the impression that there was something going on between them, but she wasn't going to make a big deal of it unless he carried it further.

She told herself it didn't matter what Brody thought. He wasn't interested enough in her to care what she did as long as she didn't do it in one of his shops and bring the wrath of Civilian Personnel down on him again.

After a few minutes of light chatter the two couples went off in separate directions, and before long, dinner was announced. Victoria lost track of Brody and Illa in the crowd.

Dinner was the standard banquet fare—good but unexciting. Wine was served with the food, but Victoria put her hand over the top of her glass and asked for coffee instead. Troy drank both his share and hers, then ordered another bottle.

After they'd finished eating, there were the usual speeches honoring the retiree, and the presentation of gifts. When it was over and the musicians began to set up for dancing, Victoria excused herself to go to the rest room. She was repairing her lipstick in front of the mirror when Illa Vaughn came out of one of the stalls.

Their glances met in the mirror, and Illa came over to stand beside Victoria and repair her own makeup. "It's a nice party, isn't it?" she said in the soft Southern drawl that identified her as a native of the area. "Gollleee," she moaned as she patted her stomach, "I'm going to have to diet for a week after all that rich food."

She was a rather full-figured woman, but the fullness was in all the right places, and Victoria suspected she just wanted to be told that she looked fine the way she was.

"You have a very nice figure," Victoria said, and meant it. "Mr. Monroe obviously likes the way you look."

Illa's face lit up with a big smile. "Oh? Has he talked to you about me?"

She clearly wanted to hear that Brody'd been praising her to others, and Victoria was almost sorry she had to disappoint her.

"No," she said carefully, "we don't know each other well enough to exchange confidences, but I've heard rumors that you two are going together."

Illa's smile disappeared and she sighed. "Don't I wish," she said regretfully. "He's about the nicest man I ever met, and also the loneliest. He's kind and considerate, and always makes me feel special, but Brody's not interested in a relationship. He dates me now and then and we have a good time together, but that's all it is—just fun and games. I think he's still mourning his wife."

Victoria hadn't been in the south long enough to be sure of its jargon. Did "fun and games" mean they slept together on occasion, or just that they enjoyed each other's company?

And what about Brody's dead wife? She hated to gossip about him, but how else could she find out?

"How did his wife die?" she asked, before she could talk herself out of it.

Illa touched up her blusher. "She was killed in a car accident somewhere on the East Coast. Brody doesn't talk about it much, but I don't think he ever got over it."

That explanation sounded reasonable. Brody seemed the type who would fall in love for life. Why couldn't she have met him earlier?

But if she had it wouldn't have done any good. When he'd graduated from high school, she couldn't have been more than four or five years old!

There were so many other questions she wanted to ask, but she steeled herself not to. She wasn't going to pry any more than she already had.

Tucking her lipstick back into her bag, she turned and smiled at the other woman. "It's been nice meeting and talking with you, but I'd better get back to Troy before he sends in the search-and-rescue team."

Illa laughed. "Yeah, you don't want to leave that handsome hunk alone for too long. Most any woman here would love to take him home. Hell, if I were a few years younger I'd be tempted myself."

When Victoria returned to the banquet room, the tables had been pushed back to make more room for dancing, and the Cajun musicians, with their violin, guitar and accordion, were playing a lively first tune. She looked around for Troy and didn't see him, but finally found him at the bar in the lounge, drinking what looked like straight whiskey and talking to several other people.

He didn't see her until she touched his shoulder. "Oh, hi, honey," he said. She thought his words were a little slurred, but there was too much background noise to be sure. "What do you want to drink? Bartender..."

He motioned to the man behind the counter, but she stopped him. "I don't want a drink, Troy, and you'd better not have any more, either, unless you want me to drive home."

He grinned like a little boy caught doing something his mama disapproved of. "Ah, come on, sweetie, I can hold my liquor. You wanna dance?"

He took his drink with him as they wended their way through the crowd to the dance floor, then set it on a table before he took her in his arms. The Cajun music had the same beat as the country rhythm of the heartland, and Troy was an excellent dancer. He didn't miss a step, and Victoria relaxed and decided he hadn't drunk too much after all.

During the next couple of hours, Victoria and Troy changed partners with several different couples. She saw Brody and Illa several times as they danced by, but neither Brody nor Troy suggested they trade off, much to Victoria's disappointment.

Finally, during one of Troy's trips outside to smoke, Brody approached Victoria as she sat at a table watching the dancers. "Come on, Tiger," he said, and held his hands out to her. "Dance with me."

She didn't question the wisdom of it, but put her hands in his and let him pull her up and into his embrace. He held her with both arms around her waist, and she put her arms around his neck as they swayed to the dreamy ballad. She wished they could hold each other like this forever.

"Where's Troy?" he asked, and pressed his cheek against hers.

"They don't allow smoking in here, so he went outside for a cigarette. Where's Illa?"

"She went out for a smoke, too."

He led her in the familiar steps as they joined the other dancers on the floor. "Are you and Troy..." He paused, and she waited for him to go on. "That is, have you been dating Troy a lot?"

His tone was strained, as though he was trying not to sound disapproving and botching it.

She tipped her head back to look at him. "Not a lot, why? Is there some reason I shouldn't date him?"

The muscle in his jaw clenched. "No, I suppose not. All the women go for him—there's no reason you should be different."

She stroked the back of his head with her fingers. "Do you want me to be different, Brody?"

She saw a flicker in his eyes. "Yes, dammit, I do."

She smiled and put her cheek back against his. "Troy's fun to be with, but he's not my type," she murmured against his ear. "I want a man who is older, more mature.

One who takes me to elegant restaurants once in a while—who enjoys plays and concerts as well as bowling.''

She turned her face slightly and kissed him on the cheek. "I want a man who will love me for the woman I am, and not just for my bust measurements."

Brody's arms tightened around her, and she snuggled against him as he lowered his head and nuzzled the side of her neck.

"I'm warning you, Vicky...." His voice was low and ragged. "Don't think that because I'm older my self-control is indestructible. It's not, so don't tempt me too far." He caressed her earlobe with his tongue. "And tell Troy to keep his hands off your bust measurements or I'll break his fingers."

The jolt of other bodies brushing against them reminded them where they were. The music had stopped and the dancers were leaving the floor.

Brody handed Victoria over to Troy, thanked her for the dance and left.

By one o'clock the crowd had thinned out considerably, and Troy was taking another of his numerous cigarette breaks. He'd been gone quite a while this time, and Victoria was irritated about being left alone so much. It made her a target for men without dates who assumed she was available. She saw another one approaching and decided this had gone on long enough.

She stood and went in search of her escort, but as she walked through the lounge on her way to the front door, she heard Troy's voice raised in argument over by the bar. "Don't give me that old runaround, fella. You can't refuse to serve me. I'll file an official complaint with the commander...."

His tone was loud, and his words were slurred. Victoria's stomach clenched as she reversed direction to go to him. She'd been right several hours ago. He was drinking too much.

"Sorry, sir," answered the placating voice of the bartender, "but it's against the law to serve anyone who is obviously under the influence. How about a cup of black coffee?"

"Black coffee, hell!" Troy raged as Victoria got close enough to see him in the dim light. He was sitting at the bar.

She hurried over and put her hand on his arm, startling him into action.

He whirled around on the revolving seat, and she stumbled back to keep from getting hit by his flying arms and legs. "What the...?"

His unsteady gaze finally settled on her and he smiled sheepishly. "Oh, hi, sweetie. Wanna drink? Barkeep, bring the lady white wine, and make mine a whiskey neat."

Again she took his arm. "No, thanks, Troy." She fought to keep her voice light. "I don't want anything more to drink. It's time to go home. If you'll just give me the keys to the car—"

"Don't wanna go home," he mumbled almost incoherently. "Not till I get my drink." He swiveled back around to face the bartender. "Hurry it up, dammit."

The bartender ignored him and looked at Victoria. "Do you need some help, miss?"

She hesitated. No way was she going to get in the car with him at the wheel, but a lot of people had gathered around them and she didn't want to make more of a scene than he already had.

"Let me see if I can get him to come peacefully," she said, then turned to Troy, who didn't seem to be aware of much that was going on around him. "Come on, Troy, they're getting ready to close up. It's too late to serve more drinks. Give me your keys and I'll drive us home. Then you can have all you want."

She was almost sure he'd pass out long before she got him home, and she had no idea how she'd get him into his apartment if he did.

His lightning mood swings changed again, and he banged his fist on the bar, knocking over an uncapped bottle of liquor and breaking a couple of glasses. "Whatsa matter? You deaf or somethin'? I said I'm not leavin' till I get another drink."

The bartender was a big man with boxer-size fists, and he'd just started to come around the bar with a determined look in his eye when a familiar voice behind Victoria called, "What in hell is going on here?"

It was Brody, and she nearly collapsed with relief.

She turned to see him pushing through the spectators, his searching gaze wandering back and forth across the shadowy haze of the room until he got close enough to see first Victoria and then Troy, who had slid off the stool at the sound of Brody's voice and stood tottering on his feet.

Brody's jaw dropped, and he looked as if he'd been hit in the stomach. "Troy!" He sounded shocked and unutterably sad. "My God, what happened?"

The bartender spoke up. "He's been drinking steadily all night, sir. I can't serve him anymore. If he won't give the lady his keys we're going to have to call a cab for them. I can't allow him to get behind the wheel of a car."

Troy squinted at Brody. "S'all right, pal," he said thickly. "Just a misss . . . misunderstanding. My girl here thinks I'm drunk." He tittered. "Ain't that a hoot? Only had a couple'a cocktails. You know I don't drink."

Brody sighed as he gestured to the bartender that he'd take care of it, then put his arm around Troy's shoulder. "Yeah, I know, but let's humor the lady. I'll drive you home in my car, and Illa and Vicky can follow in yours."

Troy sat down hard, as if his knees had suddenly given out. "Okay, we'll hu...humor her, but you be sure and tell her that I don't drink."

"I will," Brody assured him gently. "Now you sit here and wait while Illa and I go bring the cars around." He put out his hand palm up. "Give me your keys." There was no room for argument in his tone.

Docilely Troy reached in his pocket and brought out his key ring, which he put in Brody's hand. "Take your time," he said happily. "My baby and I'll have a nightcap while we're waitin'."

"No." Brody's voice rang with authority. "Remember, you're on the wagon. You don't want to ruin your good record."

It seemed to Victoria that if Troy had been on the wagon he'd fallen off hours ago, but he didn't seem to find anything wrong in Brody's logic as he grinned and nodded. "Oh, yeah, you're right. Wouldn't wanna go back..."

His voice trailed off and he didn't finish the sentence.

Twenty minutes later, Brody and Illa had brought the cars to the door and with the help of a couple of other guys, had walked Troy out to the curb and settled him in the back seat of Brody's car, where he immediately went to sleep. Victoria got into the passenger seat of Troy's white sports car, which Illa was driving, and the two-car caravan drove off the base and in a few minutes was on Highway I-10 heading back into town.

Victoria sat back in her seat and glanced over at Illa. "Do you know where Troy lives?"

Illa shook her head. "No, but we're not taking him to his apartment. We're taking him to Brody's house."

Victoria's eyes widened. "Brody's house? But why?"

Illa shrugged. "Troy's an alcoholic, and Brody's been counseling him. He'd been sober for several months until tonight. Do you know what happened to make him take his first drink?"

Victoria was numb with dismay. "No. I didn't know he had a drinking problem. I'd noticed that he always drank colas when we bowled, but when he ordered drinks to-night I didn't think anything of it.''

A disquieting thought made her frown. "Why is Brody counseling him? Is he qualified to do that?''

Illa continued to watch Brody's car in front of them. "I guess. It's probably part of his job as a supervisor. We have a branch of Alcoholics Anonymous at the depot, you know. It's more cost-effective to rehabilitate them than to fire them and train someone new.''

Victoria shivered. Had Illa meant to sound as cold and calculating as she did? Wasn't saving the person more important to her than saving money? Was that Brody's atti-tude, too?

Brody turned off the highway at Metairie, a bedroom-type community on the outskirts of the city, and Illa fol-lowed. "Does Brody live in Metairie?'' Victoria asked.

"Yes,'' Illa answered. "He bought a house here. It's a nice, family-oriented suburb within easy driving distance of the depot.''

"But he doesn't have a family....'' Victoria stopped and looked at Illa. "Does he?''

"No, but the property is a good investment. Most peo-ple looking for homes anymore either have children or plan to, so they're buying larger places. Brody's has three bed-rooms and two baths as well as a good-size lot. When he gets ready to sell it, he'll stand to make a good profit.''

"But why would he buy a house and then turn right around and sell it?'' Victoria protested.

Illa stopped for a blinking red light, then turned left. "Oh, his plans are fairly long-range. He bought the place two years ago, and as far as I know he plans on staying there for several more years. Meanwhile, it's not only go-ing up in value, but is a good tax shelter.''

Victoria nodded. "I can relate to that. I'm enjoying a tax deduction on my house, too. Where do you live, Illa?''

"I live in the heart of New Orleans," Illa said. "When my husband and I divorced, we sold our house as part of the settlement, and I rented an apartment in the French Quarter. I don't want to be bothered with yard work and maintenance upkeep."

So she'd been married and divorced. "You don't have children, then?" Victoria ventured.

"No, thank God. That's one mistake I didn't make. I'm really not the mother type." She turned to look at Victoria. "I suppose you want a big family."

Victoria smiled. "Well, I'd like to have at least a couple of babies."

Illa shrugged. "Sure, kid, go for it if that's what you want. I'm all for women doing what they think's best for them. That is, as long as they leave me alone to do my own thing."

She slowed and took a right turn onto a street lined with big oak trees, and lighted by old-fashioned-looking lamps on poles. Brody's car ahead of them swung into the driveway of a house in the middle of the block, and Illa pulled up at the curb.

Although there was a porch light on, it was too dark to see more than an outline of the one-story dwelling that was partially hidden by large bushes and shade trees.

Brody managed to half support and half carry Troy to the door where he handed Illa the key. She unlocked and opened it, and Victoria was delighted to discover that he obviously hadn't given Illa a key of her own to his home. Surely he would have if she'd made a habit of staying over.

Brody didn't follow Illa and Victoria into the living room but turned left at the hall off the entryway. "You ladies make yourselves comfortable while I put Troy to bed," he said.

"Do you need help?" Illa asked.

"No thanks, I've done this before. As soon as I'm sure he'll be okay, I'll take you two home."

"But that's a lot of bother for you," Illa protested. "Why don't I take Troy's car and drop Vicky off at her place? I can bring it back here tomorrow morning."

"It's no bother. I'm not going to send two beautiful women out alone in a city the size of New Orleans in the middle of the night. Now, if you'll excuse me...."

He turned and staggered under the weight of dragging a nearly unconscious Troy down the hall toward the bedrooms.

Victoria identified the architecture of the house as what was known in California as ranch-style—oblong and rambling. A glance to the right of the entry disclosed a darkened kitchen, and the living room faced the backyard with a wall of windows that at two-thirty in the morning revealed nothing but the darkness outside.

Brody's choice of interior decorating was strictly masculine with earth-tone carpeting, sturdy, well-built furniture and leather-upholstered sofa and chairs. A large, colorful oil painting of a sunset over a vast expanse of water graced the wall above the massive brick fireplace at one end of the long room, and a square clock of exquisite light and dark wood inlay hung on the wall at the other end.

Victoria walked over to the timepiece to examine it more closely. The wooden background was approximately a foot square, but the round face in the center was framed in gold with the sunburst pattern of the inlaid pieces radiating from it.

"Magnificent, isn't it?" Illa said from behind her.

"Oh, yes," Victoria whispered as she touched the highly lacquered wood with her fingertips.

"It contains a musical movement that plays a different fifty-note melody from Verdi's operas every hour on a four-hour turnaround," Illa informed her.

Victoria was dazzled. "It must be a museum piece. Where on earth did Brody get it? It's surely worth a fortune."

Illa hesitated a moment before answering. "He made it."

With a gasp of surprise Victoria turned to look at Illa. "Really? But that's amazing. I didn't know he was an artist."

Illa shrugged. "He says he's not. That he just dabbles in woodworking, but he also made that coffee table—" she pointed to the heavy cherry wood table in front of the sofa "—and the matching lamp table. I'm no expert but they sure don't look like 'dabbling' to me."

She was right. They were the work of a master craftsman. "Does he sell any of his pieces?" Victoria asked.

"Not that I know of. He made a rocking horse as a gift for a small child with leukemia whose father works in one of Brody's shops. It was the cutest damn thing I ever saw. I understand the kid loved it."

Victoria shook her head slowly. "Where did he learn to do this? Or is it a talent he inherited?"

"I don't know," Illa admitted. "He seldom talks about his background, and he ignores questions he doesn't want to answer. He has a workshop in the garage, and spends quite a bit of time there. I think it relaxes him."

How odd, thought Victoria. She'd never known a man like Brody before. He was friendly and compassionate, but maintained an invisible barrier between himself and others. Everybody liked him, but nobody seemed to know him well. Apparently even the women he dated were not taken into his confidence.

"Come and I'll show you the rest of the house." Illa walked through the small archway at the side of the fireplace.

"This is the dining room." She turned on the light to reveal a room furnished with a large oak dining table and four ladder-back chairs with two more standing against the opposite wall at either end of a china cabinet.

Illa continued to the next doorway. "And here's the family room." She flipped a switch to reveal a three-step drop into a sunken, long, narrow room that jutted out into the backyard and featured another fireplace in the outer end wall.

They went down the steps, and Victoria stood in the middle of the gardenlike chamber filled with huge bouquets of colorful exotic blooms and baskets of greenery. "How absolutely breathtaking," she exclaimed. "Brody must have to hire a gardener full-time."

Illa laughed. "Well, not quite. The greenery is real, but the flowers are silk."

Victoria stared at her openmouthed until she finally gathered her wits about her. "Oh, no, you're not going to sucker me. I know silk flowers when I see them." She walked over to one bouquet and reached out to touch it.

"I thought I did, too," Illa said, "but I was sure fooled by these. Brody had them custom-made. Go ahead and touch them. They even feel real."

Victoria gently rubbed one of the delicate petals between her two fingers. "You see. I knew it, they *are* real." She was a little put out with Illa for teasing her.

"No, really. I'm not kidding," Illa assured her. "Stick your finger in the vase. There's no water in it."

Gingerly, Victoria did as Illa suggested, and there was indeed no moisture. "I've never seen such perfect fakes," she said.

They settled down on the two upholstered rattan chairs. "Does Brody live here by himself?"

"He sure does, and not from necessity, either. There are a lot of women at the depot who would be more than happy to share it with him."

Victoria leaned back and closed her eyes. "Yes, I'm sure there are," she murmured, and was certain that Illa was one of them. "It must get awfully lonely for him."

Illa sighed. "Brody's the type who would be lonely in a crowd of people. He doesn't let anyone get close to him."

"Who doesn't let anyone close to him?" Brody said from the doorway as Victoria's eyes flew open and both women jumped.

Illa recovered first. "I was talking about you," she said lightly. "You're the most secretive man I've ever known."

He grinned and came down the steps to take a seat on the couch. "That's not true. What do you want to know?"

"Well, for openers," Illa drawled, "why don't you find a nice lady to share this house with you?"

Victoria was appalled that the other woman would ask such a personal question, especially in front of a third party who was practically a stranger.

His grin faded, and he looked directly at Illa. "Because I like plenty of room to move around in. Also, I value my privacy." He spoke quietly, but effectively closed the door to further conversation on that subject.

"Now," he said, smiling again, "would you two like some coffee? Or how about breakfast? I have bacon, eggs, cereal...."

Victoria would have liked nothing better than to have breakfast with him, but she wasn't going to be an unwelcome third party on his date. At least, not any longer.

"Please," she said, interrupting him, "if you'll give me the keys to Troy's car I'll just go on home. He can figure out a way to get it tomorrow. I think he owes me that much."

She strongly resented the embarrassing position Troy had put her in.

"That's a good idea..." Illa started to say, but Brody broke in, speaking to Victoria.

"I won't hear of you driving clear across town alone in the middle of the night. Troy owes you a hell of a lot more consideration than that, and I intend to tell him so as soon as he wakes up. He won't surface again for hours, though, so if you're ready to leave..." He stood up.

"But I feel so bad about ruining your evening together," Victoria protested as she rose and looked from Brody to Illa.

Illa stood, too, and made no effort to hide the resentment in her expression, but Brody smiled. "You didn't ruin our evening—it was nearly over anyway—and it's not your fault that Troy drank too much."

He turned, walked toward the door and escorted them to the car.

Illa took the passenger seat next to Brody, and Victoria sat in the back. Illa selected a tape from a box built into the console between the seats, and put it in the stereo cassette player. The throaty voice of Crystal Gayle filled the confined space and discouraged talking as they sped down the highway. Victoria huddled, miserable and silent, in the dark.

When Brody turned into the driveway of Victoria's house Illa straightened and looked around. "How come you didn't have to ask for her address and how to get here?" she demanded.

"I've been here before," he answered curtly as he stepped out of the car, then opened the door for Victoria and extended his hand to help her out.

Victoria knew Illa was angry, and she leaned down and ducked her head back inside. "It was awfully nice meeting you, Illa, and I'm so sorry to be such a bother."

Illa didn't turn to look at her but mumbled, "Yeah, same here. 'Night."

Victoria wondered if that "same here" meant she enjoyed meeting Victoria, too, or that she was also sorry Victoria had been such a bother.

"You don't have to walk me to the door, Brody," she said when he took her arm. "The porch light's on, and I left a lamp lit in the living room. I'll be okay."

He kept on walking beside her with his hand at her elbow. "I'll make sure that you are," he said as he reached for her key. "I always see my dates to the door."

She handed him the key. "But I'm not your date, and I don't blame Illa for being mad at me. I'd be furious if she horned in on a date I had with you." Her voice quavered, and she swallowed.

Brody opened the door and escorted her inside, then pushed it so that it closed but didn't latch. He put his hands on her shoulders and turned her to look at him. "Would you, really?"

She couldn't trust herself to talk, so she just nodded.

Very gently he skimmed his palms up the sides of her neck to rest on either side of her face. His dark eyes looked bruised in the dimness of the entryway. "Victoria, my sweet young tormentor, what am I going to do about you?" It was a moan.

She ran the tip of her tongue around her dry lips. "What do you want to do?"

She knew she was his for the taking. All he had to do was say he wanted her.

"Don't ask." His fingers splayed into her hair. "Don't even think of asking or I may tell you."

"Would that be so bad?"

He put his forehead against hers and kissed the tip of her nose. "It could be salvation for me, love, but for you, yes, it would be bad."

Chapter Six

Jagged streaks of lightning zigzagged across the ebony sky, followed by the rumble of thunder, as Brody sped toward Metairie and home. It had been a long night filled with wrenching emotions, and he was tired.

He'd been in no mood for the jealous tirade from Illa just moments ago when, after taking her home, he'd politely but firmly turned down her invitation to spend the rest of the night. It wasn't the first time he'd done that. She offered more often than he asked, and she'd never seemed upset the times he'd declined. But tonight—or rather, this morning—when he'd explained that he had to go home in case Troy woke up and got sick, she'd turned on him with a vengeance.

"You wouldn't have given Troy another thought if Vicky had asked you to spend the night with her," she'd said angrily. Then her eyes narrowed with suspicion. "Or did she? You sure took long enough telling her good-night behind that closed door."

He'd tried to protest, but Illa's voice had escalated. "Damn you, she did seduce you into coming back, didn't she? You're going to *her* now that you've gotten rid of me?"

Her pretty face twisted into an ugly expression. "Men! You're all alike. You'll chase after any alley cat that wiggles her tail at you, especially if she's young and sleek and purrs when you stroke her. Don't think I didn't notice that you can't keep your hands off Vicky. God, Brody, I'd have thought you'd had enough of that trouble-making little bitch."

The rage Brody felt at the insults Illa directed toward Victoria was frightening. Especially since he'd been so sure he'd managed to conquer his destructive black fury years ago. At least he'd had the good sense not to answer her, but had immediately gotten back into his car and driven away.

However, Illa was right—not about Victoria but about him. If he'd stayed in Vicky's house one more minute when he took her home, she wouldn't have had to invite him to come back. He'd have pleaded with her to let him make love with her, and, after taking Illa home, would have forgotten all about Troy lying in a drunken stupor back at his house.

Troy. Some of the rage seeped out of him as he thought of the fun-loving young man who was going to wake up with a gigantic hangover. Troy had been doing so well in his effort to stop drinking. Why had he started up again?

Brody knew that was a futile question. An alcoholic didn't need any excuse other than the terrible craving that overpowered everything but its need to be satisfied. That addiction had killed Brody's father, and it would destroy Troy just as surely if he couldn't conquer it.

Victoria slept until almost noon that Saturday, and was wakened by the raucous buzz of the doorbell. As she rolled out of bed and struggled into her robe, she vowed to re-place the noisemaker with a soothing chime at the earliest opportunity. Still half asleep, she opened the door to find Troy standing behind the screen, looking pale and dishev-eled.

Before she could gather her wits about her, he groaned. "If you're going to yell at me, please do it quietly," he said and put both hands to his temples. "My head is going to explode any minute."

In spite of her annoyance with him, she couldn't resist his obvious agony. She unlocked the screen and pushed it open. "Come in, Troy." She spoke quietly. "I'm sorry you're suffering. Can I get you some aspirin?"

He weaved over to the sofa and sat down. "Thanks, but I've tried painkillers. They keep coming back up."

He leaned over and propped his elbows on his knees, then lowered his head into his hands.

"Then what are you doing here?" she asked. "Why aren't you home in bed?"

"Brody says I owe you an apology," he said without looking up, "and obviously I do, but I swear, Vicky, I don't remember anything that happened after we finished eating."

Her anger melted in the face of his misery. He didn't need her to punish him. His own conscience and body were doing that with unrelenting force.

She went into the bedroom and got a pillow, then stopped in the bathroom where she moistened a wash-cloth with cold water and carried them both back to the living room.

She put the pillow at the end of the couch, then stroked Troy's bent head. "Lie down," she directed, and when he did, she spread the cold cloth on his forehead.

"Why are you being so nice to me?" he murmured, his eyes still closed against the daylight. "I made a real jack-ass of myself last night. Brody said I even fought you for the car keys. Jeez, I'd never have forgiven myself if you'd been hurt because I insisted on driving."

"That couldn't have happened because I wouldn't have ridden with you," she assured him. "But you could have injured or killed yourself."

"That wouldn't be any loss," he mumbled on another groan.

Troy had the powerful appeal of a sick child, and Victoria had to fight the urge to mother him, but she instinctively knew that would only drive him deeper into the morass of self-loathing.

Instead, she spoke matter-of-factly. "It would have been a loss to me, Troy. I value your friendship. Now, lie quietly and I'll see what I can do about an ice bag for your head."

In the kitchen she put ice cubes in a plastic bag and wrapped it in a linen towel. When she substituted it for the cloth on his forehead, he sighed. "That feels better," he said, and promptly fell asleep.

By two o'clock Victoria had showered, dressed in jeans and a T-shirt, eaten lunch and cleaned house except for running the vacuum cleaner, which would have wakened Troy. She was making out her shopping list when Brody called. "Vicky, have you seen or heard from Troy in the past couple of hours?" He sounded worried.

"Yes, he's asleep on my couch," she assured him.

"What in hell's he doing there?"

"I told you, he's sleeping. He's got a king-size hangover, Brody. Do you think he needs medical attention?"

Brody paused. "What have you been doing for him?"

Victoria thought he sounded sarcastic, but it could have just been concern. "There wasn't much I could do," she said. "I offered aspirin, but he said he couldn't keep them down, so I had him lie down and put an ice pack on his head. He went right to sleep. Why did you send him over here to apologize when he was so sick. That could have waited...."

"*Me* send him!" Brody roared. "I told him to go home and spend the rest of the day in bed. When I phoned later to see if he was all right, nobody answered. Obviously he was hoping to get more sympathy from you. Did he put on his suffering little boy act?"

For a moment Victoria was too startled to speak, but then she couldn't help but chuckle. "Yes, I guess he did," she admitted. "But his suffering was real, and if he was expecting sympathy I'm afraid I disappointed him badly." Her amusement disappeared as a thought occurred to her. "I didn't comfort him in my bed, if that's what you're implying."

"No, honey, that's not what I was thinking." Brody's low, husky voice sent her pulse racing. "I just don't want you to be taken in by his very real need for someone to love him. When he's drinking he'll go to any lengths to get it, and I'm not necessarily talking about sex. Do you want me to come over and get him?"

For a moment she was tempted to jump at any excuse to get Brody in her home again, but she wasn't going to take advantage of his good nature. "No, thanks, I don't think that will be necessary. He should feel better next time he wakes up, but if he doesn't, I'll call you. Do you mind?"

"You can call me anytime, Vicky." His tone was solemn. "You don't need to ask permission. In any case let me know when he leaves there, will you?"

She assured him she would, and he gave her his number and hung up.

When Victoria went back into the living room, Troy was no longer stretched out on the couch, and she heard water running in the bathroom. She hoped he hadn't been sick again, but when he came out a few minutes later, his color was better and he'd washed his face and combed his hair.

He even managed a shamefaced little smile. "I'm sorry, Vicky," he said, and looked away. "Thanks for not kicking me out on my butt when I showed up on your doorstep."

She felt a tug of sympathy but quickly masked it. "I could never turn away anybody as sick as you were. Did you find the aspirin in the medicine cabinet?"

He sat down on the couch. "Yeah, but my head feels a lot better." He grinned. "It must have been your tender-loving care."

Brody'd been right, Troy was trying to manipulate her. "It wasn't tender-loving care I was giving you, Troy," she told him firmly. "I don't feel either tender or loving toward you. I don't take kindly to my dates getting drunk and embarrassing me, to say nothing of leaving me to find my own way home."

Troy blanched and put his hands to his face. "Oh, God, I'm sorry, sweetheart." It was a moan of pure misery. "I honestly thought I could handle a drink or two. Last night was the first time I'd had any liquor in months. I'm not lying."

Again a stab of sympathy jabbed her, and she fought against the need to comfort him. "I know you're not, and I admire you for trying so hard. I know it's hellishly difficult to give up drinking once you're addicted to alcohol, and I'm not judging you, or blaming you for failing this time. I'm just trying to tell you that I can't help you."

He dropped his hands from his face and she saw the film of anguish in his eyes. "You mean you *won't* help me," he said despairingly, but she noted a hint of self-pity. "You hate me, and don't ever want to see me again."

His childishness made it easier for her to be firm. "Don't tell me what I mean, Troy. I don't hate you, and as for seeing you again, it would be difficult not to since we work side by side every day. If there were some way I could help you I'd be happy to, but you need counseling by someone who understands your problem. I know nothing about alcoholism. I don't even date men who drink a lot.''

He looked away from her. ''Are you telling me you won't go out with me anymore?''

''Yes, that's what I'm saying.'' She said it gently, but even so, he winced.

''Will you still be my friend?''

She knew he was trying to wear her down, but because she had no romantic feelings for Troy she could afford to give a little. ''Of course I'll be your friend, and I'd like for you to be mine.''

She stood up in what she hoped he'd take as a dismissing gesture. ''Now, if you're feeling well enough to drive you'd better go home. I still have to vacuum and do the grocery shopping. Oh, but you'd better call Brody first.''

Troy blinked. ''Why should I call Brody?''

She picked up Troy's wrinkled suit coat off the chair where he'd flung it earlier, and handed it to him. ''Because Brody's worried about you. When he couldn't rouse you at home, he called to ask if I'd seen you. He wants to talk to you.''

''Yeah, I'll bet he does,'' Troy muttered as he rose and put on his coat. ''Where's the telephone?''

''Go through the dining room and turn right into the kitchen,'' she directed. ''It's on the wall by the table.''

Troy wandered off, but was back in a very few minutes. ''I got Brody's answering machine and left a message.'' He looked at her hopefully. ''I told him to call me here when he comes in.''

Victoria shook her head and made no effort to keep the exasperation out of her tone. ''No, Troy, you're not going to stay here until he calls. I told you I have things to do, and I want you to go home. Call him again when you get there and leave another message if necessary.''

Troy argued, but Victoria was adamant and he finally left. She finished her house cleaning and was getting ready to leave for the supermarket when Brody phoned and asked, somewhat sharply, for Troy.

"He's not here. I sent him home."

"Oh." It sounded like a sigh of relief. "He said he'd wait there for my call."

"So he informed me," Victoria said, "but I'd already told him he had to leave. He was apparently hoping I'd relent, but I didn't. That was about forty-five minutes ago, so he's probably home by now."

Brody chuckled. "I'm glad he couldn't con you into letting him stay."

Victoria had been having doubts. "Are you, Brody?" she asked anxiously. "I've been wondering if it was the right thing to do. He acted so forlorn...."

"Vicky, giving in to Troy's 'poor little me' posturing wouldn't have helped him a bit." Brody's tone was firm. "He has to learn to accept the responsibility and the consequences for his actions. Otherwise he'll never grow up, and he'll never give up drinking."

She sighed. "I'm glad what I did was right because, to tell the truth, I simply ran out of patience with him. I guess that makes me pretty hard-hearted—"

"It makes you pretty smart, Tiger," Brody interrupted, "and since we're being truthful, I'll admit that I don't want you to feel protective toward Troy. If you feel the need to ease anyone's pain I want it to be mine."

Talk like that went straight to Victoria's heart and made it jump for joy. "I wish I could ease your pain, Brody." Her voice had a breathless quality. "But you won't let me get close enough to you to know what causes it."

For a moment there was silence on the other end of the line, and when he spoke, his tone was heavy with sadness. "I'm sorry, Vicky, I shouldn't have said what I did. I'm being as selfish and immature as Troy. You don't need the burden of a middle-aged man's sorrows. Enjoy being young and carefree while you can."

She knew that arguing with him would do no good, so she decided to play it lightly. "All right, Grandpa," she said jauntily. "If you don't want to share your elderly heartaches with me, why don't you hobble over to my house tomorrow evening and let me share my youthful happiness with you? I'm a great hostess. I have the addresses of all the best take-out food places in town. Just tell me which you prefer—Chinese, Italian or American—and I'll have it ready by six o'clock."

Brody had started laughing before she finished her little spiel. "You're a nut, do you know that?" he gasped delightedly. "It would serve you right if I took you up on that."

A warm, bubbly feeling ran through her. "Please do." She was serious now. "I'd love to fix dinner for you, and I really am a good cook."

For a moment Brody didn't answer and a feeling of impending rejection made her queasy. "I shouldn't, honey," he said reluctantly. "Much as I'd like to, I—"

She had to overcome his caution. "Are you afraid I'll seduce you?"

She'd only meant to tease him, but her voice was unexpectedly low and sexy.

"No." His voice matched hers. "I'm afraid *I'll* seduce *you.* An evening alone with you at your house is more temptation than I can handle, but how would you like to take a cruise down the Mississippi on the *Creole Queen*?"

He was actually asking her for a date! "You mean the paddle-wheel boat?"

"That's the one. Have you taken that trip?"

"No, but I'd love to. What time will you pick me up?"

Brody laughed. "Nine-thirty. They board at ten. No need to dress up. Wear something comfortable, it's a three-hour trip."

The following morning Victoria was up early, too excited to sleep. After a breakfast of tea and toast, she dressed in khaki slacks and a cream-colored blouse. Spring in Louisiana was warm and sunny, although even in May the humidity was high and the rain, which fell nearly every day, only made it warmer. She'd been warned to enjoy the pleasant weather now because it would soon turn hot and steamy.

By the time Brody drove up to her curb, she was standing behind the lace curtains of the picture window in her living room, watching for him. She chided herself for acting like a teenager waiting for her first date to arrive, but nevertheless she watched as he got out of the car and walked to the house.

She fought the urge to run outside and meet him. Not for the first time she wondered what it was about this man that drew her so strongly? Love at first sight? Surely not. She'd thought she was in love with her college boyfriend, but it had been nothing like what she felt for Brody.

Today he was wearing jeans and a navy pullover shirt just like millions of other men, but she'd be able to pick him out of any crowd. There was an aura around him that drew her to him even as he tried to push her away.

Talk about mixed messages! All the time he was saying, "I don't want to get involved," the magnetism that radiated between them beckoned, "I want you. I need you. Come to me."

The doorbell rang. She forced herself to wait a moment before walking sedately to answer it. It wouldn't do to let him know she'd been pacing the floor for over an hour.

Victoria had left the front door open in an effort to capture the fresh morning breeze. When she appeared at the screen Brody smiled the gentle, captivating smile that made her heart do flip-flops.

She unlatched the screen and pushed it open. "Hello, Brody," she said huskily.

She stepped aside to let him in, but whether by design or accident she didn't move quite far enough, and he brushed against her. She caught her breath as his arms went around her. "Good morning, Vicky." His voice was as husky as hers.

She put her arms around his neck and snuggled against him. For a while neither of them spoke, and Victoria was lost in a world inhabited only by the two of them. They swayed slightly to a symphony only they could hear.

"It's been a long night," Brody murmured against her ear.

"Yes. I thought today would never come." She wasn't just talking about the past twelve hours.

"So did I, but I should have known I wasn't strong enough to resist." He'd understood her double meaning and answered it. "Are you sure this is what you want?"

"I want whatever you're willing to give." She was incapable of being coy with him.

His hand moved against the small of her back. "In that case, how about that good-night kiss I wasn't free to claim night before last?"

"I thought you'd never ask," she whispered, and raised her face to his.

His mouth brushed across hers with a feathery lightness that filled her with sunshine. Then again, not so lightly, and the sunshine inside her sparkled. The third time his lips parted and claimed hers with a tender longing that spread the sparkling warmth into the shadowy recesses of her soul.

Victoria had never experienced a kiss like this before, so sweet and so loving. Brody made no effort to deepen it and unleash the passion that would be welcome later, but not yet. First she wanted to be courted. To know the joy of discovering his likes and dislikes, his needs and his frustrations, his dreams and, yes, even his nightmares.

She moaned softly, and her arms around him tightened as he tilted his head and repositioned his mouth over hers. His breath was warm and fresh, and his lips were just rough enough to cause an exciting friction when they rubbed against the softness of hers. She was boneless and pliable in his embrace, and she felt buoyant, as though she would float off and get lost in the brightness of the sunshine he'd sparked in her if he didn't hold her close.

His hand roamed slowly over her back as he again shifted the angle of the kiss. Each time he did that it was like starting over again and finding a new facet of his lovemaking. If he affected her this strongly the first time their lips touched, what on earth would he do to her soaring emotions when he got her into bed?

The very thought made her shiver, and she stroked his shoulders through the lightweight cotton of his shirt. Always before when he'd held her he'd worn a coat, but this time she could feel the heat of his flesh under her palm, and also where her breasts pressed against his chest.

He was more muscular than she'd realized, and very strong. If he ever set free the full force of his passion with her it would be an awesome experience.

Long before she was ready, he raised his head and looked at her. His face was as flushed as she knew hers must be, and his eyes were dark with desire.

"It's time to leave, sweetheart," he murmured unsteadily, in a voice gravelly with suppressed emotion.

"Must we?" Her fingers still caressed his shoulders.

His muscles flexed under her touch. "Yes, we must. Otherwise we're going to rush into something that neither of us is ready for yet."

He was holding her against him, and Victoria found she couldn't stop herself. "It seems to me that you're more than ready," she blurted, then shyly hid her face against his chest.

He hooted with laughter and swatted her gently on the tush. "Brat! I think you enjoy tormenting me."

She raised her head to protest. "Oh, no, Brody..." Then she saw the amusement in his expression and smiled. "I'm sorry. I shouldn't have said that."

He hugged her quickly then released her. "Of course you should have said it. It's true, and there's no way you could have missed the obvious. I'm always physically ready when I'm close to you, but I'm carrying around a lot of emotional baggage that I'm not willing to share—and you're not ready to deal with. Until we come to terms with that, we're going to behave like brother and sister."

Now it was Victoria's turn to laugh. "I think it's against the law for brothers and sisters to behave the way we do with each other."

"Yeah, well," Brody muttered as they walked out the door and closed it behind them, "then we're going to have to clean up our act."

The two-story cruise vessel, *Creole Queen*, an authentic replica of a nineteenth-century paddle wheeler, was being readied at the Canal Street dock alongside the glass-enclosed Riverwalk mall, a twentieth-century, air-conditioned shopping center housing over one-hundred-and-forty specialty shops and cafés. While Brody bought the tickets, Victoria lingered in the spectacular circular fountain area, studying the colorful mosaic crests that formed the backs of the cement benches facing the pool and the spectacular fountains.

Within minutes the boarding began. A photographer took a picture of each person, couple or family who boarded, and Brody put his arm around Victoria and hugged her close as they smiled for the camera.

Upstairs on the top deck, they claimed the last table along the white metal railing at the bow of the boat, a vantage point that offered an excellent view of both the wide Mississippi River and the New Orleans skyline to the right.

The sun that had been shining so brightly earlier had disappeared behind heavy gray clouds. In California, Victoria would have expected an immediate drop in temperature, but not in this semitropical city that was surrounded on all four sides by water. Here the clouds intensified the humidity, but did nothing to quench the heat.

Once the huge red paddle wheel began turning and they were underway, the breeze on the river was cool. Brody and Victoria pushed their chairs close together and held hands as the guide pointed out the three towering steeples of St. Louis Cathedral, described as the jewel of the Vieux Carré, the weather-beaten warehouses that lined the docks for miles and the wide variety of vessels, tugboats, block-long barges, maritime crafts and other ships that sailed up and down the wide, deep waterway.

As they continued their leisurely trip downstream, several plantation houses were visible on shore, but by the time they reached the Chalmette National Historical Park, the battlefield where the battle of New Orleans took place during the war of 1812, and docked, it had started to rain.

Along with the others, Victoria and Brody moved to the covered bar area in the middle of the deck. "Oh, darn," Victoria said. "I hope this shower will be over in time for us to go ashore. What's that building just on the other side of the levee?"

"That's the old plantation Beauregard-Keyes House," Brody explained. "It was built shortly after General Andrew Jackson's victory over the British. I think part of it is used as a visitor's center. Actually, you can get a more panoramic view of the battleground from here than when you're standing on it." He gestured toward the lush, green meadow. "A battlefield isn't very interesting unless there's a battle going on."

"I suppose you're right," she said, but her tone betrayed her disappointment.

Just then the captain's voice came over the public address system. "Sorry about the rain, folks, but we're making arrangements for the park ranger to come aboard and tell you about the battle. If you'll assemble in the cabin on the lower deck you'll find it cool and dry, and you can have lunch while she talks."

Brody took Victoria's arm and linked it with his. "Now see, you aren't going to miss anything after all. She'll give you all the gory details while you eat."

Victoria made a face at him as they started downstairs.

Lunch was a light, informal meal served buffet-style, and both Brody and Vicky chose Cajun chili, hot and delicious.

Victoria was enthralled by the ranger's account of the bloody battle between the American and British armies. It was fought in January of 1815, several miles east of town at Chalmette, on the bank of the Mississippi. The British were badly defeated when they marched straight into the American entrenchments prepared by General Jackson. American artillery and sharpshooting riflemen mowed down two-thousand British soldiers, including the commanding officer, General Sir Edward Parkenham.

But Victoria wasn't prepared for the shocker at the end of the story. "The victory at New Orleans had no military importance," the ranger informed them, "because it was fought two weeks *after* the treaty of peace had been signed at Ghent, Belgium. If there had been telegraphic communication with Europe at that time, the battle would never have been fought."

"That...that's criminal," Victoria gasped, as the ranger's words echoed in the shocked silence. "All those people were killed for nothing!"

The ranger shook her head sadly. "It's a very great tragedy," she corrected gently, "but not criminal. At that time it took about six weeks to get messages across the ocean, and neither the American nor the British forces had been notified that the war was over. I think we should all be thankful for the tremendous advances that have been made in the field of communications since that time."

When the *Creole Queen* returned to the Canal Street dock, the photographs that had been taken earlier were displayed for sale on a large easel. Victoria and Brody joined the crowd that surrounded it, and soon picked out their picture. "Oh, I like it," she said excitedly as she reached for it. "Look, Brody, it's really good, isn't it?"

The photographer had caught them in a happy, carefree mood with dazzling smiles and their arms around each other.

For a long moment he studied it thoughtfully. She was beginning to think he wasn't going to answer when he finally spoke. "Yes, it is. I hardly recognized myself with that big smile on my face, and the beautiful girl in my arms."

He wasn't smiling now but looked almost regretful.

She touched his cheek with her fingers. "I'm not a girl— why do you always think of me as one?"

He took her hand in his and kissed her palm. "Because you're so young and sweet and innocent. You have your whole life ahead of you, and with a little luck it can be a good one, but be very sure of what you want. With your drive and determination you just might get it, and if it turns out to be wrong for you, it could leave scars that never heal."

Chapter Seven

On the drive home, Victoria held the folder containing the five-by-seven-inch, color photograph. Brody had bought her the picture, but refused to expound on his cryptic remarks about her future happiness.

His words and his tone had chilled her, but when pressed for an explanation, he'd said merely, "Your enthusiasm for life is marvelous, and I don't want to see it dimmed by mistakes." That left her even more confused.

Back at the house, Victoria unlocked the door. "I made devil's food cake with chocolate frosting last night," she told Brody as they walked into the living room. "Want some?"

"I never turn down chocolate cake," he informed her. "It's my favorite food."

"Great. Do you want coffee, iced tea or milk with it?"

"Milk, if it's good and cold."

"Oh, it is." She opened the folder she carried and stood the picture on the fireplace mantel. "There, how does that look?"

"It looks nice. Can I help you cut the cake?"

"Sure, if you want to."

She led him into the kitchen with its cobblestone pattern linoleum and yellow ruffled curtains.

"You have a pretty house," he said as he glanced around the room. "Do you rent or own?"

She laughed. "You could say I own it, although it'll be thirty years before I can burn the mortgage and call it mine."

She reached into the cupboard, brought out two glasses and handed them to him. "You get the milk and I'll cut the cake."

They carried their snack into the living room and sat side by side on the couch. Brody took a bite of the cake and chewed slowly. "Any chance I can take a rain check on that offer of cooking dinner for me sometime?" he asked after he'd swallowed, and speared another bite with his fork. "If this cake is any indication, you are a fabulous cook."

"It's my grandmother's favorite recipe, and the offer still stands. How about this evening?"

He swallowed his second bite. "Not tonight, but soon. Tell me about your grandmother. Is she still alive?"

Victoria blinked. "My grandmother?"

Brody nodded. "I want to learn more about you and your family. Do you mind?"

His confession turned her insides to mush. Did that mean he was more than casually interested in her? "I have two grandmothers. The one who supplied the recipe is in her late seventies and suffers from arthritis. The other one, my mom's mother is sixty-four, looks ten years younger and even I have difficulty keeping up with her. She's a widow who teaches school, is president of the teachers' union, plays golf at least once a week and has a gentleman friend who would like to marry her if he could convince her that she wouldn't have to give up her cherished independence."

Brody laughed. "Obviously she's the one you take after. Is she as lovely as you are?"

"Hey, that's a loaded question," Victoria protested. "I can't answer it without being immodest, but the pictures I've seen of her at my age look remarkably like me."

He sobered. "Good genes. It runs in the family. You'll undoubtedly have beautiful children."

She leaned forward to put her empty plate on the coffee table. "Do you want beautiful children, Brody?" She tried for a light tone, but her voice was soft and shook slightly.

He looked startled. "I... No..." His voice was gruff. "That is, I'm too old to start a family."

She hadn't expected that answer, and her tongue ran away with her tact again. "Why do you say that?"

He put his plate on the coffee table, too. "Because it's true. I have no intention of getting married again anytime soon, if at all, and when or if I do, I'll be old enough to be a grandfather. It's not fair to saddle a child with an old man for a father."

A stab of anger brought Victoria to her feet. "Dammit, Brody, why do you keep referring to yourself as an old man? I know men ten years older than you who still don't consider themselves middle-aged! Do you plan to spend the rest of your life alone, with no wife and no children?"

Brody also stood. "Yes," he snapped. "That's exactly what I expect to do. Why shouldn't I? I'm self-sufficient, I don't need a wife to look after me and the world is overcrowded as it is. The zero-population people are delighted with folks like me who are willing to forgo the so-called joys of parenthood."

He turned away and combed his fingers through his hair. "Don't try to push your values on me, Vicky. I've lived a hell of a lot longer than you have, and I know what I do and don't want. The one thing I'm sure of is that I don't want another family. The first time around nearly destroyed me.''

He turned and stalked out of the house, leaving Victoria staring after him, sick with shock and remorse.

On Monday morning Brody rolled out of bed long before the alarm would go off and stumbled down the hall toward the kitchen to make a pot of coffee. No use trying to sleep any longer. He'd tossed and turned most of the night, but every time he closed his eyes, the image of Victoria's face, white and stricken, tormented him.

You're a bastard, Monroe. There's no excuse for you taking out your festering rage on that poor sweet child who would never knowingly hurt you. She was only making conversation. She had no way of knowing that she was trespassing into your private hell. You could have simply changed the subject as you do with other people. It wasn't necessary to blast her with the white hot heat of an injustice that has nothing to do with her.

Those thoughts had stirred up others he'd dealt with long ago but couldn't seem to bury. Was he going to have to pay all the rest of his life for a fleeting moment of stubborn pride that had shattered his world and left him alone and bereft?

Hadn't he given up enough? Did he also have to forfeit any chance of future happiness?

You do if it's taken at the expense of Vicky's happiness. Come on, man, she's too young for you. She's only eight years older than Adriana.

Adriana! My God, that's right. Adriana was sixteen now, almost seventeen. And that would make Patricia thirteen. Why did he always think of them as little golden-haired girls with laughing brown eyes?

Probably because it was the only way he could think of them at all and stay sane. To focus for long on his inability to be with them as they grew up was unbearable.

In the kitchen he turned on the light, then put coffee and water into the electric pot and turned it on. Almost immediately, the water started dripping into the ground beans in the basket and filtering into the glass carafe as coffee. Simple.

It was easy to be a bachelor. With electrical appliances to do almost everything from making coffee to cleaning the house, and nutritious frozen dinners that could be warmed in the microwave in minutes, who needed a woman cluttering up his life?

Certainly not Brody. He had everything just the way he wanted it: plenty of room to spread out in, privacy, quiet when he needed it and a stereo system and two televisions when he didn't, plus the luxury of doing what he wanted, when he wanted, without inconveniencing anybody.

The last thing he needed was a relationship. So why was he letting a kid like Victoria Chambers torment him during the day and plague his dreams at night?

Let her? Hah! He didn't seem to have much choice. He'd been trying to get her out of his life, and out of his mind, ever since she'd come to him with her complaint of sexual harassment, but he couldn't leave her alone. If she didn't seek him out, he found a way to go to her and still square it with his conscience.

The coffee stopped dripping, and he poured some of it into a mug and took it with him into the family room. The sky was just beginning to get light, and he didn't bother to turn on a lamp but sat in his favorite chair in the semi-darkness.

If only he'd had enough self-control yesterday to resist the overwhelming temptation to kiss Vicky!

That kiss had been his undoing. He was going to be paying for it for a very long time, but no male between the ages of ten and death could have resisted. She was so soft and warm and caring, and the sweet eagerness of her response had simply overwhelmed him. He'd needed that kiss so badly, and if it haunted him for the rest of his life it would be worth it.

Now, though, it was time to stop thinking about his needs and start being more concerned for hers. He was the last thing she needed in her life. He'd bring her nothing but sorrow and despair, and he wouldn't, couldn't, do that to her.

Inadvertently he'd already set the means in motion for disillusioning her. He'd panicked when she'd asked if he wanted children and said hurtful things to her. He owed her an apology, but once that was given he'd close the door on their friendship.

And this time he'd make sure it stayed shut!

Dawn in the Lake Pontchartrain area on this Monday morning was decidedly unwelcome by Victoria. Her sleep had been intermittent during the night, and now that it was nearly time for the alarm to ring she felt bleary-eyed and exhausted.

Twice she'd gotten up and watched television, hoping it would bore her into slumber, but she'd hardly noticed what was happening on the screen. Her mind had seemed incapable of focusing on anything but Brody and his totally unexpected, and unexplained, anger yesterday when she'd asked him if he wanted children.

What could possibly have set him off like that? If she'd trodden on a sore spot it wasn't her fault. How could she avoid his bruises if she didn't know where they were?

There was something else she hadn't caught at the time, but that she'd picked up on during the many replays her unrelenting mind had subjected her to. Why had he said he didn't want *another* family? Brody and his wife hadn't had children, had they?

Dammit, why was she letting him treat her like a troublesome child? She didn't deserve his wrath, and she wasn't going to take any more of it. If he wanted to make up, he'd have to agree to some new ground rules.

She turned off the alarm and sat up in bed. But what if he didn't want to make up? Victoria was well aware that she'd been the aggressive one in this . . . this what? It was more intense than a friendship, but hardly a romance. He'd only kissed her once, but, oh, my, what a kiss. It had curled her toes and made her an instant addict.

Could she survive if she knew he'd never kiss her again?

She groaned and wearily got out of bed. It was her own fault. He'd made it plain that he didn't want to get involved with her, but she'd gone right on responding to his unspoken need rather than to his spoken wishes.

Well, he'd finally gotten through to her this time. He'd been right all along. He was old enough to know what he wanted, and he obviously didn't want her, neither in his bed nor in his life. She should be grateful that he cared enough about her not to take advantage of her silly schoolgirl infatuation.

In spite of her resolution not to, Victoria couldn't help but hope Brody would contact her at work that day. All of her senses were tuned to him. She heard everyone who came into the shop and always looked up eagerly. Each time the phone rang on the foreman's desk, she strained to hear and waited to be summoned to take a call.

By the end of the day her nerves were raw, but there'd been no sign of Brody. She chastised herself all the way home for caring, but the first thing she did when she got in the house was to check the answering machine for messages. There were none.

Neither did he call during the evening. By the time she climbed into bed, she was so exhausted that she fell into a deep sleep, but it was punctuated by tormenting dreams that kept her in a state of turmoil. Frightening dreams whose content she couldn't remember the next morning.

Brody didn't contact her at work the next day, either, and in defiance she went out to dinner and a movie with a couple of the other women in the shop. When she got home around ten o'clock, the red light was blinking on her answering machine, but whoever had called hadn't left a message.

She turned off the machine and took a shower, then curled up in bed and cried herself to sleep.

That night there were no dreams, and she woke up feeling better.

There was no sign of Brody the third day, either, but Victoria had given up hoping, so she wasn't as disappointed. It was long past time to get herself together and stop moping.

She picked up Chinese food on her way home, and had just finished eating when the phone rang. It startled her so that she dropped her tea cup in the saucer and broke them both. So much for her ability to remain detached about Brody Monroe.

She reached for the telephone on the wall above her, and her hand shook as she said, "Hello."

"Vicky, it's Brody." His tone was tense.

Her hand tightened on the phone, but she took time to breathe before she answered. "Yes, Brody?"

She was pleased to note that, in spite of her trembling hands, she sounded cool and collected.

Brody was anything but calm. He'd put off calling her until the strain began affecting his work, and now he was a mass of jangled nerves.

"I need to talk to you. Would it be inconvenient for me to come over now?"

She hesitated so long that he had to bite his lip to keep from shouting at her.

"Just what do you want to talk to me about?"

The muscles in his stomach knotted. Could she really be as unaffected as she sounded? "I think you know," he said gently. "I owe you an apology."

Again she hesitated. "You don't owe me anything, Brody. I shouldn't have pried into your affairs."

It was all he could do to keep his voice from shaking. "Look Vicky, I'm not going to argue with you on the phone. I'm coming over there. Please wait for me."

He hung up before she could answer and hurried out to the car. This stalemate was tearing him apart. He had to apologize and then end it with a clean break before it drove him stark, raving mad.

Victoria went through the motions of cleaning up the kitchen, repairing her makeup and combing her hair, in a daze made up of part excitement and part dread.

What did Brody want of her? He'd said he owed her an apology, but she didn't want him to feel he *owed* her anything. An apology meant nothing if he was just going through the motions.

For the first time since Sunday she made the effort to really look at herself in the mirror. The anguish she'd been suffering had taken its toll on her. Even with makeup, she couldn't hide the dark circles under her eyes or the lines of strain around her mouth. Even her hair had lost some of its bounce and hung limply on her shoulders.

She picked up her brush and ran it vigorously through the thick, auburn locks. She wasn't going to appear at the door looking like a deserted waif. That would bring out Brody's protective instincts and he'd feel sorry for her.

Pity was the last thing she wanted from him, and she'd be darned if she was going to let him think she couldn't get along without him.

She sighed as she brushed the shine back into her hair. It would be a lot easier to convince him of that than it would be to convince herself.

Victoria had been practicing breathing exercises and reviewing her assertiveness training for fifteen minutes by the time Brody rang her doorbell. This time she wasn't going to let him reduce her to a quivering mass of runaway emotions. She'd be sociable, friendly up to a point, but if he wanted more than that he'd have to make the moves.

She opened the door, unhooked the screen door and said, "Come in, Brody," in a clear, crisp voice that gave no hint of her inner turmoil.

He opened the screen door and walked in, but this time she'd been careful to step back far enough that there was no chance of them accidentally touching.

For a moment he just stood there looking at her with such an anxious expression, it nearly broke her heart. "I...I'm sorry if I've come at a bad time," he said in that gentle tone of his. "Were you going out?"

She'd worn a dressier outfit than usual to work that day because she'd taken an extra hour off at noon to attend a luncheon bridal shower in honor of her next-door neighbor's mother, and she hadn't changed her clothes when she got home.

"No, I'm not going out," she said as she moved on into the living room. "Would you like some iced tea, or maybe a soda?"

He shook his head. "No, thank you. Could we sit down?"

He motioned toward the sofa, but she headed for the occasional chair. "Yes, of course," she said as she seated herself, leaving the couch to him.

He lowered himself onto it and sighed. "Vicky, I don't blame you for being mad at me. I was way out of line with some of the things I said to you Sunday. I'm sorry—"

"I'm not mad at you," she interrupted, "and you were right to be angry. I shouldn't have been so nosey. It's none of my business whether or not you want children."

He leaned forward and raked his fingers through his hair in that endearing gesture she knew so well. "Honey, there was nothing wrong with your question."

She clasped her hands in her lap to stop herself from reaching out to him. "Obviously there was or you wouldn't have gotten so upset. I...I guess I never learned how to be tactful. I lived in Sacramento all my life and never considered anybody a stranger. I've always been open with people and nobody's ever objected before, but I must have seemed meddlesome and grasping to you."

"No!" It sounded like a cross between a moan and an oath. "There's nothing wrong with you. You're the most compassionate and generous person I've ever known. Don't blame yourself for my shortcomings. I'm the one who's impaired."

She shook her head. "You're not impaired, Brody. You're kind and gentle, and all you've ever asked of me is that I respect your privacy. I didn't mean to push my values on you, but that's what I was doing and I'm sorry—"

Before she could finish, Brody jumped up and turned away from her. "Victoria! Don't!" Each word was a cry of torment as he bent forward and crossed his arms over his waist.

"Brody!" She was on her feet and at his side with her arm around his shoulders before she had time to think. "What's the matter? Are you sick?"

He turned and then she was in his arms, her body pressed full length against his and his face buried in her hair. "Yes, I'm sick." His voice was low and unsteady. "Sick with the longing to hold you without fear, to kiss you without guilt, to make love to you without betraying you. Oh, Victoria, I need you so badly."

Vicky heard what she wanted to. *Longing to hold you, kiss you, make love to you, need you badly,* were seared in her mind, and the rest simply didn't register.

She raised her face to his and whispered, "I need you, too," just before his mouth covered hers in a bone-jarring kiss that was never meant to be tender. That had no beginning and no end, but effectively sealed their souls together, for better or for worse, until death and beyond.

When at last they tore themselves apart, Victoria's head was spinning. She rested it on Brody's shoulder, and he picked her up in his arms and carried her to the couch.

He sat down with her on his lap and cradled her against him. She could feel his heart hammering beneath her. "Sweetheart, did you hear what I said before the world exploded around us?" he murmured in her ear.

"Yes," she said contentedly as she unbuttoned a few buttons on the sport shirt he was wearing and put her hand inside against his bare chest. "You said you needed me."

"Oh, that feels so good," he purred as her fingers stroked him. "Did you hear what else I said?"

"Mmmmm." It was a mewling sound of pleasure when his hand settled on the side of her breast. "You said you wanted to hold me, kiss me and make love to me."

"Right on all counts." He cupped the full rise of her breast, then lowered his head and kissed it. "How do I get you out of this dress?"

She started unbuttoning the rest of his shirt. "It has two pieces. The top has a zipper in the back."

He unzipped it and pulled the garment over her head, then removed his shirt, leaving him bare to the waist. Victoria made no attempt to hide her admiration as her gaze roamed over him. He had a physique any man could be proud of—muscular and strong with a covering of dark brown body hair that sent little trills of excitement up her arms as she rubbed her palms through it.

He reached in back of her to find the fastener for her bra. "Do you mind?" he asked huskily as he trailed kisses across the uncovered flesh above the satin and lace.

She knew she wouldn't deny him anything. "Please do."

He quickly disposed of the encumbrances and buried his face in her softness.

She put her arms around him and held him, loving the feel of his bare skin. His cheek was smooth with no prickly beard, and she knew he'd shaved for the second time that day before coming to see her. How like Brody to be so considerate.

He raised his head and brushed his lips across one nipple, then the other, making her shiver with delight. "I apologize for calling you a girl," he said. "I was wrong. You're all exquisite woman."

He caressed one rosy nipple with his tongue, then took it in his mouth and continued to stroke it lovingly while Victoria tightened her arms around him, urging him to continue.

For a long time they sat there loving each other with their lips, their tongues and their hands, and it was pure heaven, but as she became more and more aroused she realized that all their touching was above the waist. Not once had Brody's hand wandered over her derriere, her thighs... She swallowed at the thought.

One thing she knew for sure, it wasn't because he wasn't as aroused as she was. Nor was she unaware that every time she shifted he shuddered and dug his fingers into her bare flesh.

So what was holding him back? Didn't he know how ready she was? She'd told him she wasn't a virgin, but maybe he was afraid she'd think he was moving too fast.

During their next soul-searing kiss, when his tongue was driving her crazy, she took his hand from her breast and moved it to the middle of her nylon-clad thigh. His whole body tensed, and he clutched her leg with such force that she winced.

Immediately he pulled away from her and put his hand on neutral territory. "I'm sorry, sweetheart," he said anxiously. "I didn't mean to hurt you, but my self-control is in shreds. I'd better get out of here before I—"

"Get out? You mean leave?" Victoria's tone was incredulous. "But I thought . . . I mean you said . . ."

He tumbled her back into his embrace, but kept his hands on her back. "I said I wanted to make love with you, and you must know that I do. I doubt that you have any idea just how much I want that, but it can't happen tonight, love. There are too many things you don't know about me, and I'd be a real bastard if I took advantage of your innocence."

Victoria was crushed. She didn't understand any of this, and she fought to hold back tears of frustration and embarrassment. Was he just playing with her? Teasing her?

No! Brody wasn't that cruel. She'd bet her life on it. So what was there in his past that drove him to reject her, even though he admitted that his desire—no, not just desire, his *need* for her was crucifying him?

In spite of her efforts a sob shook her, and his arms around her tightened. "Don't cry, Vicky." He lowered his head and kissed her on the temple. "If you do, I'll break down and cry with you, and that won't solve anything. We need to talk."

He was silent for a few minutes, as though pulling his thoughts together again, and with an effort Victoria held back the sobs that clawed at her throat.

When he spoke again, she could tell by his voice that he'd once more regained control of himself and the situation. She admired his iron will, but shuddered to think what it must have cost him.

"Tomorrow is Thursday, and my schedule at work is flexible. Is there any chance that you could take leave?"

She tried to assemble her scattered thoughts. "I . . . Yes, I think so. Our work load has been pretty light lately, but—"

"Then would you be willing to take the afternoon off and spend it with me? We'll go somewhere for lunch, then drive out to my place where we can have all the time and privacy we need."

"You know I will," she said.

He tipped her face up to his and kissed her. "God, it's so hard to leave you," he groaned.

"Then stay," she pleaded. "Darling, there isn't anything you can tell me that will change the way I feel about you. Your past isn't important. I want you now."

He drew a ragged breath and moved her off his lap, then stood. "I wish that were true. I'd sell my soul to make it true, but unfortunately we've come too far now to dodge the consequences. My past will determine your future. I can't let you make decisions blindly without knowing what you're getting into."

He picked up his shirt and put it on without bothering to button it, then reached out his hands to her. "Come see me to the door and tell me good-night. I can't stay here any longer without giving in to the temptation that's driving me crazy, and if I did that to you I could never live with myself."

She took his hands and let him draw her up beside him. Reaching for the top part of her dress, she put it on, then walked with him to the door. Victoria had so lost track of time that she was surprised to note that it wasn't totally dark yet.

They went out on the porch together, and Brody put his arms around her and kissed her again, hard but quick. "I'll come over to Electro-Optics tomorrow at noon and get you," he said, then turned and jogged out to his car.

Victoria stood on the porch and watched as he backed out of her driveway and drove out of sight. She had to fight the urge to run after him, to stop him and make him understand that she loved him no matter what he'd done in the past, to bring him back and seduce him, if necessary, into making love with her.

She had the most awful feeling of foreboding, a gut-wrenching fear that if she didn't succeed, there would be no future at all for the two of them together.

Chapter Eight

The following morning Victoria requested the afternoon off on emergency annual leave to attend to personal business. It was granted, and when the lunch-break whistle blew, she slipped out of her smock, put on her jacket and hurried out of the shop. To her surprise Brody was waiting for her.

He was wearing brown slacks and a gold blazer with a burgundy, green and gold paisley tie. When he saw her, a smile of both admiration and welcome lit his face, and it was all she could do not to throw herself into his arms.

Instead, she gave him an answering smile. "How did you get over to this end of the building so quickly?" she asked. "You must have left before the whistle blew."

"I did," he admitted unrepentantly. "I couldn't wait."

He took her hand and tucked it in the crook of his arm, and she snuggled as close to his side as she could get without being too obvious. "I've made reservations at Arnaud's in the French Quarter. Is that all right with you?"

The only thing Victoria really wanted was to be with Brody. She didn't care where, or if, she ate, but Arnaud's, the grande dame of Vieux Carré restaurants, was renowned for its French and Creole cuisine. It was also elegant and expensive, and she was glad she'd worn her navy blue suit this morning and brought a cotton smock to substitute for the jacket while she worked.

"That's great," she said, and squeezed his arm. "I've never been there."

They walked out of the building, and Brody headed for the parking lot across the street although he had a reserved parking space in front. "We'd better take both cars," he said. "That way we won't have to come back and get yours after lunch. Yesterday, when I said we'd go to my house later to talk I forgot that my cleaning lady comes on Thursday afternoons. We wouldn't have any privacy there, so do you mind if we go to your place?"

She'd been looking forward to being alone with him in his beautiful home, but the important thing was that they be together. "Of course I don't mind," she assured him as they headed toward her car.

When they reached the red Toyota, Victoria unlocked the door and slid behind the steering wheel. Brody leaned in to talk to her. "Do you know how to get to Arnaud's? It's on the Rue Bienville. Drive over to where I'm parked and then follow me."

"I'll try to stay with you," she promised, "but if we should get separated I can find my way."

He put his hand under her chin and tipped her face up to his. "I don't care if the whole damn army depot is watching," he growled. "I want a kiss."

"Oh, so do I," she murmured, just before his lips covered hers and made her forget everything else.

The French Quarter, or Vieux Carré, formed the original settlement of New Orleans, and Victoria never tired of exploring it. It was a magical place, a flamboyant architectural montage of intricate ironwork, timber, brick and plaster, and was alive with history and that hybrid of French, Spanish and African musical rhythms known as jazz.

Arnaud's was everything she'd imagined and more with its mosaic tile floors, ceiling fans and leaded glass windows reminiscent of days gone by. They ordered oysters on the half shell as an appetizer, charcoal-broiled redfish and crusty French bread for the entrée and *beignets* and café au lait for dessert.

It was after two o'clock by the time they finished eating, and afterward they strolled through the antique stores on Royal Street and admired the many works of art around the perimeter of Jackson Square where sidewalk artists set up shop.

They laughed and teased and walked with their arms around each other—like a man and woman in love. Victoria was so caught up in the joy of it, that for a little while she managed to forget that they were just killing time, trying to put off the moment when Brody would reveal the secrets of his past and possibly shatter their budding love affair.

Like all fantasies, though, this one had to end, and she was jolted back to reality when Brody suggested, gently but firmly, that it was time for them to go home. The foreboding that had plagued her from the time he'd left last night until he'd come for her at noon and banished it, sneaked back and blew a cold draft across her quivering nerve ends.

What could he possibly tell her that would make any difference in the way she felt about him? Brody was a good man. If he'd done some hell-raising as a teenager . . . well, what man hadn't?

Or maybe he was going to tell her that his wife hadn't wanted a family and he'd had a vasectomy. Could that be why he reacted so strongly when she'd asked if he wanted children? She thought about it for a moment. That would be a disappointment—she'd always wanted babies—but if the surgery couldn't be reversed they could adopt. If he truly didn't want children, as he'd indicated Sunday, then she could adjust to that, too.

She wasn't looking for a stud to sire her offspring; she wanted to spend the rest of her life with Brody Monroe. If that meant scrapping some of her dreams, well, so be it. At least she had her priorities straight.

Victoria got to the house first, and just had time to take off her suit jacket and hang it up before Brody arrived. The silk blouse she wore underneath was a navy, white and red print.

She heard him drive up, and met him at the door. The happy, relaxed expression he'd had all afternoon had been replaced by one of anxiety, possibly even dread.

As soon as the door closed behind him, he took her in his arms and cradled her against him. She nuzzled the pounding pulse at the side of his throat. "I've been waiting hours for you to hold me." She sighed contentedly.

"Don't think it's been any easier for me," he murmured. "My arms ached for you. All night and all morning I kept telling myself I wasn't going to touch you again until after you'd heard what I have to say. I meant it, too, but then you came to me this noon looking so beautiful, and so desirable, and I couldn't even wait until we got away from the depot to claim a kiss." He rubbed his cheek in her unbound hair.

She stroked the back of his neck. "Would you like another?"

"Oh, God, yes," he muttered, and captured her mouth.

Their tongues tasted and explored as he moved his hand up to cup her breast, sending warm ripples of delight all through her. He nipped gently at her lower lip and surprised her by the erotic sensations the strange caress aroused. She returned it, and he moaned as his other hand roamed over her bottom.

Raising his head slightly, he rained kisses on her closed eyelids, her temples and down her jaw to the sensitive hollow below her ear. "This has got to stop," he said huskily. "You know that, don't you?"

She angled her head to make her throat more easily available to his enticing lips. "Not on my account it doesn't." Her voice was little more than a whisper. "As long as you keep on kissing me, I don't care what happened in your past."

He accepted the invitation of her bare throat and fondled it with his mouth. "Ah, but there's the rub," he said sadly, and straightened up. "Kissing doesn't last, but past mistakes do. Now, stop tempting me almost beyond endurance and let's get this over with."

His tone was gravelly with strain, and she realized just how painfully difficult this was for him. "All right," she said, as she stepped out of his embrace, "but why don't you take off your coat and tie? You'll be more comfortable."

He shook his head. "No thank you. I'd better leave them on. If I start taking clothes off I probably won't stop until we're both nude and on fire with no hope of putting it out."

They went into the living room, and Victoria sat down on the sofa, expecting Brody to join her, but he took a seat across the room. He didn't relax, but sat straight and leaned forward. "Only three people in New Orleans know the whole truth of what I'm about to tell you. It's not something I want to talk about, even after all this time."

"Brody, your secret's safe with me," she assured him, eager to relieve his anxiety. "I won't tell anyone."

He looked at her and smiled softly. "I know you won't, honey. I trust you implicitly, although it's hardly a secret. It's all a matter of public record in the state of New York."

She frowned. "Public record? I don't understand."

He hesitated a moment, then took a deep breath and let it out slowly. "It's simple." His voice was devoid of emotion. "Eight years ago I was convicted of killing my wife, and I spent the next three years in a state prison."

His admission hit Victoria gradually, like a blow coming at her in slow motion. Her first reaction was confusion. Obviously she'd heard him wrong. His words were put together in a way that didn't make sense.

She replayed them again in her mind. *Eight years ago I was convicted.*

Convicted? Yes, she was sure he'd said that, but convicted of what?

Of killing my wife.

The blood seemed to drain from her head in a gush, and she clutched the arm of the couch as the room began to tilt. *No! No! No! He couldn't have said that!*

Her mind was playing tricks on her. Brody wouldn't do such a monstrous thing.

Her eyes were wide open, but the light around her was going dark when she felt strong hands on her shoulders and heard Brody's voice above the racket in her head. "Vicky, sweetheart, are you all right? Oh, damn, I'm an idiot! I shouldn't have flung it at you like that."

He put his arms around her, and she realized that he was sitting on the sofa beside her, holding her head against his chest and rocking her gently. She closed her eyes and leaned into him. Brody would protect her. He wouldn't let anyone shock her so cruelly. . . .

Get real, lady. Brody's the man you need protection from. He just told you that he killed his wife!

That brought her to her senses, and she pulled away from him and sat up.

He made no attempt to detain her. "Do you have any brandy in the house?"

She nodded, still befuddled. "Yes, in the kitchen cabinet."

"I'll find it." He got up and left the room.

Victoria collapsed back against the sofa and realized that she was shaking. She wasn't prepared for this. She hadn't even allowed herself to consider that Brody just might know what he was talking about when he warned her that he had an unsavory past.

How could she have been so blind, deaf and just plain childish as to think she was Cinderella and he was Prince Charming! That when he discovered the glass slipper fit her they'd live happily ever after?

Grow up, little girl. Prince Charming only lives in a fairy tale, and you've just been catapulted into the real world. It's time to stop swooning and find out what actually happened.

Brody returned with brandy in a juice glass and handed it to her. "Drink this," he ordered, obviously not intending to accept a refusal or excuse.

The glass shook in her hand, but she tipped it up and took a swallow. She choked as it burned its way down her throat, but then took another sip as she straightened up and made an effort to pull herself together.

Brody was hovering over her. "Will you be all right?"

She nodded and took another sip from the glass, then handed it to him. "Here, you drink the rest of it."

He raised it to his mouth and drained it, then walked over to the chair and sat down again. It was the only time she'd ever seen him take a drink of anything alcoholic.

"I think you'd better tell me what happened," she said, battling to keep her voice steady.

He lowered his head. "Yes, that's what I'm going to do, but first you'll need some background." He was silent for a moment, then looked up. "My wife, Gloria, and I both grew up in the town of Verner's Crossing, in upstate New York. It's a small county seat with a population of around ten thousand and was founded about a hundred and fifty years ago by Gloria's forefathers."

He spoke in a monotone, as though reading from an essay. "She was Gloria Verner, debutante daughter of the mayor and granddaughter of the publisher of the area's only newspaper. Her uncle was the leading banker, and her mother and her aunt were the women you had to stay on the good side of if you wanted any social life, which all the women in town did."

Again he hesitated, but then he caught her gaze with his. "On the other hand, my parents ran a sleazy boardinghouse on the wrong side of town, and my dad was a drunk."

Victoria had been too badly shocked by his earlier revelation to absorb anymore, and, although she quickly tore her glance from his and looked away, she knew her dismay had shown plainly in her expression.

He gave a self-derisive chortle. "You're right, I wasn't exactly the man the Verners would have chosen for their beautiful and spoiled daughter. When they found out we were seeing each other during our last year of high school, they were outraged. They ordered her not to see me anymore, but that just made her all the more determined. Up to then they'd never denied her anything, and she was willful and undisciplined."

Victoria had a question, and a need to know the answer. "How... how did you feel about that? I mean, were you a... a bad influence on their daughter?"

Brody's bark of laughter was bitter. "Well, hell, yes I was. My ancestors didn't fight in the Revolutionary War, and my parents were disgustingly common. Why, my mother wasn't even a member of the Ladies' Literary Society, and my dad spent most of his time getting smashed in a crummy bar."

Vicky could hear the raw pain behind his sarcasm, and she couldn't bear it. "Brody, please don't do this. That's not what I meant. I wanted to know if you ever cut school, or drove recklessly, or...or tried to seduce their teenage daughter?"

"Of course I tried to seduce Gloria." He sounded angry. "So did every other guy who took her out. That's what seventeen-year-old boys do, but every time she said no I stopped.

"As for skipping school or driving recklessly, no, I did neither," he went on. "I carried an A-average all through high school, and I didn't even have a car. I was known as a hothead because I got into a lot of fights, but that only happened when someone made nasty remarks about Dad.

"Anyway, Gloria finally wore her dad and mother down, and we continued to date, but they insisted that she go out with other boys, too. As soon as we graduated, they sent her to visit relatives in Florida for the summer, and the next fall they enrolled her in an exclusive women's college in the Midwest. I didn't have money for college, and I would have been drafted, so I joined the navy."

"You were in the navy?" He'd never mentioned that to Victoria before. She was beginning to realize just how little she did know about this man who had stolen her heart, but didn't really seem to want it.

"Yes," he said. "For three years. That kept us apart, but we wrote letters and she called me several times a week when I was stateside. When my enlistment was up, we eloped. Ken and Laura, Gloria's parents, were furious, but there was nothing they could do. They didn't want to lose their daughter, so they accepted me as part of the family and tried to make the best of it."

Brody leaned back in the chair and closed his eyes. For what seemed like a long time he said nothing, and Victoria wondered if he was just getting his thoughts in order, or if he was trying to gather the strength to go on.

She could see how difficult it was for him. He was pale and tense, and sometimes his voice broke and he had to clear his throat. Also he was giving her facts, but not sharing his feelings with her.

How had he felt about Gloria? Had he loved her? Victoria would assume so, but he hadn't said he had. Had Gloria loved him? Or had they both just been rebelling against her parents' unjust prejudice and then couldn't back down gracefully?

Victoria wasn't going to make it more difficult for Brody by asking these questions, but she was aware that he was only skimming the surface of his torment. For one thing, he'd thrown out the shocker about his father being a drunk as though he were talking about someone else's dad. He hadn't even softened the description by using the term *alcoholic*. It had just been a blunt statement of fact before he'd gone on to something else.

It must have been awful for him growing up as an object of pity, or contempt, and rejected by the so-called betters of the town. The thought made her sick to her stomach, and she was battling an overwhelming desire to go to him when he opened his eyes and straightened up again.

He smiled that disarming little smile and shook his head slowly. "Don't do it, sweetheart," he said, and she knew he'd been able to read her thoughts. "If you come over here and touch me I'll never finish the story, and you need to know the ending."

She knew he was right, but she ached to help him get through the ordeal. "I do want to know all of it," she said, and let the love she felt for him come through in her tone. "But, darling, I don't believe for one moment that you killed your wife. I'd bet my life on it."

His face contorted with emotion, and he gripped the arms of the chair. "Dammit, Vicky...." he blurted, then pushed himself to his feet and hurried into the bathroom, shutting the door behind him. But not before she'd seen tears glistening in his eyes.

She stood and began to pace. She wasn't handling this well at all. When she'd reacted with shock, he thought it was disgust, and when she had tried to comfort him, she had only made things worse.

Her own growing-up years had been so different. Her family was comfortable financially, her mother had always been there when the children needed her and Victoria and her sisters and brother had been leaders in the exciting extracurricular activities at school. She'd never known the kind of misery that Brody had been subjected to.

She was standing at the window with her forehead pressed against the glass and her thoughts turned inward when she heard Brody come back into the room. She turned, and he put his hands on her arms and looked at her. His eyes were red-rimmed, but he was in control once more.

He didn't pull her to him but leaned forward and kissed her lingeringly. His face and hair were still damp from being splashed with water, and his lips were warm and clinging. She put her hands on either side of his waist and tried to move closer, but he held her away.

"Thank you." His voice was rough with emotion. "Your unquestioning faith in me is the most precious gift anyone has ever given me. I . . ." His voice broke, and he kissed her again.

She put her arms around his neck, and this time he gathered her into his embrace and deepened the kiss. "It's easy to have faith in you," she murmured against his mouth.

"I wish I'd had you on my jury," he said.

She leaned back to look at him. "Jury?"

He nodded. "The jury that found me guilty of vehicular manslaughter."

She blinked. "But that's—"

"Yes, Gloria was killed in an automobile accident. They said I was drunk and lost control of the car."

"But you don't drink!" Her tone was loud, incredulous in the silent room.

"I did then," he said tonelessly, and put her away from him. "Let's sit back down and I'll tell you about it."

Once again they took seats across the room from each other, and Brody continued his story. "After we were married, we moved back to upstate New York and both enrolled at SUNY. Gloria's parents continued to pay for her schooling, and the government paid for mine under the G.I. bill."

He took a deep breath, and although he tried not to let on, she knew he was watching her closely. "A year later, Gloria graduated, and shortly after that, our daughter, Adriana, was born."

Victoria felt as if she'd been punched in the stomach, and it took her a few seconds to catch her breath. "You have a daughter?"

He continued to watch her carefully. "Yes, honey, I have two daughters. Adriana is sixteen and Patricia is thirteen."

She could only gape at him in disbelief. Brody had *two* children? "But you never mentioned... Illa said you didn't have a family. Where... where are they?"

His gaze hardened. "Illa doesn't know about them," he said impatiently. "Neither does anyone else around here. As for where they are, well, I'm coming to that."

Victoria wilted. Apparently there was no end to the shocks he had in store for her. No wonder he hadn't wanted more children. He already had two that were nearly grown! But where were they?

She made an effort to subdue her driving need to know the answer to that question. "I'm sorry. Go ahead. I'll try not to interrupt again."

"No, I'm the one who's sorry." He spoke gently this time. "I know this is difficult for you, but it's the only way I can do it. Just try to bear with me."

He seemed to relax a little as he leaned back and continued his story. "After the children were born, Gloria's parents grudgingly accepted me as a son-in-law. They adored their granddaughters, and since I was the girls' father they couldn't ignore me any longer and hope I'd go away. By that time my father had died of cirrhosis of the liver, and Mom died the following year."

The bitterness in his voice was like a knife in Victoria's heart. She longed to comfort him, but he didn't want that, and she'd promised not to interrupt.

"After I got my degree, I went to work for an air force base near Verner's Crossing," he continued. "Gloria and I were happy enough, but we did quarrel about my drinking."

Vicky couldn't stifle a gasp, and Brody looked at her. "No, sweetheart, I'm not an alcoholic like my father. I had a beer now and then and mixed drinks on social occasions, but liquor of any kind was forbidden in Gloria's family. They were all teetotalers, which is fine, but they were thoroughly obnoxious about it. They were absolutely certain that I was going to end up like Dad, and they never missed a chance to tell me so."

He shifted position and once more sat straight and tense. "I should have given in to them. It wouldn't have been any hardship, but I saw it as just another way they could remind me that I wasn't good enough to be a member of the Verner family, even by marriage, and I was damned if I was going to give them the satisfaction of knuckling under."

He paused, and looked past her in a sightless gaze. "That sin of pride cost me everything I held dear," he said quietly in a voice that was flat and empty.

Victoria couldn't stand the suspense any longer. It was tearing her apart.

She leaned forward and concentrated on keeping her voice from trembling. "Brody, I have to know. Were you drunk when the accident happened?"

He shifted his gaze to her, and it was no longer sightless. It was tormented.

"Yes, Vicky, I was legally intoxicated. My blood alcohol level was one point above the legal limit. But I wasn't driving. Gloria was."

Chapter Nine

Victoria was battered by the twin blows of consternation and relief without time to catch her breath in between. It was all coming at her too fast. She didn't have time to recover from one shock before Brody delivered another.

Her head whirled, and her thoughts were a jumble of discordant impressions.

Brody has no family, but his wife bore him two daughters. He doesn't drink, but he was intoxicated when his wife was killed. He was convicted of vehicular manslaughter, but his wife was driving the car when the accident occurred.

My God, he expected her to understand riddles that even a Sphinx couldn't untangle!

With a cry of sheer vexation she brought her legs up to curl under her on the couch, and dropped her face in her hands. She didn't want to hear any more. Her mind wouldn't absorb it. She needed time to sort out what he'd already told her.

A moment later, Brody hunkered down in front of her. "Here, honey, drink some more of this."

She raised her face and saw that he was offering her the juice glass, once more filled with brandy. She shook her head. "No, I need to clear my brain, not befuddle it more."

He took her hand and put the glass in it. "A few sips won't hurt you, and it'll make you feel better."

His face was white and pinched with concern, and she knew he was only trying to help.

Raising the glass to her mouth she took a swallow. It didn't burn quite so much this time, and she took another sip before handing it back to him. "Drink the rest—you look like you could use a little bracing up, too."

He took it but set it on the coffee table. "I'm all right. I lived through all this, and most of it is behind me now. I've managed to come to terms with it and find a measure of peace, but I hate what the telling of it is doing to you. We don't have to go on, you know. Why don't you just write me off and forget about the rest? I won't blame you."

He spoke so earnestly, and she knew he meant what he said. If she asked him to leave and not contact her again he'd comply with her wishes. But how could he? Didn't he love her even a little bit?

Sending him away wouldn't spare her the problems that loving him would bring. She could cope with them, but a future without Brody would be a lonely, barren hell on earth.

She put her hands on either side of his head and stroked his temples with her thumbs. "Brody, I've told you before that I don't care what sins you've committed or what laws you've broken in the past. I haven't changed my mind, so let's have no more about 'writing you off.' Don't you know how much I love you?"

She leaned forward and kissed him, then drew his head between her breasts and held it there.

A shudder convulsed him as his arms went around her waist and clasped her in a hard, almost desperate, embrace. His trembling continued as he fought for control, and she held him and stroked him until he was calmer.

Why did it shake him up so to be told that she believed in his innocence? And again when she said she loved him. It was almost as if no one had ever trusted or loved him before.

She trailed kisses in his hair and caressed his back and shoulders, and eventually he lay quietly in her embrace. When he finally spoke, his words were muffled against her breast. "For such a little thing you pack a real wallop. That makes twice this afternoon that you've nearly unmanned me."

She smiled and rubbed her cheek in his hair. "There's nothing unmanly about showing your emotions," she assured him tenderly.

"Maybe not, but I've never let mine get so out of hand before." He kissed the breast he was speaking against. "You mustn't love me, Vicky."

He'd changed the subject so unexpectedly and spoken so softly, that it took her a minute to comprehend. When she did she was puzzled. "Why not?"

"Because I'll break your heart."

He pulled away from her then and stood. "Don't confuse compassion or affection for love. You're very young yet, but someday you'll meet the man who is right for you. Then you'll know what I'm talking about."

Victoria was both hurt and indignant. He was treating her like an adolescent again. Telling her she didn't have enough sense to know when she was in love.

She wanted to argue with him, but something in his expression and his manner stopped her. If he didn't want her love, she wasn't going to force it on him. She'd embarrassed herself enough already by blurting it out and being repulsed.

Instead she merely nodded. "You're probably right," she agreed. "I do tend to be impulsive. I've thought I was in love before, and I no doubt will again. Now, please tell me why you were charged when Gloria was the one who was driving."

For a fleeting moment she thought she saw a look of painful regret cross his face, but then he walked away.

You can't have it both ways, chum, she thought. It'll be a cold day in Hades before I admit my feelings to you again.

Brody didn't sit down. Instead he walked to the fireplace and stared into it. He devoutly wished that he'd never met Victoria Chambers. He'd been making headway in his battle with the demons of his past, and for the first time he'd managed to put them behind him.

He'd come to terms with the loneliness, the occasional nightmares and the bleakness of his future. He'd learned to live in the present and not think of what had gone before, or what lay ahead. Then Vicky had come into his life with her sweet, loving nature and her enthusiastic zest for living, and shot his tenuous complacency all to hell.

She'd walked into his office on that fateful day such a short time ago and brought sunshine, joy and laughter with her. She was his light, his warmth and his buffer against despair, but now he'd been placed in the impossible position of having to disillusion her and send her away from him. He wasn't sure he could stand the pain.

Dammit, hadn't he suffered enough? He'd lost his wife and his daughters. Why did he have to lose the one woman who could make him whole again, too?

"Brody, would you rather not talk about the accident?" Victoria asked, and jolted him out of his self-pitying fog.

He focused his gaze on her, and saw the concern in her beautiful face. For a moment, he was tempted to take what he wanted and forget about the consequences. Tempted to engulf her in his arms and make love to her until they were both exhausted.

He knew she'd give herself to him, freely and openly and without reservation. That knowledge made the temptation excruciatingly urgent, but it also made the act unthinkable. It wasn't just sex he wanted from her. He also wanted the love she'd so endearingly offered him. Wanted it so bad that it was a hunger in his soul, but he couldn't accept it, now or ever.

The best he could do was try to protect her from himself.

He forced his thoughts back to the story of that horror-filled night of the accident. "I'm coming to that," he told her. "Gloria and I had been married nine years, and the girls were eight and five on that night we attended a party to celebrate a friend's promotion to vice president of one of the local banks."

Brody could still see the young, well-dressed crowd mingling in the cheerfully decorated home. Colorful balloons with long ribbon streamers hovered near the ceiling and were fastened to the backs of chairs as toast after toast was proposed and drunk.

"There was lots of food and champagne, as well as a full-service bar, and I was enjoying drinks with the rest of them. Gloria started fussing at me from the first one, and kept it up all evening."

He tried to shut out the nagging sound of his wife's voice, and the look of disgust on her pretty face that telling about it brought to mind so vividly.

"Actually, I didn't drink all that much," he continued. "I knew I had to drive home, and mostly I nursed each one along for quite a while before taking another, but Gloria was irritating me so that I had more than I would have otherwise just to let her know that I could damn well hold my liquor."

He plowed his hand through his hair and began to pace. "A pretty stupid way for a family man to act, I admit, and I've regretted it every minute for the past eight years."

"Is that why you don't drink anymore?" Victoria asked.

He stood still and looked at her. If he let himself, he could drown in those expressive emerald eyes. "Yes. The first time we went out together and you were surprised when I didn't order a drink, I told you that alcohol makes me sick. It's the truth. Ever since the accident, I get violently ill if I take more than a swallow or two."

His nerves were too jangled to stand still, and he started pacing again. "To get back to the story, by the time the party started breaking up, Gloria and I were quarreling angrily. She said I was too drunk to drive. I knew my head was clear and my hands were steady. Back then I had a high tolerance for alcohol, and it took a lot more than I'd consumed that night to slow down my reflexes."

He made a bitter sound in his throat. "Since then, I've learned that's what every drunk thinks when he gets behind the wheel of a car.

"Everyone there heard Gloria say she wanted to drive and ask for the keys," he continued. "They also heard me refuse to give them to her. We exchanged heated words for a few minutes until I finally convinced her to get in the car on the passenger side. I called goodbye to the group who had collected on the lawn on their way to their own cars, slid in behind the steering wheel, started the engine and drove off."

Again Victoria interrupted. "But you said you weren't driving—"

Subconsciously he clenched and unclenched his fists as the tension in him built. "I wasn't. We'd only gone a couple of blocks when Gloria started to cry. I could see that she really was frightened, and I felt like a heel. I grudgingly pulled over to the curb and we changed places."

Brody was sweating, and he found it hard to breathe. "She was driving when she lost control of the car and veered across the line, running head-on into the pickup coming toward us."

His knees felt shaky and he slumped back down in the chair as a replay of that grinding crash exploded in his mind.

Victoria had finally reached the limit of her endurance. She couldn't bear to sit across the room and watch Brody struggle to control himself while he relived the tragedy that had killed his wife and shattered his life.

She crossed the room and sank to the floor beside him. Once more he was staring into space, lost in painful reminiscence, until she rested her head on his thigh. His muscles beneath the sheer wool of his slacks contracted, and she caressed his knee with her palm. "If you don't want me close to you, you'll have to send me away," she said softly.

He caught his breath and tangled his hand in the thickness of her hair. "Fat chance," he muttered in a voice heavy with anguish. "How about sitting on my lap?"

Her heartbeat quickened. "I'd love to."

He helped her stand, then settled her comfortably across his thighs and cradled her against him. She put her arms around him and her head on his shoulder. He relaxed to a degree and leaned against the high upholstered back of the chair.

"You realize, don't you, that you've just scattered my thoughts all to hell?" he demanded tenderly.

"Mm. That's where they belong. I'm not going to let you put yourself through this any longer." She nuzzled the side of his throat, and he leaned into the caress as though afraid she might stop.

Instead, she spoke with her mouth against his flesh. "There are only two more things I need to know. Were you injured in the crash? And where are your daughters?"

"No, I wasn't injured except for some nasty-looking cuts and bruises. Neither of us had remembered to fasten our seat belts, and we were both thrown out of the car. I was thrown clear, but . . ." He paused and started again. "But it rolled over on Gloria."

For once, Victoria was speechless. The horror of such an accident was almost too much to comprehend. How terrible it must have been for Brody to live through!

They sat huddled together in the chair, each occupied with his own thoughts, until at last Brody spoke. "The two men in the pickup were seriously injured but nothing life threatening. There was no way to tell who was driving my car, but since everyone at the party had seen me at the wheel when we left and the alcohol level in my blood was above the legal limit, I was charged and convicted of drunk driving and manslaughter."

Victoria was incensed by the injustice. "And your little girls? What happened to them?"

She could feel the muscles knot in his stomach and arms. "I was sentenced to four years in prison, and Gloria's parents petitioned for and received custody of Adriana and Patty. They've had them ever since."

Stunned, Victoria sat up and looked at him. "But why?" It was a cry of disbelief and confusion. "You'd served four years in prison for a crime you didn't commit. Surely the law couldn't take your children away from you forever."

"I served a little over three years with time off for good behavior," he corrected her, "but three years is a long time in a child's life. Ken and Laura never doubted that I was guilty as charged. I'd just proven what they'd known all along, that I'd end up being a drunken bum like my father.

"They were bitter and vindictive. They never brought the girls to see me, and they asked me not to write or phone them. The kids were old enough to know that I was in prison for killing their mother, and Gloria's parents never let them forget it. By the time I got out, they'd adjusted to their new life and were happy with their grandparents.''

Victoria wanted to scream with frustration. ''You mean they still think you were driving that car?''

Brody shook his head sadly. ''Sweetheart, *everyone* still thinks that I was driving the car. After all, I was tried and found guilty. Being freed only meant that I'd paid my debt to society. For the rest of my life I'll carry the stigma of being an ex-convict who killed his wife and did time in prison.''

''But that's so unfair!''

He shrugged. ''Not if you accept the prosecutor's version of what happened. We'd attended a party where there was drinking, my wife had been telling me all evening that I was imbibing too much, she accused me of being too drunk to drive but I wouldn't give her the keys and a couple of dozen people saw me get behind the wheel and drive away just minutes before the accident. The jury made up of men and women I'd lived among all my life was out less than two hours before convicting me.''

''But didn't you tell them that you'd stopped and changed places with Gloria? That she was driving?'' It seemed so simple to Victoria. Surely those people knew that Brody wouldn't lie.

''Of course I did,'' he admitted. ''I also told them that something happened to her just before she lost control of the car. She sort of stiffened and then fell forward across the steering wheel. It happened so fast that there was no time for me to react before the two vehicles collided. I suspect that she suffered either a stroke or a heart attack.''

Victoria was doubtful. ''But she was young....''

Again he shook his head. ''Strokes and heart attacks aren't limited to the elderly, and Gloria had always been high-strung.''

"Well, then, surely—"

"Honey, think about it," he said patiently. "That's exactly what anyone in my position who was desperate for extenuating circumstances would say. Actually, I think it hurt my case because it sounded as though I was trying to get myself off the hook by putting the blame on a dead woman who couldn't defend herself. The prosecutor even accused me of lying both in his cross-examination and in his summation. Obviously, the jury agreed with him."

Reluctantly, she had to admit that he was right. Still . . . "Couldn't the doctor tell? I mean wouldn't a stroke or heart attack show up in the autopsy?"

He winced, and his face went even whiter. "The autopsy was inconclusive." His tone was ragged. "The injuries were too severe. . . ."

A sob seemed to be torn from deep within him, and he bit his lip and looked away.

"Oh, dear Lord," she whispered, and once more snuggled into his embrace.

His arms tightened around her, and for a long time they just held each other, both too shaken to talk.

Vicky's mind was in chaos as a picture of that gory scene played across it. What a monstrous experience to have to live through. How had Brody ever survived it? No wonder that in eight years he'd never been able to talk about it.

A wave of guilt and remorse slammed through her. Now, because he wanted to be fair to her, he was living it over again, and it was nearly killing him. She wanted so badly to make him happy, and so far all she'd done was cause him pain.

He was right. She wasn't mature enough to give him what he wanted—a calm and understanding lover who would soothe him and give him the peace of mind and soul he needed so badly. Instead, she bumbled along saying things that upset him, doing things that made him angry and embarrassing him by proclaiming her undying love when all he wanted was friendship and sex.

Well, there was one thing she could do for him, and that was put an end to the torture he'd been enduring all afternoon on her account. She was still curious as to why he hadn't fought for custody of his daughters, or maybe he had and lost, but she wasn't going to ask him.

She didn't have to. He told her without any prompting. "Ken came to the prison the day before I was released," he said, as though they'd never changed the subject, "and told me that he and Laura had no intention of giving up my children. He pointed out that I had nothing—no job, no money. I'd spent everything I had to defend myself. I had no home or family, and a record that would make it difficult to find employment and regain any of these things. I had no way to take care of two little girls, and he vowed to fight me in court if I tried to get them back."

Victoria swallowed the rage that threatened to choke her, but managed to hold her tongue and not interrupt.

"For once I had to agree with him. Much as I wanted my children, it would be months, maybe years before I could take care of them properly. I had agreed to let him keep them until I was on my feet again, but I wanted to see them, have visitation rights.

"He said if I had any feelings for them at all I'd leave them alone. That they barely remembered me, and if I came back it would just upset them and stir up the gossip all over again. I didn't want to cause them any more grief, so I signed papers giving them indefinite custody."

This time the rage overwhelmed her, and she sat up again. "You mean you never see them?" Victoria couldn't believe that anyone could be so vindictive as to not let a father see his own children.

Brody closed his eyes. "No, I don't. I saw them once shortly after I signed the custody papers, but they didn't see me. I went to Verner's Crossing on a Saturday and spent the day in the tree-shaded park across the street from the Verner home. I was lucky. They were in and out of the house several times that day. They even played in the park for a while...."

His voice broke, and Vicky stroked his cheek. He reached up and took her hand in his, then brought it to his lips and kissed her palm. "That was five years ago, and I haven't seen them since, although I've arranged for a private investigator, a woman who has children of her own, to do a thorough check on their well-being four times a year."

He brought her hand to his chest and held it there. "It makes Ken furious, but he doesn't dare complain to the courts because I made it clear that if he did I'd fight him for custody. He knows better than to push me any further."

In spite of her good intentions not to ask more questions, she felt it was imperative that she ask one more.

Again she cuddled into his embrace. He held her without passion, but with a need that went far beyond desire. She trusted him implicitly and didn't for a minute doubt but that his version of the accident was the truth. She'd meant it when she told him she'd bet her life on his innocence.

"Brody, do you mind if I ask just one more question?"

"Ask me anything you want to. I'll tell you whatever you want to know." He sounded tired, or maybe *weary* was a better word. Bone weary.

"Now that you have a good job, a home and the respect of everyone who knows you, why haven't you regained custody of your children? Surely the court would give them back to you. You're a fine, upstanding citizen, and you'd be a loving father."

He took a deep breath and let it out, but when he spoke, it had nothing to do with her question. He put his fingers under her chin and lifted her face to his. His eyes were shadowed, unreadable, as his gaze roamed over her features.

"Kiss me once more, Vicky," he said unsteadily, then waited for her to respond.

If this was his way of avoiding her question she was more than willing to give him what he asked for. She hadn't meant to pry, but she had every intention of seducing him if he didn't make the first move.

She shifted slightly so their mouths touched and clung. A sound from deep in his throat, like a moan of desolation, sent a chill of foreboding down her spine. His arms tightened around her, and her caressing hands roamed over his shoulders and back, seeking the smooth warmth of bare flesh and finding only the rough weave of his blazer.

Too soon he raised his head and looked at her. Her apprehension increased. "I . . . I wasn't finished yet. . . ."

He almost smiled. "Neither was I, love, but I'm afraid that's all we're going to get." He lifted her to a sitting position. "Now get up and go back and sit on the sofa, and I'll answer your question."

She rubbed at her arms and was surprised to find that they were covered with goose bumps even though it was almost uncomfortably warm in the house. "Why can't I stay right here?"

"You know why. I can't think when I've got you in my arms, and I need all my wits about me to make you understand what I'm about to say."

Her apprehension exploded into full-blown panic. "Brody—"

Before she could say more, he clasped her under the arms and stood, in effect dumping her off his lap. "No, Vicky." He spoke in his most commanding tone as he led her over to the couch. "No more delaying tactics."

Her knees gave way when they reached their destination and she sank down on the soft cushion. Brody stepped back but didn't resume his seat.

"I had a lot of time to think while I was getting reestablished in the outside world," he told her, "and eventually I was able to see that Ken was right when he said Adriana and Patty were better off with Laura and him than they would ever be with me."

Vicky opened her mouth to protest, but Brody gave her a stern look and she closed it again.

"Even though I had no trouble getting rehired in civil service, it was three more years before I was in a position to take care of the girls. By that time I'd been out of their lives for over six years, and they'd been thoroughly indoctrinated against me. I was a father in name only, and they'd heard all their grandparents' prejudicial accusations against me. It really wouldn't have been in their best interest for me to insist on taking them away from the two people who were truly more mother and father to them than grandparents."

"But what about your best interests?" Victoria demanded. "You'd lost so much. You were entitled to claim your children."

Brody moved restlessly around the room. "My best interests were strangled along with justice when the jury found me guilty. I've been a felon from that day on and will be until the day I die. There are few 'best interests' in a prison cell, and I learned not to expect them. I also learned to do what I was told and not make waves if I wanted to get out at the end of my term reasonably unscathed."

He turned to glare at her. "I'm an ex-con, Vicky, and that stigma will follow me all the rest of my life. Most places won't hire me, almost no clubs will admit me to their membership, I can't get a permit to carry a gun should the need ever arise and if I had a wife and children, they'd be subjected to the same discrimination just because they were mine."

Victoria's head was swimming again. Subconsciously, she'd totally ignored the fact of Brody's incarceration. She'd concentrated on the accident and the trial, but she'd pushed aside the horror of his living for three long years locked up in a state prison!

Through the fog in her brain she heard Brody's voice as he continued. "I won't put anyone I care about through that. Adriana and Patty don't need a father with a record of killing their mother when driving while drunk. They were very young and partially protected from the scandal when it happened, and now it's behind them. The town's had a lot of other juicy gossip to gnaw on since then, and their grandparents' standing in the community guarantees them a place in polite society."

He ran his fingers through his hair. "The best thing I can do for them now is to stay out of their lives."

Victoria wasn't so sure of that. "You think that having a social position in a snobbish little town is more important to them than being reunited with their father?"

Brody didn't hesitate. "Yes, I do. At their age, peer acceptance is vital. A lot of kids are raised by grandparents these days, but damn few of them have fathers who are labeled as killers. Both girls are healthy, happy and doing well in school. They go to Sunday school every week and are active in youth activities."

Victoria had to admit that a lot of what he said was true, but she wondered if they were as happy as he seemed to think. Surely they missed their father. It must have been devastating for them to lose both of their parents. If they'd had a close, loving relationship with Brody, and knowing him she was sure they had, they must have been terribly hurt when they never saw or heard from him even though they knew he was in prison. When he didn't come for them once he was free they must have thought he'd deserted them.

She looked up to find Brody standing at the window, his hands in his pockets and his shoulders slumped. He looked so . . . so melancholy, and she longed to go to him, put her arms around him and help ease the grief he felt over the loss of his daughters.

Before she could move, he spoke again. "The reasons I gave up my children are also the reasons why I have no interest in a long-term relationship with a woman, or marriage. You have no future with me, Vicky, even if we become lovers. I have all the usual male urges, and you are sweet and empathetic and sexy. I yearn to take you to bed and let you make me forget for a little while, but I won't love you, I'll never marry you and I'll never give you children."

Victoria was too numb by now to feel anything. Her emotions had apparently blown a fuse somewhere along the line, and she could only watch in silence as he turned around and looked at her.

Chapter Ten

Brody stood by the window, looking at Vicky. The damage he'd done to her was nakedly visible. She looked battered, even though he hadn't laid a hand on her. He'd done it with words.

It took all the determination he could muster not to let the anguish he was feeling show on his own face.

You bastard, he thought. You had to go for the jugular, didn't you? You could have been a hell of a lot kinder and gotten the same meaning across.

No, that wasn't true. He knew Victoria too well to believe that. She was one of the most compassionate people he'd ever known, and the story he'd just told her was the thing soap operas are made of. The fact that it was true made her all the more vulnerable to him. He'd expected revulsion, but he'd gotten sympathy instead. It was unusual that someone so young understood what he'd gone through. She'd believed his improbable account of the accident without question, and she'd done all he'd let her do to comfort him.

That wasn't what he'd intended. It had been his experience that people didn't want to be involved with ex-cons. That's why only the people in charge of hiring him at the depot knew about his prison term. It's also why he'd been so callous in telling her he'd been convicted of killing his wife.

He hadn't expected the intensity of her shock, or her willingness to stay around and hear the rest. The last thing he'd wanted was her pity, and when she said she believed he was innocent, he'd been reduced to tears.

No, this young lady had a depth to her that was frightening, and she was too loyal to desert him now. He was going to do whatever he had to do to keep her away from him.

If she knew how much he wanted her and what sending her away was costing him, she'd never go.

Why in hell hadn't he put a stop to this attraction between them when he first became aware of it? He'd known it was special and therefore to be avoided at all costs. He was the supervisor, the adult, the man in charge. He should have left her alone once he transferred her out of his shop.

He'd managed to walk away from his own children for God's sake; why hadn't he been able to do the same with Victoria? Surely she wasn't more important to him than Adriana and Patty.

Her big green eyes were filmy with tears, and her face looked ravaged, but she didn't cry. His whole body ached to go to her, hold her, promise her anything if she'd just live with him and be his love, his wife, the mother of his children—both to Adriana and Patty and to the ones they would have together.

But that was impossible. He'd known it all along, but still he'd continued to see her, spend time with her, thrill to the gentleness of her touch, the sexy timbre of her voice and her sensitivity to his moods.

Then he'd made his biggest mistake. He'd kissed her. He hadn't intended to. It was not only unwise; it was forbidden. He'd been so positive that his control was absolute, that he was strong enough to resist a little temptation.

A *little* temptation? He'd never felt one so powerful before in all his life. He'd walked into her house the day they'd taken the cruise on the river, intending to say something light and conversational, but then he saw her standing there radiating sweetness and beauty. Before he was aware of reaching for her, she was in his arms, her mouth moving under his, and he wasn't sure he'd ever be able to let her go.

As it turned out, he was right. He hadn't been able to let her go, and now they were both paying the price.

One lone tear escaped and rolled down her cheek, and he knew he had to get out of there quick. If he didn't, he was going to break down and take her in his arms again, plead for her forgiveness and take her home with him.

He made one last massive effort to remain cool and slightly aloof. "I'm sorry, Vicky," he said, and was relieved that his voice was steady. "I should never have let things between us go this far. I never meant for you to be hurt."

She said nothing, just watched him as he walked across the room and out the door.

For a long time Victoria just sat there, Brody's words replaying again in her mind.

I don't love you, I'll never marry you and I'll never give you children.

That was plain enough for anyone to understand. His voice had been firm and clear. He'd left no room for doubt but that he'd meant what he said. So why was he so tormented, acting as if each word were like the thrust of a knife in his heart, as it was in hers?

That's wishful thinking, you idiot. You'd shot off your mouth and told him you loved him. He was just embarrassed about having to tell you that it wouldn't be reciprocated. He's a nice man, and it upset him to know he was hurting you.

She sighed. That was probably it. He may not love her, but he did care about her. Otherwise he wouldn't have held her and kissed her and told her he wanted her.

Oh, come on, Victoria. Face it. He's male, and males have physical needs that even the most gentlemanly of them can't ignore. You fuel his fire, but all he wants is for you to go up in smoke with him for an hour or so. He admitted as much. He doesn't have any deep and lasting feelings for you. He spelled it all out—I don't love you, I'll never marry you . . . I'll never give you children.

She stood and went into the kitchen, trying to get away from her nagging thoughts. There was something wrong with the way she was remembering his unflinching statement, but she couldn't put her finger on it.

Her mouth and throat were dry, and she saw that her hand shook as she poured water into a glass and drank it. Brody obviously assumed she wouldn't come to him on his terms. He hadn't even asked her to make up her mind and let him know.

Well, he was right. She hadn't been capable of such a shallow, one-sided relationship with any of the other men she'd ever known. The one she'd given herself to in college had loved her at the time. They'd planned to marry eventually, and when the infatuation had ended it had been by mutual consent.

But with Brody . . . ? Brody was special. They were on the same wavelength. They tuned in to each others' thoughts and moods . . . or was she just kidding herself? She'd been so sure that he felt as close to her as she did to him. The electricity positively vibrated between them when they were together, but she must have misread the signals. It was probably just overeager sexual energy on his part.

The glass, which she'd forgotten she still held, dropped from her nerveless fingers and shattered on the tile of the counter. It startled her, and when she tried to pick up the pieces, a large jagged one lacerated her hand and the tile turned red with blood.

She stared at it, feeling nothing as her mind reeled. Maybe it was symbolic. Shattered glass, shattered romance, shattered dreams, bleeding heart.

The cut was deep, and when she couldn't make it stop bleeding, she wrapped it tightly in a towel and drove herself to the emergency room at a nearby hospital. The cut needed two stitches and her whole hand was bandaged afterward.

When the doctor finished and helped her to a sitting position on the table, he asked her if there was someone with her.

"No," she said. "I live alone, and I was able to drive all right."

He glanced through the papers he held in his hand. "I'm afraid I'll have to argue that point with you. You're exhibiting mild symptoms of shock. Nothing to worry about if you follow my instructions, but I can't let you drive a car."

"That's ridiculous. I feel fine," she said, although now that she was sitting up, she realized she was light-headed.

"No, you don't," the doctor insisted. "Look at you. You're trembling."

She put out her hand and saw that it was true.

"But how am I going to get home?" she wailed, uncharacteristically on the verge of tears.

"I'll have the reception desk call a cab for you. You can leave your car here and have someone drive you over in the morning to pick it up."

There wasn't much she could do but agree, although she knew it wasn't just the wound that caused her symptoms. She'd been subjected to more shocks that day than most people suffered in a year.

By the time she got home she was too drained and exhausted to do anything but fall into bed.

When the alarm buzzed the next morning, Victoria woke from a deep, dreamless sleep. Although her hand throbbed painfully, she felt rested and better able to cope with all that Brody had told her yesterday.

She plugged in the coffeemaker, then showered with one hand while keeping the bandaged one out of the water. Fortunately she was right-handed, and it was the left one that had been injured so it only slowed her up a little.

While eating granola for breakfast she again went over in her mind the story of Brody's background. Outrage still burned through her at the injustices that had plagued him through most of his life. First being ostracized for the sins of his father, then being punished for his wife's misfortune and finally losing his daughters because of a crime he didn't commit.

He'd apparently expected Victoria to be repulsed by his past and accept his offer of an easy way out, but instead it had made her more determined to give him the love he needed so badly. If it had only been his past that he wanted to protect her from, she'd have banished his doubts and they'd have spent last night making love.

But his objection to a relationship with her went beyond that. He didn't want her in his future, either. All he was willing to give her was the now. Today. Tomorrow. Next month. However long it took to dull the desire he felt for her. Maybe she could even hold him until next year, but eventually he'd be sated. Then he'd gently ease her out of his life and be alone again until some other woman incited his inconvenient lust for a short while.

She'd be an idiot to go into a relationship like that with her eyes wide open. Somehow she knew that if they ever made love she'd be his forever whether he wanted her or not. No modern, intelligent and independent woman would settle for such an outdated arrangement.

Yeah, sure, woman-of-the-nineties—you've got it made with your own house, your own car and a well-paying job that used to be open only to men. So how come the thought of a future without Brody Monroe feels more like an empty hell than a joyous heaven?

A glance at the clock warned Victoria she'd better call a cab and get on her way if she intended to stop at the hospital and pick up her car before she went to work.

Even so, she got caught in a traffic tie-up and was just two minutes short of half an hour late when she pulled into the parking lot at the depot. Thank goodness she'd worn slacks and walking shoes this morning, because she hit the ground on a dead run. If she made it to her desk before the clock on the wall reached eight-thirty, she might be able to talk the foreman out of docking her an hour's wages.

She tore into the building and was sprinting through the Test Equipment and Repair section, where she used to work, on her way to Electro-Optics when she collided with another body, nearly decking them both. They clung to each other in an effort to regain their balance, and the other body found its voice.

"Dammit, why don't you look where you're going...?"

It was Brody. She recognized the feel of him and his voice even before she managed to focus her eyes. It figured. With almost four hundred people working in this end of the building, it was her luck to run into the one man she didn't want to see.

He recognized her and stopped in midsentence. "Vicky! What's the rush? Where are you going in such a hurry?"

They were still standing in the open area with their arms around each other, and for just a second his grip on her tightened before he released her and stepped back. Their gazes meshed, and she saw dark circles under his eyes.

She was the first to look away. "I'm so sorry," she said, still breathless from the exertion. "I had to stop at the hospital to get my car and I'm late. I was hoping—"

"The hospital?" His tone had become louder, more strident. "Why was your car—"

It was then that he saw her bandaged hand. His eyes widened with concern. "Oh my God, what happened to you?"

Gently his fingers circled her wrist, and he held her hand up so he could examine it. "Victoria, answer me. What happened to you between the time I left you last evening and this morning?"

"I...I dropped a glass on the tile and it broke," she said, then went on to tell him about the incident. His face seemed to grow whiter with each sentence.

"The doctor said I was exhibiting mild symptoms of shock, and he wouldn't let me drive the car home so I left it there and took a cab," she concluded. "I took another cab back this morning to pick it up, and that's why I'm late."

"Why didn't you call me?" Brody's voice was thick with anxiety.

"There was no need to disturb you—"

"Disturb me!" he shouted. "It would have disturbed me a hell of a lot less last night if you'd called on me for help than it does now knowing you had to go through it alone with no one to take care of you!"

He lowered his voice, but didn't release her wrist. "I never should have left you alone after the shocks I'd given you. I just wasn't thinking straight—"

She reached out and put her uninjured palm on his cheek. "Brody, it wasn't your fault. It was just an accident, and I'm fine now. Don't look so stricken."

He put his hand over hers and pressed on it, deepening her caress. "I can't help how I look. I *am* stricken. The thought of you being injured and going to the hospital all by yourself is almost more than I can..."

His voice broke, and he took her hand from his face and tucked it into the crook of his arm. "Come on, I'm taking you to the dispensary."

He turned them around and started for the door, practically dragging her along with him.

"I don't need to go to the dispensary," she tried to tell him. "The doctor at the hospital fixed it up."

He pushed open the door and headed for his car. "I want a second opinion, and I'm not going to let you come back to work until the doctor assures me it's safe."

He opened the door on the passenger side and helped her get in, then went around and slid behind the steering wheel.

"I won't be a hazard to the equipment," she assured him. "I work with my right hand. I won't break anything."

Brody had started the engine, but now he turned in his seat to face her and cupped her chin with his hand, raising her face to his. She could have cried at the bleakness that looked out of his eyes.

"You don't have a clue, do you?" he said softly. "Sweetheart, I don't give a hoot in hell about the equipment. It's you I want to keep safe."

He leaned over and planted a quick hard kiss on her mouth. "Now, please, sit back and shut up and stop driving me crazy before I really do wreck the damn car this time."

The dispensary was another flat rectangular building situated just inside the main gate. A nurse cut the bandage off Victoria's hand, and Brody, who had insisted on staying with her, caught his breath as he looked at the angry laceration in the fleshy part of her palm. It was held together with two dark sutures and looked more painful than it actually was.

"It seems to be healing nicely," the nurse said, "but I'll have the doctor examine it just to make sure."

She left the room, and Brody took Victoria's hand in his, careful not to touch the wounded area. "It looks sore," he murmured tenderly. "It's still so raw. You should wait until it's had more time to heal before you come to work."

He raised her hand to his mouth and kissed the soft flesh next to the cut, sending twitches of pleasure all the way up her arm to her shoulder. The door opened just then, and Brody quickly released her and stepped back as the doctor walked in. He flashed Brody a wide smile. "Morning, Brody, what have we got here?"

Brody smiled, too. "Hi, Ray. This is Victoria Chambers. She's cut her hand, and I don't think she should come back to work for a while. What do you think?"

The doctor took Victoria's hand, palm up, and looked at it, then at her. "Good morning, Victoria," he said pleasantly. "How did this happen?"

She recounted last night's experience while he was examining the injury. "The only reason I went to the hospital was because it was bleeding so much," she concluded, "but that stopped when it was stitched together. There's really no reason for me to take off on sick leave. It might slow me up a little, but I can get the job done."

"You work in one of Brody's shops, do you?" he asked.

"No," she admitted. "I used to, but I recently transferred to Electro-Optics."

The doctor looked at Brody and raised one eyebrow. "Oh. So how come Paul Osmond didn't send her up here?"

A quick flush colored Brody's face. "Because I saw her first," he snapped, and made no further effort to explain.

A teasing grin played at the corners of the doctor's mouth. "I see. Well, since you're such a Good Samaritan you can take her down to Paul and tell him she has my permission to come to work, but he's to put her on light duty until I see her again on Tuesday of next week."

The nurse rebandaged Victoria's hand and gave her a card noting the appointment on Tuesday.

Brody chatted with the nurse, but once they left the dispensary he was quiet and didn't speak again until they were back in the maintenance building. Victoria, always finely tuned to his moods, knew that it wasn't a peaceful silence. He was probably upset by the doctor's teasing. After all, he was trying to get rid of her, not make it obvious to everyone at work that he was temporarily attracted to her.

At the foot of the stairs that led to the offices, he stopped and turned to her. "I've got to get back to the office," he said in a coolly professional tone. "Be sure to tell Paul what the doctor said about putting you on light duty. Tell him to call either me or the dispensary if he has any questions."

He started up the stairs, and she'd just turned to continue on to Electro-Optics when he called softly to her. She turned back to see him standing just above her, looking down.

"Vicky, please, for my sake, take care of yourself." There was nothing impersonal about his tone this time. It was filled with concern and bordered on pleading.

She hoped her love for him was shining in her eyes for him to see. "I will." Her voice was husky with emotion. "And Brody, please take care of yourself, too. For my sake."

She choked on the last word and took off on a run for the other end of the building.

* * *

Victoria got through the day with only a slight clumsiness in handling the night-vision devices she'd been working on, but by quitting time her hand throbbed and she was exhausted. Apparently the events of yesterday had taken more of a toll on her than she'd realized. When she got home, she lay down on the couch to rest for a few minutes and promptly fell asleep.

It was a dream. She knew it was because she had wakened enough to feel the nubby texture of the rose-flowered upholstery that covered the sofa on which she was stretched out full length. Also the scent of the crushed rose-petal potpourri she kept in a small crystal jar on the lamp table permeated the scene that was playing out in her twilight sleep.

In the dream she was sitting on the same sofa. And Brody was standing by the window in a replay of yesterday's live action. This time he was pointing his finger at her, and his voice was strident as he thundered, "I won't love you. I won't love you. I won't love you."

The words reverberated inside her head, the different syllables rising and swelling as they ran into one another and bounced off the side of her skull. "I won't love you. I won't love you."

Victoria bolted upright, her eyes wide open and her heart hammering in her chest. She was gasping for breath as momentarily the words continued to batter her. "I won't love you. I won't, I won't, I won't."

That was it! The clamor abruptly ceased, and her mind was once more clear. That's what had bothered her about her memory of Brody's unwavering assertion. He hadn't said "I *don't* love you." He'd said, "I *won't* love you."

Don't meant do not. I do not love you. A fact that cannot be disputed.

But *won't* meant will not. I will not love you. Not a fact but an avowal. An open declaration that he would make every effort not to love her, but also an admission that it was possible he could fail in that effort.

Victoria felt a rush of relief that was more puzzling than comforting. It was such a small difference, and Brody was a strong-willed man. If he vowed he wouldn't love her, she knew he'd make every effort to put her out of his mind, and his life.

But could he put her out of his heart? Few people could turn their feelings on and off at will, and he'd shown in so many ways that he did care about her. Like this morning....

When he saw the bandage on her hand, he didn't shrug and suggest that she probably should have the injury looked at in the dispensary. Instead he'd dropped everything to scoop her up and drive her there, then stayed with her until he was sure the cut wasn't serious and it was all right for her to work. Even though she was no longer assigned to his shop and wasn't his responsibility.

That wasn't the reaction of a busy supervisor to an employee with a minor injury that had already been treated. She was pretty sure he hadn't even considered the fact that he was out of line until the doctor had subtly pointed it out to him.

And then there'd been that kiss. Oh, God, that quick, sweet, passionate kiss.

She sighed and rubbed the sleep from her eyes. So what did that prove other than that he was attracted to her? He'd admitted that much, but he'd also told her loud and clear that he didn't welcome that attraction and didn't intend to act on it.

Brody'd been through hell. He'd earned the right to peace of mind and soul. If she truly loved him, wouldn't she want what was best for him, even if it meant breaking her own heart?

But was putting her out of his life best for him? Or was it one more painful sacrifice he felt he had to make because of a crime that in truth wasn't a crime at all but an accident. An accident he wasn't responsible for.

It had been a long day for Brody, and his nerves were rubbed raw. He'd hardly slept the night before, and he was tired and hungry and his head ached, but even now that he was home he couldn't relax.

At least half a dozen times since his early morning encounter with Vicky he'd had to forcibly restrain himself from going down to Electro-Optics to see how she was. To make sure Paul, her foreman, had given her light duty as instructed, to convince himself the work wasn't too hard for her with just one hand operational, to hover over her like an overprotective lover and keep her safe from further harm.

He muttered a bitter oath and dropped down in the leather recliner in the family room. Why did he find it so difficult to break off this entanglement? He hadn't had any problem with others over the years. Even telling Victoria about his past, a thing he'd never done before, hadn't seemed to revolt her.

But dammit, it should have! She deserved so much better than anything he could give her. He couldn't start another family. He'd had one and lost it. He couldn't let himself care that much again.

Vicky was too young to understand the consequences of being married to a convicted felon. He never knew when his past might catch up with him and be made public again. She had no idea of the slights, the prejudices and the indignities the families of an ex-con could be subjected to, and he was determined that she'd never find out through personal experience.

Again his thoughts turned to the nasty-looking cut on her hand. How had she survived the day? Had it been awfully painful? That damn doctor should have sent her home and told her to take a few days off. Would she be all right tonight all by herself?

His stomach twisted into knots. Maybe he should call her, just to make sure she got home okay. He'd feel better if he could talk to her.

The hell you would, Monroe. If you hear her voice on the phone you'll spend the night in an agony of frustration. Wanting her. Needing her. Go mow the lawn, or scrub the floors, or anything to take your mind off her.

And keep your damn hands off that telephone!

Victoria didn't wake up the next morning until after ten o'clock, but that didn't surprise her. She'd spent most of the night pacing the floor, trying to decide what to do about her star-crossed relationship with Brody Monroe.

She loved him—there was no doubt about that. But he didn't love her. At least if he did, he wouldn't admit it. He did need her, though, and neither of them denied that. He needed her sexually, but he also needed her companionship, her cheerfulness and, yes, even her love.

Although he'd probably never admit it, he was desperate for someone to believe in him in spite of his conviction, to love him without reservation, to accept him for what he was and not for what he thought he should be.

She could give him all that and more, but how long could such a one-sided affair last? Could she really give up all hope of a man to love her unequivocally? Of a secure and respectable marriage? Of children? These things were not frills. They went to the very core of her future, and she couldn't give them up lightly. Not even for Brody.

It had been three o'clock before she finally knew what she had to do and had gone to bed. She'd slept soundly with no more dreams.

Thank goodness it was Saturday and she didn't have to go to work. She did have to see Brody, though, and the sooner the better. If this situation wasn't resolved soon she'd go out of her mind.

She got out of bed, dressed in a blue denim skirt with a matching blouse emblazoned with hand-embroidered Indian designs and ate breakfast. No matter how it turned out, she was going to need all the strength she could muster today.

The drive to Metairie seemed to take forever. Victoria's courage ebbed with every turn of the wheels. Had she made the right decision? How would Brody feel about it? Was she securing her future, or was she throwing it away?

It was twenty minutes after eleven when she pulled up in front of Brody's house. His car wasn't in the driveway, and her stomach roiled. Still, that didn't mean he was gone. It was probably in the garage.

Quickly she got out and walked up to the front door. Her hand shook as she pressed the bell. She could hear it chime inside the house, but there was no sound of footsteps approaching.

She waited for what seemed like an eternity, then pressed it again. Still no footsteps, but within seconds the door opened and Brody stood behind the screen. He was dressed in faded jeans and a gold T-shirt, and his eyes widened with surprise.

"Vicky." It was a cross between a statement and a question.

Her throat felt raspy, and she cleared it. "Good morning, Brody." Her voice was as raspy as her throat. "Do you mind if I come in?"

Chapter Eleven

Brody unfastened the screen door and held it open for Victoria. She walked into the entryway and noticed that it was thickly carpeted. That was why she hadn't heard footsteps from outside.

"Vicky, what are you doing here?" He asked anxiously. "Your hand? Is it—"

"No," she assured him. "It's fine. It hardly even hurts now. I . . . I came to talk to you."

It occurred to her that maybe she was interrupting something. "Is this a bad time? I should have called. I didn't think—"

"It's all right. I was just weeding the flower beds in the backyard." He held up his hands and looked at them. They were covered with damp soil. "Look, why don't you go on into the living room and sit down while I clean up a little?"

"Fine. I . . . I'm sorry to interrupt—"

"Vicky." His tone was firm. "You didn't interrupt anything. I'm happy to see you."

He didn't look happy. He looked...wary, as if he didn't want to hear what she had to say. Was he afraid she'd tell him that she didn't want their relationship to continue? Or was he upset because of the possibility that she did want to be his lover?

"There's coffee in the kitchen," he continued. "I just made it fresh. If you'd like to pour us each a cup, I'll be with you in a minute."

He went down the hall to the left, and she entered the kitchen at the right. It was a narrow oblong room that faced the front street, and though small, it was arranged to make use of every inch of space. The hardwood cabinets were stained a golden brown, and the stove, refrigerator and sink were almond.

The coffeemaker was on the counter, and she found mugs in the cabinet above it. She filled the mugs, added cream to hers and found a small tray to carry the cups on since it was awkward for her to handle a cup in her bandaged left hand.

Instead of going into the living room as Brody had suggested, she turned in the other direction and went down the three steps into the family room. She'd only been here once before, but she'd been greatly impressed by the gardenlike setting. It was so cozy and peaceful with a lived-in look. More inviting than the formal living room.

In the light of day she could now see through the large windows that the backyard looked like a private park with big old shade trees, flowering bushes and beds of colorful flowers. She put the tray on the coffee table and sat down on the beige-and-green-upholstered rattan sofa.

A moment later, Brody's voice calling her name broke the peaceful silence of the house. His tone was strident, and she jumped up and hurried toward the living room. "I'm right here, Brody," she said, as she crossed the dining room to the archway into the living room. "Is something wrong?"

He turned, and she saw a look of relief cross his face before he spoke. "Oh. I'm sorry if I startled you," he said. "I . . . I was afraid you'd changed your mind and left."

It was obvious that his nerves were still strung almost to the breaking point, and she walked over to him and tucked her arm through his. "I wouldn't do that without telling you first," she assured him. "I was in the family room. Do you mind if we talk in there?"

She could feel the tension in him as they walked together back into the other room and sat down on the couch, he at one end and she at the other.

Victoria handed him his mug and noticed that his hand was unsteady when he took it. She really had upset him by coming here so unexpectedly. She'd known how unnerving it had been for him to tell her about his past, and then again when he'd learned of her injury. She should have had the common courtesy to call first and let him set a day and time for this discussion.

Dammit, couldn't she ever do anything right? Why was she such a walking disaster where Brody was concerned? If she could only remember to think before she spoke or acted.

He took a long swallow of his coffee, then put the mug down and turned to her. "What is it you want to talk to me about, Vicky?" His voice was calm now. "I assume it has to do with . . . with what I told you Thursday. Don't feel bad. Just come right out with it. I won't blame you."

She blinked. Blame her? He'd anticipated that she was going to break off their budding relationship. Was that what he really wanted? Or was he just trying to make it easier for her?

Either way, she was going to get it over with as quickly as possible before they both came unstrung. "I . . . I've thought about this a lot. Actually it's been hard to think about anything else, and I know exactly what I'm doing. Really I do, Brody, so if you...if you still want me..." She saw his eyes widen and hastily added, "Strictly in the physical sense, of course." Her voice gave way, and she had to stop to take a breath. "What I'm trying to say is I'd very much like to make love with you, and I won't expect any kind of commitment."

There. It was out, and she realized that her whole body was damp with perspiration. She looked away from him and took deep breaths in an effort to still her pounding heart.

For a moment Brody didn't speak, and when he did it was just one word. "Why?"

Her heart nearly jumped into her throat, and her head raised of its own accord to face him. "Why?" she gasped.

His mouth was set in a tight line. "Yes, why? Why do you want a relationship that will never go anywhere? If you were fifteen years older and divorced with a couple of kids I might understand, but you have your whole life ahead of you. Why do you want to throw away your best years with a middle-aged ex-con who has no future?"

Vicky hadn't expected this reaction, and she had no idea how to respond. She wasn't going to tell him again that she loved him. She'd told him once and gotten it flung back in her face. Besides, he was too sensitive and perceptive not to know how she felt about him.

Since he obviously didn't want to accept her love, she wasn't going to humiliate herself by being a nuisance.

"Brody, I'm over twenty-one and reasonably intelligent," she said, more than a little annoyed. "I was under the impression that you told me about your past so I could make an informed decision as to whether or not I wanted to become intimate with you. Well, I've made it, and I don't know that I have to give you my reasons for it as long as I'm not making any demands on you."

She got up and walked to the window, where she stood with her back to him, looking out.

"But that's the problem, sweetheart," he said gently from behind her. "You will be making demands on me. Demands I cannot fill. You feel sorry for me, don't you?"

She was startled by the sudden change of subject, but she knew what he was getting at. "Of course I feel sorry for you," she said carefully. "Anyone would. You got a raw deal, but that's not why I want to make love with you."

"I think it is." He sounded as cool and reasonable as an attorney arguing a point of law. "You have a very compassionate nature. You can't stand to see anyone hurting, and I've had a lot of pain in my life. You want to kiss it and make it go away."

What he said was true, but she resented his assumption that it was only pity that motivated her. "If I could do that I would and gladly," she said through clenched teeth, "but I'm not silly enough to think that's possible."

She heard him get up and walk across the room to stand just behind her without touching. "But it is possible, and you know it. I can almost forget when I'm holding you, and when you kiss me..." He caught his breath, and it was a moment before he continued. "But pity is a poor basis for a relationship. You don't really believe me when I say I won't love you, marry you, or give you children."

She gasped and opened her mouth to protest, but he didn't give her a chance.

"You think that once the pain is gone I'll change my mind, but it doesn't work that way. My prison record will always haunt me, and I'll never start another family. It wouldn't be fair to you, or to me, or to any children we might have."

Her defenses crumbled, and she knew she'd been defeated. The only thing she could do now was to get out of there before she broke down and made an even bigger fool of herself.

She straightened her shoulders and turned to him, but couldn't bring herself to lock her gaze with his. Instead she looked past him, praying all the while that her voice wouldn't betray her when she spoke. "All right, Brody, I'll go. I can see I was mistaken. You weren't giving me a choice after all. You never had any intention of having an affair with me—you were just trying to get rid of me as kindly as possible."

She took a deep breath as she felt tears behind her eyes and sobs choking her throat. "I guess I'm not very perceptive. You should have come right out and told me to get lost. I'm sorry I've put you through so much. I won't bother you again."

She turned around and walked away with as much dignity as she could manage with tears streaming down her cheeks.

She made it to the dining room before Brody called to her. He didn't raise his voice, but the anguish in it stopped her even more effectively.

"Victoria, you are dearer to me than my own children. I managed to give them up. I don't seem to be able to do that with you. If you still want me, I'll cherish you until you want out of the relationship. Then I'll step aside and let you go. That's the best I can offer you. It's all I have left."

The sob she'd been holding back escaped, and her shoulders shook as she slowly turned around to face him. He was standing in the family room at the bottom of the steps, looking shaken and uncertain, as though he thought she might refuse.

With tears still spilling down her face, she walked slowly toward him. Their gazes clung, and when she got to the arch he put out his hands. Silently she took them and walked down the steps and into his arms.

She buried her face in his chest and let the sobs and the tears take over. He just held her close and let her cry, but she was aware of the jerkiness of his breathing and the effort he was making not to break down with her. Theirs really was an ill-fated union. Was there any possibility that they could be happy together? Victoria hoped so, because she knew there was no chance that she could ever be happy without him.

For a long time they stood wrapped in each other's arms until finally her sobs lessened, her tears dried up and Brody got his own emotions under control.

He reached in his back pocket and handed her a handkerchief. "Here, sweetheart," he said. "Dry your tears, and I give you my solemn vow that I'll never make you cry again."

Victoria knew that was a vow he'd never be able to keep, given the temporary nature he insisted on for their liaison, but she wasn't going to think about that. He'd been right when he said she believed she could change his mind. That's exactly what she was counting on. She'd make him so happy that he wouldn't be able to live without her.

She dried her eyes and blew her nose, then looked up at him with a tentative smile, uncertain of what to do next. "Does this mean we can sit on the sofa and neck?" she blurted out, then reddened when she realized how blunt it sounded.

A grin split Brody's face and he hooted with laughter, breaking the tension. "Damn right it does," he said emphatically, and scooped her up in his arms.

He walked to the couch and lowered her onto it, then sat down beside her and once more cuddled her to him. "This is going to take a little getting used to for me," he said as he rubbed his cheek in her hair. "For so long I've had to stifle all the sharp, urgent impulses that tormented me whenever I was with you. There were times when I didn't think I could stand one more minute of the temptation to touch you, hold you, caress you here—" his hand moved up to cup her breast, making her catch her breath as she felt her nipple harden "—and here..." His hand moved to her hip and kneaded it gently, sending pinpricks of fire to her core. "And especially here." He lowered his head and brushed his lips back and forth across hers until she was lost in a swirl of sensations.

There was no more talking for a while as he planted light kisses at the corners of her mouth, her closed eyelids, her chin, then back to her mouth. This time he claimed it with a mastery that told her his control was not as absolute as it had seemed. She opened to him without hesitation and welcomed his eager, caressing tongue that probed, explored and tasted her as if he couldn't get enough.

Through the haze of pleasure, she remembered that she'd never liked French-kissing with other men, but with Brody it was deeply intimate and wildly exciting. When he broke it off, she moaned with disappointment.

He pressed her cheek against his chest. "You like that, do you?" he asked huskily.

"Oh, yes," she answered with a sigh.

"So do I. Oh, darling, you can't possibly know how much I like that, but we're pretty combustible together and I want to make this last as long as possible."

He gathered her heavy hair to one side and kissed her nape, sending tingles down her spine. "I want to make love to you, not just have sex. Do you understand?"

She could have cried again, but this time from pure happiness. She probably knew what he was saying better than he did, or at least would admit to himself. He was telling her that he cared enough about her to want the commitment of true intimacy, not just quick relief.

Her arms tightened around his neck. "I know what you're saying." She raised her head and nuzzled his throat. "That's what I want, too. I want to hug you, kiss you, stroke you and make you forget all the heartache...."

She felt him shiver as she nibbled on his earlobe. "Victoria," he groaned. "You're no help at all. Just listening to you talk about it is doing unmentionable things to me. How about changing the subject?"

She allowed herself a secret smile as she rubbed her right palm across his shoulder and down his chest to rest against the hard pectoral muscles under his T-shirt. "All right," she agreed. "What do you want to talk about?"

"I don't want to talk about anything," he said raggedly as he unfastened her skirt and tugged at her blouse. "I just want you to keep on doing what you're doing."

"You mean this?" She bit his other ear. "And this?" She fingered the hard nub of his nipple through his thin shirt and felt his heart pound.

The blouse came away from the skirt, and he muttered, "Put up your arms." She did, and he pulled the garment over her head and flung it to the other end of the sofa, then pulled his own shirt off and did the same with it.

She was wearing a blue satin-and-lace low-cut bra, and he traced the pattern of the lace on her flesh above it with his finger, then leaned down and trailed tiny kisses along the same path. The tender roughness of his lips sent a rush of heat that filled her breasts and made them feel heavy and pliable.

"You have the breasts of an earth goddess," Brody murmured, as he ran his hands over her bra. "Intended to nourish and replenish, and so beautiful."

Victoria had always been self-conscious about the fullness of her bosom, but now she was thankful for it. She stroked his back with her fingers. "If they please you then I'm happy."

He raised his glance to hers. "Please me?" He lifted both hands and tangled them in her hair on either side of her head. "Don't you know that everything about you pleases me? The auburn highlights in your dark hair, the sweet innocence that sparkles in you wide green eyes, the lushness of your body, the loving warmth of your disposition, and most of all, that magical smile that is made up of equal parts of sunshine and stardust.''

He leaned forward and kissed her lightly on the lips. ''The one that lifts me out of the deepest pit of despair when it shines on me, and casts me into the darkest inferno when it's withheld because I've hurt you.''

Victoria knew she couldn't speak. The lump in her throat was too big a barrier. Nobody had ever said such touchingly beautiful things to her before. What could she say in return? Nothing. She didn't even try. Instead she tightened her arms around him and took his mouth with hers. She put everything she was feeling but couldn't say into that kiss—her love, her gratitude, her compassion, and hoped he'd understand.

Apparently he did, because without breaking it off, he put one arm under her legs and stood. He didn't miss a step as he carried her through the dining room and living room and down the hall to a bedroom where they tumbled onto the bed, still clinging to each other.

The jolt forced their mouths apart and they both laughed. ''So much for taking it slow and easy,'' Victoria teased.

Brody smoothed the tangled hair back from her face. ''My God, woman, what did you expect?'' His tone was light, but he was trembling. ''I didn't know you were going to set fire to me right there in the family room.''

She stroked the back of his head. ''All I did was cuddle up and kiss you.''

''That's all it took.'' He sounded as awestruck as she felt as he lowered his head and took her nipple in his mouth.

He explored it with his tongue as he moved to lie partially over her with his knee between her thighs, making her stunningly aware of the intensity of his desire for her. She clutched his nude shoulders and arched against him with a flaming need of her own, and when he began to suckle at her breast, she felt the pull all the way to her groin.

She cried his name, and he pulled up her skirt and caressed her bare thigh as he shifted his mouth from one breast to the other. The pleasure he kept building in her was so intense, it bordered on pain. She tried to shift her body further under his, but when she rubbed her hip hard against his throbbing shaft, he groaned and clenched her thigh between both of his as he raised his head.

"We...we'd better get our clothes off," he said, his voice gravelly with frustrated need.

"Yes," she whispered, but made no move to release him from her embrace, or herself from his.

Her questing hands slid slowly over his broad back from his shoulders, downward past the indentation of his waist, and on to the band of his jeans. When her fingers slipped under the denim and started working their way around to the front, he caught his breath and tensed but raised his hips slightly so she could wedge her hand between them and unfasten the button.

She couldn't avoid the turgid bulge that strained beneath his zipper, and when her hand brushed over it he bucked against her and clenched his fists into the fleshy part of her buttocks.

She quickly removed her hand. "I'm sorry," she said anxiously. "Did I hurt you?"

He didn't answer for a moment, but then his hold on her relaxed and he rolled over. "Vicky, my darling," he said breathlessly. "Don't you know anything about men?"

She turned on her side to face him. "Well, I—"

He looked at her and grinned. "Never mind, it's all right. You didn't hurt me. Quite the contrary, it felt so good that I almost..."

He reached for the hand she'd been using and kissed it. "Let's just say my control is severely tested when you put those little hands on the more...uh...sensitive parts of me, and it would be best if we each take off our own clothes."

He sat up and pulled her up beside him. "On second thought, I want to undress you."

He bent over and took off his shoes and socks, then stood and unzipped his jeans, sliding both them and his briefs down his legs to where he could step out of them.

Victoria sat there fascinated. She couldn't tear her gaze away from him. He might be pushing forty, but there wasn't an ounce of flab on him. His shoulders, arms, chest and legs rippled with hard, firm muscles. He could compete with any college man for hunk-of-the-month, and stark naked he was absolutely magnificent!

He touched her shoulder and snapped her out of her trance. She blinked, and realized that she'd been staring.

He smiled as he hunkered down in front of her. "What's the matter, love?" His voice was soft. "Didn't you ever see a naked man before?"

She shook her head. "Never one as beautiful as you."

He looked both startled and pleased as he leaned forward and kissed first one breast, then the other. "I'll treasure that remark always," he murmured, and bent to unbuckle her sandals and remove them.

Putting them aside, he reached around her waist to unzip her skirt. "Now stand up."

She did, and he pulled the skirt and half-slip down to pool in a circle at her feet. Then he reached for her panties, and suddenly she was shy and uncomfortable about removing that last barrier. She burned for his possession, but was embarrassed to have him see her totally naked.

She put her hands over his at her hips. "Brody, please."

He looked up at her, puzzled. "Do you mind if... that is, I'm uncomfortable about stripping completely in front of you."

She looked away and felt the hot flush in her face and neck. Now she'd really done it. He kept saying she was too young for him, and she'd just proved him right. He probably wouldn't even want her now. He preferred his women to be sophisticated.

He caught her hands and tugged gently. "Sit down, Vicky."

She did, making room for him between her knees. He moved his hands to the top of her thighs and rubbed them slowly from the knee to the hip and back again. Her muscles tightened all the way to her waist, and a rush of liquid heat made her squirm.

"If you hadn't told me differently, I'd be convinced you're a virgin," he said tenderly.

Again she felt the blush. "I'm sorry. I know I'm behaving like a ninny...."

He leaned forward to touch his mouth to her navel, sending ripples of desire through her. "Don't ever apologize for being innocent. It just makes you that much more dear to me."

He laid his cheek against her silk-covered stomach. "You're a sweet and loving enigma. A study in contradictions."

His thumbs were stroking up and down the inside of her thighs as he talked, concentrating her attention on the turmoil deep in her most intimate recesses.

"There are times when you seem to know just what to say to me, where to touch me, how to look at me, to drive me right over the edge," he continued, his voice thick with passion. "Then at other times such as now, you're so charmingly unsophisticated and naive...."

He started trailing kisses down her belly. Spasms of fire rocked her, and she grabbed him on either side of his head and stiffened. "Brody!" It was a cry of both resistance and pleasure. "Oh, Brody, please..."

He stopped his descent but continued the kisses. "Please what?" His tone was blurred with desire. "Please stop? Or please continue?"

She clutched her hands in his hair. "I don't know," she moaned. "Just do something. I think I'm going to…to fly apart."

She was in too much of a fog to know how he managed it, but then they were both on the bed and he was hovering over her. She felt his hands stripping off her panties, exposing the area that was now so eager to welcome him.

He kissed her, hard, but then raised his head and looked at her. "You're not protected, are you?"

She shook her head, incapable at this point of worrying about whether she was or not. She wanted Brody's babies.

"I'll take care of it," he said, and moved away from her.

He returned a few seconds later and lay down beside her, then rolled to his side and ran his hand gently across her stomach. Her muscles clenched, and he leaned down to follow his hand with his mouth.

She writhed under his nibbling kisses, and his hand lowered to cup the throbbing, wet heat of her. His fingers probed and tantalized until she dug her nails into his back and cried out with overwhelming need.

Then there was no more waiting as Brody positioned himself over her and joined their mouths and then their bodies in a union that melded them together in a rocking rhythm surpassing anything Victoria had ever imagined.

She locked her legs around his undulating hips and gave herself up to the convulsive cadence of his thrusts that drove deeper and deeper until they released her earthly ties and sent her rocketing to the heavens. It was like the fourth of July, but she wasn't *watching* the fireworks, she *was* the fireworks exploding into myriad pieces of color and design.

For a long time afterward they clung to each other, united in both body and soul, and hovering between heaven and earth. The celestial sphere where Brody had taken her was magical, a fantasy of sensations too rapturous to describe, too powerful to deny.

When he finally lifted himself off her, she clutched at him in protest. He put his arms around her and rolled over so that he was on his back and she was lying on top of him. "I'm too heavy for you, sweetheart," he said anxiously. "I don't want to crush you. I . . . I didn't mean to be rough. I've never lost control like that before. If I've hurt you I—"

She snuggled against him and laid her cheek on his chest. His heart was still pounding. "You didn't hurt me," she assured him. "It was—" She rubbed her thumb across his nipple. "It was wonderful beyond description. I didn't know it could be like that."

His hands roamed over her buttocks. "Neither did I," he murmured huskily. "Believe me, Vicky, neither did I. I suspect that you've bewitched me. I don't know any other way to explain the exhilaration. . . ."

She kissed the hollow at the base of his throat. "Don't even try. It's like attempting to explain a miracle. Let's just be thankful for it."

His arms tightened around her. "I'm thankful for you. I don't know whether you were sent to me as a punishment or a reward, but with rewards like what just happened I can survive a lot of punishment."

"You've more than atoned for any sins you may have committed, my darling," she assured him. "From now on I'm going to make up to you for all the sins committed *against* you."

She twined her legs with his and covered one flat nipple with her mouth. She caressed it with her tongue, then repeated the fondling on the other side. "Do you think we can do that again soon?" she asked lovingly as her unbandaged hand skimmed down his side to his hip.

"Slide down a few inches and find out for yourself."

She did, and he was once more rigid. "You're going to make an old man of me before I'm forty," he moaned.

"I'll do my best," she promised.

He chuckled. "This time we'll make it last."

She sat up and straddled his hips. "Don't count on it."

It was a glorious weekend; they spent most of it in bed. And by Sunday evening they were both sated and exhausted as Victoria dressed to go home. They knew they'd never make it to work the next morning if she spent the night with him again, but she hated the thought of leaving him. For the past thirty hours he'd managed to put aside the cloying shadows of the past and had been truly and completely happy. It showed on his face, in his voice, his laugh, the way he touched her, kissed her, loved her.

She wanted him to stay that way, happy and content, loving her with his body for now, but surely later with his heart, too.

Victoria and Brody were together in his bedroom, he sitting on the edge of the bed tying his shoes and she standing at the big mirror over the double chest of drawers and combing her hair, when the phone rang. Brody reached for it on the bedside table. "Hello," he said. Then after a pause, "Ursula? Is something the matter?"

The change in his tone from mild interest to concern caused Victoria to look up. She could see him behind her in the mirror. He'd snapped to attention and she could feel the tension in him from across the room as he listened.

"Oh, no," he said. "When...? But you told me she was in good health."

Victoria put down her comb and turned around. Had something happened to somebody in one of Brody's shops?

After a rather lengthy pause he spoke again. "Yes, I'm sure he is, but how are they taking it? Who's caring for them?"

The anxiety in Brody's voice transmitted itself to Victoria as he stood up. This wasn't just a work-related problem, but what else could it be?

She wondered if she should leave the room, give him privacy, but before she could act, he spoke once more. "Look, Ursula, I'll catch the first flight out of here to La Guardia, but don't tell anyone you've talked to me or that I'm coming. I don't want that old man pulling any more of his wiliness on me. I'll be there sometime tomorrow, and thanks for calling."

Brody put down the phone and just stood there with his back to her, staring off into space.

Victoria was thoroughly alarmed. She crossed the room and put her hand on his arm. "Brody. What's the matter? Where are you going?"

He turned to look at her, and all signs of happiness were erased. He had a dazed look about him. His face was colorless, the lines of strain had returned to the corners of his eyes and mouth and he looked at her with eyes dulled with shock. "That was Ursula Hildebrand, the private investigator who reports to me on my children's well-being. She told me Laura Verner, their grandmother who's been raising them, died yesterday afternoon.

"I have to go to Verner's Crossing and get my daughters."

Chapter Twelve

Victoria arrived at the New Orleans International Airport more than an hour early to meet Brody's incoming flight, then had all that time to kill before he got in.

It had been five days since that telephone call had blown away their sensual fog of happiness and sent him scurrying halfway across the country to reclaim the daughters he'd given up over eight years ago. At least that had been his intention, but when he'd called her for the first time last night to ask her to meet his plane, he's said he'd be arriving alone.

She was an emotional wreck. Brody had been too distraught and too busy before he left to give her more than sketchy details about what had happened. It seemed that the investigator he employed had learned of Laura Verner's death by reading it in the newspaper the day after she'd died at age sixty-two of a heart attack. Ursula then investigated and found that Mrs. Verner had been taken to the hospital early Saturday morning and died before noon.

The funeral had been scheduled for Wednesday, and now it was Friday afternoon and Brody was finally coming home.

Victoria had stayed close to the phone after work all week, expecting him to call. It wasn't until last night that he did, and then he'd been too hurried and out of sorts to say more than that he was returning without the girls late the next afternoon and he'd tell her all about it then.

What had happened? Most important, how had he been received by his daughters? Were they glad to see him? And what about Mr. Verner? Brody had told her that his father-in-law was in his early seventies. Surely he'd be willing to give up his granddaughters now that his wife was dead and Brody was well able to take care of them. Or was he still determined to fight Brody every step of the way?

New Orleans International was a large airport, and Vicky walked down numerous corridors and past various shops before she finally found the gate Brody's plane was arriving at.

She found a seat and opened a book she'd brought with her, but she couldn't keep her mind on what she was reading. No one here knew that Brody had children. If he took custody now, how would he explain their absence after all these years without also going public about the time he served in prison?

Also, what about Adriana and Patty? How would they react to such a drastic change in their lives? Wouldn't being uprooted from the town where they'd been born and raised, and transplanted across the country to a city the size of New Orleans, be a wrenching experience for them? Especially when they were still trying to cope with the death of their grandmother.

And, most frightening for Victoria, how would the presence of two teenage girls affect Brody's new and tenuous relationship with her? Obviously she'd be the one who was expendable if there were any problems.

She closed her book and stood up, too nervous to sit still. She knew she was being selfish. She should be delighted that Brody might finally be reunited with his family. Hadn't she assured him that she was mature enough to handle any difficulty his past might present?

But, dammit, she'd expected to have more time alone with him before she had to confront those obstacles.

She paced up, down and around the aisles between the chairs in the big open waiting area until finally Brody's plane taxied up to the gate and unloaded its passengers. Victoria spotted him as he came up the ramp carrying his suitcase and looking haggard and rumpled.

He saw her and quickened his pace. When he reached her, he dropped his case and swept her into his arms with a hug that nearly took her breath away. "God, but it's good to see you," he muttered, as the other disembarking passengers smiled and walked around them. "It's like coming out of the dark into the sunshine."

He kissed her, quickly but thoroughly, then picked up his luggage and with his other arm around her waist hurried her out of the airport and to the parking lot. Her anxiety vanished. He was obviously glad to be back with her. For now that was enough.

On the way to Brody's house they talked of inconsequential matters—his flights, the weather, what was happening at work—but when they got home, he closed the front door behind them and again took her in his arms. She clasped him around the waist and lifted her face for his kiss.

It was warm and eager, and told her more eloquently than words how much he'd missed her, but he made no attempt to deepen it. He seemed content for now just to hold her and let her caresses work their magic on his battered psyche. That was fine with her. It was a sign that he didn't just need her for sex.

With their arms still around each other they walked into the family room and sat down on the couch. She snuggled into his embrace and he rained kisses on her face and throat, but his hands roamed only to her hip and her breast and settled there.

"I'm so glad you're home," she said with a sigh.

"So am I, love." The relief in his tone was genuine. "But I have to go back before long. I'm going to have to fight Ken for custody of my daughters."

"But why?" she protested. "He's too old to raise two young girls all by himself."

Brody swore. "Don't tell him that. He says I'm not fit to raise my own children and he'll prove it in court if I try to take them away from him."

"Oh, darling," she murmured, and cuddled closer. "I'm so sorry, but what about the girls? Surely they're old enough to decide where they want to live."

He nodded. "They are, and they want to stay with him. Neither of them wants anything to do with me...."

His voice broke, and her fear for her own future if Brody's children came to live with him melted in the heat of anger directed at Brody's vindictive father-in-law and ungrateful kids. "I don't understand. Surely they'd rather be with their own father—"

"Honey, they don't recognize me as their father." Brody had regained control of his voice. "Patty was only five when I was sent away. She hardly remembers me, and Adriana was old enough to think of me as the father who deserted her."

Victoria bolted upright. "You didn't! You—"

"Of course I didn't," Brody agreed, "but she wasn't mature enough at the time to make the distinction between *going* away and *being sent* away, and neither of her grandparents ever bothered to point out the difference. Also, of course, both girls are certain that I killed their mother in that accident."

"That's vile!" Vicky cried, incensed by the Verners' treachery. "Those people had no right to turn your children against you."

Brody pulled her back into his arms and cradled her against him. "Victoria, my beautiful and volatile defender. I absolutely adore you, do you know that?" His voice was thick with emotion. "You're the rock that keeps me from drowning in despair, the whip that drives me when I'm tempted to give up, and the life-giving heat that warms me and gives me a reason to go on. Without you, I..." He buried his face in her shoulder and didn't attempt to finish.

Victoria held him and stroked his nape. She was utterly speechless. He'd taken her totally off guard with his beautiful declaration of...of what? Like? Certainly. She knew he cared a great deal for her. Adoration? That's what he'd said. *I absolutely adore you.* But *adore* could mean several things. Spiritual love for a deity? That hardly seemed likely. The exaggerated expression of care for an inanimate object such as, "I adore pizza"? She hoped not.

Or had he meant what she wanted him to mean? *I love you.* Unfortunately she knew Brody well enough to know that if that's what he'd wanted to say he'd have said it. He knew that's what she wanted to hear.

She felt so ungrateful, so greedy, to be analyzing the tender feelings he'd admitted having for her. If only she could just accept them and be content, but for both their sakes she had to assume he meant that she was very special to him, and to be happy with that.

"I adore you, too," she murmured, and meant exactly what she said. She loved him more than she loved herself. More than she'd ever love anyone else. Surely that must qualify as adore.

He shivered and nuzzled the side of her neck, then raised his head and rested his chin in her hair. "I consulted an

attorney in Albany, New York, who's going to represent
me," he said, picking up their conversation once more.

"Why Albany?" she asked. "Is that where your suit will
be heard?"

"No, that'll take place in Verner's Crossing, but the
lawyers there are under the spell, or the thumb, of the
Verner family and I doubt that any of them would be im-
partial enough to really go against Ken. Especially now
that he's a bereaved widower and everyone feels sorry for
him."

"What about the lawyer who defended you at the
trial?"

"Norman Jackson," he said bitterly. "He's a good ex-
ample of what I was saying. He and I went to school together, and his parents weren't much better off than mine.
He really had to struggle for his education, and I thought
he'd be sympathetic to my plight."

Brody paused for a moment. "Actually, he was. I think
he believed my story, but he was also tired of grubbing for
everything he got. He wanted to make it big, fast, and he
knew that getting me off when it was well-known about
town that Ken Verner expected a guilty verdict would get
him stuck in a rut he'd never get out of. Let's just say he
didn't work very hard in my defense."

Victoria was beginning to understand that right or
wrong had little to do with the Godfather of Verner's
Crossing, but she couldn't bite back another protest.
"That's malpractice. He could have been disbarred."

Brody shrugged. "He didn't actually do anything
wrong. He just wasn't as aggressive as he should have
been. I'm not going to give him another chance to earn
Ken's gratitude at my expense."

She rubbed her palm over his chest, loving the feel of his
muscles under his shirt. "What happened when you got
there?"

His hand on her hip caressed her gently. "I rented a car at La Guardia Airport and drove to Verner's Crossing, then rented a room at a motel and went to the Verner house. My intention was to offer my condolences, introduce myself to my daughters and wait until after the funeral to talk to Ken about my plans for their future, but he was furious."

Victoria could hear the agitation in Brody's voice. "He threatened to have me thrown out. I told him if he did I'd get a court order forcing him to let me visit my own children."

Brody chuckled, but it was a hollow sound. "I don't know whether I could have done that or not, but he obviously thought I could so he backed down and let me stay. Adriana and Patty didn't even know me, and when I told them who I was, they..." He stopped to clear his throat. "They refused to talk to me."

Again righteous indignation brought Victoria up straight. "That's not fair! They could at least have given you a chance—"

"Honey, don't blame them. They've never heard my side of the story, and it's been eight years since they've seen me. Also, they were in mourning for their grandmother. It was like losing their mother all over again. It was the worst possible time for me to come barging into their lives."

Barge into their lives, indeed! It was all Victoria could do not to tell him just what she thought of his precious daughters, but she knew he was right. It wasn't their fault. They'd been brainwashed by their grandparents, but it made her furious to know they'd hurt him so callously.

She shut her eyes and settled back into his embrace, then changed the subject. "Have you filed for custody yet?"

He stroked his fingers through her hair. "Yes. I spent that afternoon at the house even though I wasn't welcome. I didn't want the girls to think I was running out on them again. The next day I drove to Albany and consulted an attorney who is well-known and respected in the area for his defense of the underdog. I checked, and he's still winning most of his cases.

"He seemed impressed with my story, and said he'd look into it and let me know in a day or two. On Thursday he called to say he thought I should have my children and he'd represent me. He filed the papers this morning, and asked for an early court date. He'll let me know when he gets it."

Victoria dropped her hand to Brody's thigh. "Then he thinks you have a good chance of winning?"

Brody wanted his daughters badly, and she could understand that, but what would happen if he had to force them to live with him against their will? Wouldn't that be more painful for him than leaving them where they were?

He covered her hand with his and pressed it into the firm flesh through his slacks, then held it there. "He's optimistic, but by no means certain. For one thing, the suit will be heard by a judge in Verner's Crossing which is solidly Verner territory. For another, when I got out of prison I did give the kids up...."

"But he pressured you, and you had no way to care for them!" She tried to pull away, but he held her against him.

"That's true," he admitted, "but I never petitioned to get them back. At the time I thought I was doing what was best for them, but now..."

"Doesn't the fact that their grandmother is no longer alive to care for them mean anything?"

He moved her hand up and down his leg. "Not really. Don't forget, I don't have a wife, either. No matter which of us gets them, there'll be no woman in the home."

He stopped moving her hand and removed his. "The biggest obstacle is the girls themselves. They don't want to come to New Orleans and live with me, and they'll tell the judge that."

He looked and sounded so discouraged that it nearly broke Victoria's heart. Brody was the most wonderful man she'd ever met, kind and gentle, with a brilliant mind and the guts to not only survive all the terrible things that had happened to him, but to start from nothing and make a new life for himself and his children.

Only, now his kids had rejected him without even taking the time and effort to get to know him. Where did they get off thinking they were too good to live with their own father?

Victoria had to bite her lip to keep from saying what she was thinking. It wouldn't help Brody, and would only make him resent her for daring to suspect that they were self-centered snobs.

There was only one way she knew of to distract him and make him happy for a little while. If that made her a convenient sex object rather than a loving soul mate then she'd risk it. Right now he needed her as a temporary escape from an unbearable impasse, and she wasn't going to let him down the way his own family had.

She began kneading his thigh with one hand while reaching for his top shirt button with the other. "It seems like you've been gone forever," she murmured huskily, "and I've missed you like crazy."

She moved her caressing hand ever so slowly up his leg as she lowered the other hand to the second button. The muscles in his thigh jumped, and she felt his heartbeat speed up as she unbuttoned the third one.

"Is there any chance we could take up where we left off last Sunday?" she asked, her tone low and seductive as she kissed him on the throat just before he put his hands under her arms and lifted her onto his lap.

He hugged her close and buried his face in the side of her neck. "Like I said." His voice was rough with passion. "I absolutely adore you."

Their lovemaking started gently with sweet kisses and tender caresses, then built slowly through teasing, to eager, to erotic, and finally culminated in an explosion of passion too long suppressed that rocked them and left them gasping.

It was in the middle of the night that Victoria woke in Brody's bed, cradled in his arms, and knew what it was she could do to help him get custody of his daughters. It was as clear to her as if she'd been lying awake wrestling with the problem for hours.

It was the obvious solution. She was surprised that it hadn't occurred to him. Or maybe it had and he'd been reluctant to mention it. She knew it wasn't something he'd accept easily, but it would give him a big advantage over Ken Verner. At first it might seem like a sacrifice, but Victoria was certain that he'd recognize it as a blessing in the long run.

She wanted to wake Brody and tell him about it, but he was sleeping so peacefully that she didn't have the heart to disturb him. He'd admitted that he'd had trouble sleeping while he was gone, and she'd seen the signs of exhaustion in his face. He'd been through such an emotionally brutal experience that she wasn't going to interrupt his rest to plunge him back into it.

They woke early Saturday morning, but it was nearly noon before they finally got out of bed, sated but not exactly rested. "I don't think I'll ever get enough of you," Brody murmured as he came up behind her when she stood at the stove scrambling eggs, and cupped her breasts with his hands while he nibbled her neck.

"Brody," she said with a throaty giggle. "You're insatiable."

"Only with you, sweetheart," he acknowledged, and nibbled on her ear.

She was as insatiable for him as he was for her, but they'd just gotten dressed, and besides, she was eager to tell him about her solution to one of his problems.

"You'd better go sit down at the table and let me feed you," she teased, "or you're going to run out of steam."

He laughed happily and pressed his groin into her bottom. "As you can see there's no danger of me running out of much of anything."

She turned her head and accepted his quick kiss. "Okay, buddy boy, that does it," she said airily. "No more hanky-panky until you eat your bacon and eggs and then take a trip to the nearest pharmacy."

"Yes, ma'am," he muttered, and grinned as he swatted her playfully on the derriere before taking his place at the table.

While Brody had been gone, Victoria had gotten a prescription for birth control pills, but the doctor warned her it could be a couple of weeks before she was completely safe and advised her to use double protection until then.

She waited until they were having their second cup of coffee before she broached the subject of his custody suit. She hated to drag him back into that quagmire, but surely once he heard her solution he'd be greatly relieved.

Putting down her mug she cleared her throat. "Brody..." she began, and realized her stomach was filled with butterflies. "I think I've discovered a way to give you a better chance of winning your custody suit."

He stopped with his cup halfway to his mouth and stared at her, his smile gradually dimming. "Oh?"

The butterflies were increasing. "Yes. You could... That is, why don't you ... why don't you get married?"

The last five words all ran together, but he heard her loud and clear. He slammed the mug down so hard on the table that the coffee sloshed over the sides, but he didn't seem to notice. "Married?" There was a dangerous edge to his voice.

This was going to be more difficult than she'd expected. "Yes. We could get married. Then you'd have a wife—"

"I told you before, that's not an option." His tone left no room for argument, but Victoria wasn't easily dissuaded.

She picked up her napkin and mopped at the spilled coffee. "I know, but now things have changed," she insisted. "Think about it, darling. If you had a wife you could prove that you can give the girls a normal, stable family life with both a father and a mother."

"A *mother!*" he roared. "I couldn't introduce you as Adriana's stepmother. You're only eight years older than she is!"

Victoria winced but didn't back down. "So what? The woman who's been raising her was almost fifty years older than she was. Why am I too young if Laura Verner wasn't too old?"

"She was too old, dammit, but I didn't have a choice then." He picked up his own napkin. "Here, let me do that," he said, and finished wiping up the coffee, then got up and walked over to toss both soiled napkins into the sink. "I made it clear to you before we ever made love that I wasn't going to marry again. You said you understood, so why are you bringing it up now?"

Victoria had expected some resistance, but she hadn't thought he'd be so dead set against it. "That was before you knew you'd be fighting for custody of your children," she reminded him. "You said yourself that you'd have a better chance of getting them if you were married."

He looked at her with exasperation. "That's not what I said. I said neither Ken nor I had a woman in our lives who could fill the role of mother so we were even on that score."

She had to admit that his version was closer to the truth of what he'd said than hers was. "But surely you'll agree that being married would be a plus in your favor. Think of it as a . . . a business arrangement. You need a wife, your children need a mother and I... Well, I'm applying for the job."

She couldn't believe she was doing this. Actually bargaining with a man to marry her. What had happened to her independent spirit? Where was her pride? Her dignity?

She hung her head and swallowed the knot in her throat that had formed too late to keep her from speaking out and making a fool of herself. There was no sound from Brody. He was probably as embarrassed as she was.

Then she felt his fist under her chin lifting her face up to him. She tried to resist, but he put his hands on either side of her head and tilted it so she was looking at him. His expression was grim, but his eyes were filled with tenderness. "Vicky, are you deliberately trying to drive me straight out of my mind?"

His voice was hoarse, and his fingers tangled in her hair as his thumbs rubbed her temples. "Do you honestly think I'd let you *sell* yourself to me in marriage just so I could get my children back?"

She blinked and ran the tip of her tongue over her dry lips. "Well, I—"

He leaned down and kissed her mouth. "No, don't say it. I may be a bastard, but even I wouldn't do a thing like that."

He reached down and swept her up in his arms and carried her to the living room, where he sat down in the rocking chair with her on his lap. "Now let's get one thing straight," he said, as she settled into his embrace. "I'm not going to involve you in this fight for my kids. It's my problem and I'll handle it."

Victoria felt sick. "I see," she said tightly. "You want me in your bed but not in your life."

Brody swore and sat her up so he could look at her. "That's a low blow, and I'm not going to respond to it. Don't play games with me, Victoria, I'm an expert at it. I survived three years in prison mostly by my wits. And don't think I'm going to be moved by your implication that I'm using you. You're not simpleminded. You understood my position before we ever got intimately involved, and I'm not going to defend it now.''

Victoria realized that she'd made a whopping blunder. She never should have brought up the subject of marriage. At least not until she'd had time to plan how she'd present it to him. Now he was furious with her, and she may have blown their whole relationship.

Brody moved her off his lap, then rose and walked across the room to the wall of windows that looked out over the oblong covered porch with its thickly padded patio lounges and white lacy iron tables.

He stood with his back to her as he spoke, and his voice was cold and biting. ''If marriage is what you want, then you never should have gotten involved with me. I told you that. I even put myself through hell explaining why I wouldn't marry you. You said you'd accept me on my terms, and I believed you. I don't know why you'd want to be married to me, but if you thought you could change my mind you're badly mistaken.''

The finality of his tone sent a chill through Vicky, and she shivered in apprehension. Why did she cling to this one-sided romance? Brody didn't really need her. Now was the time to get out of it. He wouldn't mind. He couldn't have opened the door wider for her departure without actually kicking her out.

She couldn't take much more of this emotional roller coaster ride—up in the stars one minute, down in the pits the next. It was too dizzying. She couldn't get her balance between the two extremes.

She took a deep breath and willed her voice not to break. ''I'm sorry. I didn't mean to upset you. I wasn't playing games or trying to force you into anything. It seemed like a way to gain an advantage over Mr. Verner, but obviously you don't think so."

She took a few steps in the direction of the bedrooms. "Now, I really must be getting home."

Quickening her pace, she hurried into the bedroom and picked up her purse. When she got back to the entryway, Brody was standing there looking shaken.

"Vicky." He put out his hand to her but she moved back, and he dropped it to his side. "Don't leave. I thought you were going to spend the weekend."

She shook her head. "I don't think so. Please let me by."

Quietly he moved away so she could get to the door without touching him. She opened it and walked out, then hastened down the walk to the curb, got in her car and drove away without looking back.

Brody leaned against the wall and wondered how much more of this punishment he could take. Not that he didn't deserve it this time. He'd beat the hell out of any man who treated one of his daughters the way he'd just treated Vicky.

Why had he overreacted so violently? She was only trying to help.

He pushed himself away from the wall and walked dejectedly through the living room and out the sliding glass door onto the porch. Sitting down on the edge of one of the chairs, he propped his elbows on his knees and lowered his head to run his fingers through his hair.

He knew exactly why he'd overreacted to Victoria's suggestion. It was because her willingness to marry him even knowing of his prison record was too damn attractive to resist. If he hadn't rejected it violently he'd have caved in and begged her to be his wife. She'd given him the perfect excuse with which to soothe his conscience. After all, what caring father wouldn't grab at any straw to get custody of his children?

And what kind of a bastard would he be if he married this naive young woman who had become dearer to him than his own happiness, and doomed her to being the wife of an ex-convict? She had no idea what she'd be getting herself into. She needed a man nearer her own age with a flawless background who would give her children.

Not someone who was always looking over his shoulder, wondering when his grim past was going to catch up with him and bring disgrace to everyone close to him.

Chapter Thirteen

After leaving Brody's house, Victoria couldn't bring herself to go home. She knew if she did, she'd be constantly tuned for the sound of the telephone or the doorbell, and would alternate between relief and despair when neither rang. Instead she spent the afternoon shopping at the huge new mall on the outskirts of Metairie and tried not to think.

She finally understood what Brody had been telling her all along. She was a cute kid, a loving companion and great in bed, but that was all he wanted from her. God forbid that he'd have to introduce her to his children, or worse, the judge presiding over his custody case.

She was a potent distraction, for which he was grateful, but certainly not the type to help raise his daughters.

Well, what had she expected? She'd been behaving like a love-struck adolescent ever since they'd met, melting all over him and practically begging him to make love to her.

No wonder he thought she was too young to be a stepmother to his daughters. She was, if not too young then certainly too immature, and it was time she grew up and started acting like an adult.

She bought two pairs of hideously expensive designer jeans that she didn't need, three breezy summer dresses that were too dressy to wear to work, and a bright green sweatshirt with a sequined Mardi Gras mask on the front, a garment designed strictly for the tourist trade. She signed the sales slips without looking at them, and knew she'd hate herself when the bills came in.

Oh, well, the mindless activity had probably saved her sanity, and she'd start acting like an adult tomorrow.

On her way home she stopped and picked up a double cheeseburger and a large order of fries. It was dinnertime and she was in no mood to cook. Or to eat, either, for that matter, but she was going to choke down every bit even if it killed her. She was through letting Brody affect her appetite.

Victoria saw the blue Oldsmobile parked in front of her house as soon as she turned onto her street. Brody's car! Her heart started pounding before she could remind it that he wasn't going to affect her that way anymore.

What was he doing here? How long had he been waiting? Surely he'd said all he had to say to her this morning.

She drove past him and turned into her driveway and parked. Now what? Dammit, he'd given her an unmistakable out and she'd taken it, so why was he sitting in his car in front of her house now?

She put her hand to her chest hoping her heart would get the message and slow down, but it paid no attention to her and kept right on thumping joyously away. Well, she'd deal with it later; now she was going to be coolly polite but nothing more.

She got out of the car and saw him coming toward her with her overnight suitcase in his hand. Her foolish fantasies died a very painful death.

So that's why he was here. In her agitation earlier she'd left without taking her things, and he didn't want her to have an excuse to come back after them.

"Hello, Brody," she said, when he came up to her while she was leaning into the car gathering up her numerous packages. She was pleased to note that none of her inner turmoil sounded in her voice. "What are you doing here? How long have you been waiting?"

He didn't attempt to touch her, nor did he hand her the case. "Not long. Here, let me help you."

"I can manage," she said, as she slung the long strap of her purse onto her shoulder and picked up the last sack. "You can carry the suitcase to the house if you don't mind."

He followed along behind her as she led the way to the door.

Without asking, he took the keys from her and opened the door, then stood back to let her precede him. He shut the door behind them, and she turned to face him.

His expression was carefully neutral, but she saw the regret in his eyes and steeled herself against it. "Thank you for bringing my suitcase back," she said formally. "I'm afraid I forgot it when I left. I'm sorry you had to come all the way over here to deliver it. If you'll just set it down on the floor I'll get it after I've dumped these packages in the bedroom."

"I didn't come to bring it back," he said firmly. "I brought it along so you'd open the door and let me in. I want to talk to you, but first let's get rid of this stuff." He walked away from her toward the back of the house where the bedrooms were. She didn't want to be in her bedroom alone with him, but he left her no choice but to follow.

"I . . . I think we said all we had to say to each other this morning." She hoped her tone wouldn't betray her surprise.

"Not quite," he answered softly as he set her small piece of luggage on the floor by the dresser, then reached out to relieve her of some of the numerous packages that were threatening to spill out of her arms. He put them on the bed. She dumped the others with them, retaining the white one with the food in it, then turned and hurried into the kitchen.

"If you're going to stay awhile then you'd better have something to eat." She opened the cupboard door and took down two small plates, all the while berating herself for her folly.

Victoria Chambers, you're a sniveling masochist! Why else would you have this compulsion to feed the man who bites you? It's true he lost weight during the week he spent in Verner's Crossing, and he looks gaunt and pale, but that's not your problem. He's a grown man. He knows enough to eat when he's hungry. Just hand him the sack, if it'll make you feel better, and tell him to go home.

Ignoring her own good advice, she reached into the sack and put the hamburger and fries on one plate, then handed it to him. "Here," she said gruffly, "go sit at the table and eat this while it's still warm."

"Vicky, I can't eat your dinner," he insisted.

"It's all right, I'll fix myself a tuna sandwich. I'd rather have that anyway."

She reached into the sack again and brought out a large plastic cup with a lid on it. "You can have the cola, too," she said, and handed it to him. "I'll have milk."

She noticed that his expression had changed from neutral to shuttered, as though something had shattered inside of him and he was determined not to let it show on his face.

Without thinking, she reached up and caressed his cheek. "Brody? What's the matter? What did I say...?"

He didn't answer, just silently set the plate and glass on the counter, then reached out and drew her into the circle of his arms and stood there holding her.

She relaxed against him and knew that trying to resist was a waste of energy. They were joined at the heart whether they wanted to be or not. They could only get so far apart before they snapped back together like a rubber band or a yo-yo.

After a few minutes Brody rubbed his cheek against hers. "I've never had anyone take care of me before," he said softly. "My mother was too swamped with trying to keep a roof over our heads and food on the table, my dad was too drunk to notice me and my wife was too busy with the children to give me much attention. When you do things like making sure I eat and get enough sleep and kiss away my hurts, it... it overwhelms me."

Victoria thought of her own loving, care-giving parents and could have cried for all Brody had missed, but before she could say anything, he continued. "I carried on this morning like an insensitive jerk and drove you away, and now when I've come to apologize and beg your forgiveness you're giving me your dinner, even before I've told you why I'm here, because you don't want me to be hungry."

"What happened this morning was my fault," she said. "You're right. You made it very clear that marriage was out of the question. It was wrong of me to suggest such a thing. You're also right when you said that the custody of your children is none of my business...."

He tensed. "That's not what I said...."

She put her hand to his mouth. "No, please, let me finish. I've always been an extremely determined person, even as a child. If I want something I go after it, and I usually get it. I guess that gave me an exaggerated sense of power, but I have to admit that I'm way out of my league with you."

A burst of nervous laughter broke through her tenuous control. "I probably have been playing games with you. One upmanship, I believe it's called. The harder you resisted me, the stronger I came on to you."

"That's not true. . . ."

Again she silenced him. "You're a bright man, Brody. You saw right through me to the spoiled, self-centered brat I've become. I can see why you don't want me as a stepmother to your daughters, but you're not totally blameless. You keep sending me mixed signals. Like today. Your words were kind but the message was clear. *You're welcome in my bed, but don't expect me to share any other part of my life!*"

"Vicky, no!"

"Yes!" She was as vehement as he was as she pulled herself out of his arms and stood facing him. "But there are limits to what I'll do to get my own way. I won't be any man's personal whore—not even yours—so I left assuming everything was over between us. Now I come home and find you waiting on my doorstep wanting absolution."

His face was chalky as he stared at her. "You're an expert at pulling my strings, Brody. You coldly push me away one moment, and melt me with sweet words and hot kisses the next. You keep me constantly off balance. I don't know what you want of me, and I don't think you do, either."

She closed her eyes and slumped against the cabinet, her emotions shredded and her energy depleted. That should do it. She'd set him free. He could leave without feeling guilty about walking away from her, and she could try to get on with her life without him.

She listened for his footsteps as he walked toward the door. Instead she felt his hands clasp her upper arms, and her eyes flew open. He was looking at her with a mixture of disbelief and tenderness. "You're wrong," he said softly. "Wrong about everything, but especially when you say I don't know what I want of you."

He moved his hands gently up and down her arms. "I know exactly what I want of you, my darling. I want you to marry me."

Victoria blinked, and felt shock waves all the way to her toes. Good Lord, the man must be intent on pushing her over the edge. Or maybe she was hallucinating and only hearing what she wanted to hear.

No, that couldn't be it because she didn't want him to propose marriage just because he knew he'd hurt her feelings and wanted to atone. The only answer she could think of to give him was the one he'd given her when she'd told him she wanted an intimate relationship with him even though he'd been in prison and wouldn't marry her.

"Why?" The word came out garbled, and she cleared her throat and tried again. "Why have you changed your mind? This morning you were positively brutal in your eagerness to let me know that you emphatically *did not* want to marry me."

He winced and dropped his hands. "I know, but I'm not as strong as I thought I was. I can't bear the thought of losing you—not yet."

It was her turn to wince. "What do you mean 'not yet'?"

"I mean that if you are lucky there will come a time in the future when I can let you go, but right now I can't. I need you too much."

"If *I'm* lucky!" She didn't know whether to laugh or throw something at him. "I'm not the one who's putting limits on our relationship."

He jammed his hands in his pockets and turned away. "I know, but it's you who stands to lose any chance for happiness if you marry me. I'm trying to protect you from that.''

She was more exasperated than flattered. ''Brody, you're not making sense. Just what is it that you're proposing?''

He reached out and took her hand. ''Let's go in the other room and sit down, and I'll tell you.''

His hand was warm and strong, and she resisted the urge to squeeze it as they walked into the living room and sat down on the couch. She wasn't going to encourage him until she found out what he had in mind. Knowing Brody, it was probably something she didn't want to hear.

Pulling her hand away, she folded it with her other one in her lap. She didn't look at him but kept her gaze focused on the oil painting of one of the area's graceful old southern mansions. It was one she'd bought from a local artist in Jackson Square and hung on the wall opposite the couch.

''You were right when you said being married would give me a better chance of regaining custody of my children,'' he began, ''but that's not why I want to marry you. What I hadn't thought of before was that an illicit relationship with you would put me at a distinct disadvantage with the court.''

Vicky felt as if he'd slapped her, and her gasp of pain caught his attention.

''Oh, sweetheart, I'm sorry,'' he said anxiously. ''I'm handling this badly. We're not doing anything wrong, but in the eyes of the judge it could seem as if we were. Especially since I'm asking him to let my teenage daughters live with me.''

''Are you telling me that you don't want to see me anymore?'' She couldn't keep the hurt or the anger from her tone.

"No, dammit." He sounded as hurt and angry as she had. "What I'm saying is that I don't want to sneak around about it, which is what we'd have to do if the girls come here. You deserve better than that. We all do."

He was only making it sound worse. "Yes, I do deserve better than that, but marrying me just so we can legally make love is a pretty shaky foundation for a lifetime commitment."

"Dammit, Vicky, you're being deliberately obtuse," he roared in frustration. "I don't want to marry you just so I can legally make love to you. I'm not an animal. I can control my sexual desires. What I can't control is my deep-seated need for you as a part of me, like my heart, or my soul."

He looked at her with all the torment he was feeling mirrored in his face. "I love you so much that sending you away is no longer an option. If I'm forced to make a choice between you and my own children, I'll drop the custody suit and let Ken keep the girls."

This time the shock was totally disabling. She couldn't move, speak or think. All she could do was stare at him, her eyes wide and her mouth open. She'd always hoped that someday he'd admit that he loved her, but never in her wildest dreams had she expected him to choose her over his daughters.

He reached out and put his hand under her hair to stroke her nape. "What's the matter, love? Didn't you ever suspect how I felt about you?"

His touch restored some of her senses, and she managed to blink and moisten her dry lips with her tongue. "You . . . you said you didn't love me. Wouldn't love me." Her voice sounded hollow.

"I lied." His gentle fingers unknotted her shock-tightened muscles. "At first I believed it, but even after I knew better I continued to lie to you. It's not in your best interest to be married to me, Vicky, and...well...you mentioned a foundation for a lifetime commitment, but that's not what I'm asking of you."

It wasn't possible for him to shock her more than he already had, and this time she simply rolled with the punch. "But you said you wanted to marry me."

His hand at the back of her neck guided her head down to his shoulder, and he settled her comfortably in his embrace. Now that she was cuddled against him she realized that he was trembling.

This was as difficult for him as it was for her! She put her arms around his waist and held him as he was holding her.

"I know this is just going to confuse you more, sweetheart," he said, "but try to understand. I do want to marry you. Very much. But I don't want you to be married to me."

He was right; she was hopelessly confused, but she'd been that way for some time now, so it didn't make much difference. "You can't have it both ways," she reminded him.

"Maybe I can," he said, "but only if you'll agree."

She was pretty sure she'd agree with anything he wanted, whether it made sense or not. "Tell me about it."

He tightened his arms around her as if he were afraid she might pull away from him. "All right, but I don't think you're going to like it. Just remember, you're under no obligation to go through with this."

Victoria was too numb to react, but she wondered if there would ever come a time when she and Brody could just talk to each other without one of them shocking the hell out of the other.

"I'd like for us to be married as soon as possible," he began, "but first we'll have a prenuptial agreement drawn up—"

"That's all right," she interrupted, anxious to reassure him. "I won't make any claims on your money or your property. I understand that those things rightfully belong to your children. I'm well able to support myself."

"That's not what I'm talking about," he said firmly. "As my wife you'll be entitled to half my estate, and that's the way it will be. It's the *terms* of our marriage that will be set forth in the agreement. It will state that you're free to leave me at any time once the custody suit is settled, and that I will not attempt to restrain you or contest a divorce."

"You're making arrangements to dissolve the marriage even before it's taken place?"

He nodded. "Yes. I'd have continued to lie about not loving you, but you were blaming yourself for our problems and it was affecting your self-esteem. I couldn't allow that, but nothing else has changed. I'll always be a convicted felon—"

"Brody, for heaven's sake, will you forget about the past! I don't—"

"My past is not that easily forgotten," he muttered, and stared off into space. "It will always follow me wherever I go, and when it's exposed, things can get ugly indeed."

Damn! Now she'd done it again. When would she learn not to speak before she thought?

She snuggled closer and nuzzled the pulse in his neck. "Oh, darling, I know," she said contritely. "I must have sounded like an insensitive clod, but you've paid your supposed debt to society. You were freed from prison, why can't you free yourself from that awful experience and get on with your life?"

He shivered when her tongue replaced her lips and roamed over his skin, but his voice remained firm. "Look, honey, we've been through this before. I don't see any need to rehash it. You're too young to be burdened with my problems. I know it sounds like a contradiction, but I love you too much to let you make a lifetime commitment to me, and I won't father more children to be tarred with the clinging shadow of my mistakes.''

He paused, as if gathering the strength to go on. "I'm sorry, but if you won't sign the agreement then we'll have to stop seeing each other.''

Victoria knew he meant it. If anything, he was even more determined than she was when he thought he was right. "Are you asking me to take vows before God that I don't intend to keep? I don't think an arrangement such as you're proposing is even legal.''

He tensed, and once more she knew she'd caused him pain. "You must know I'd never ask you to do anything you can't square with your conscience,'' he said sadly. "We don't have to be married by a minister in a church. We can have a civil ceremony if you prefer.

"As to the legality of the agreement, I'm not sure whether it's legally binding or not. We'll consult an attorney and have him draw it up, but between the two of us it will be morally binding. We're both too honorable to go back on our word once it's given. It can be used as a declaration of intent if not a legal document.''

Victoria knew they'd reached an impasse. She could either give in to his request, or try to live without him. Since the latter was impossible she really had no choice. She'd sign the blasted paper and hope he'd continue to love her too much to send her away.

"All right, Brody,'' she said with a sigh. "I love you, and I suppose I'd do almost anything to be with you, so I'll marry you on your terms, but just so there won't be any misunderstanding there's one thing you should know.''

He looked at her quizzically as she raised her head and kissed him. "I'll never voluntarily leave you, so when you want me out of your life you'll have to send me away.''

A shiver ran through him, and he lowered his face till it was almost touching hers. "We'll see," he whispered before capturing her mouth, and her soul, with his own.

Victoria and Brody were married the following weekend at her parents' home in Sacramento, California. It was a small, intimate wedding performed in the rose garden that was her mother's pride and joy. The huge blossoms were a bright splash of color against which they repeated their vows.

Victoria's family, although startled by her sudden decision to marry a man they'd never met, warmly welcomed Brody with open arms. If her parents were dismayed by her insistence that a justice of the peace officiate instead of their own minister, they didn't argue.

The bridal couple spent their wedding night in San Francisco at the Fairmont Hotel high atop Nob Hill. From their window they had a stunning view of the city—Fisherman's Wharf, Coit Tower, the bridges, the bay, none of which interested them nearly as much as their absorption in each other.

After a night that was more romantic than even Vicky had dreamed possible, they boarded a plane in the morning and flew to Hawaii where they spent the next ten days in a paradise of their own making. They shut out everything but the fact that they were on their honeymoon, and spent mornings sightseeing, afternoons on the beach, evenings sampling the islands' night life, and nights...

Oh, those wonderful, fabulous, glorious nights!

By the time they got back to New Orleans, they were fully rested, deeply tanned and totally carefree.

That blissful state lasted until they remembered to listen to the messages on Brody's telephone answering machine.

It was the last one, obviously recorded within the past few hours, that shattered their calm.

"Brody, this is Farley Davidson calling from Albany, New York. We have a court date for the custody hearing on Thursday, August eleventh at ten o'clock in the morning. Let me know as soon as possible if this is okay with you."

The eleventh of August. Just a week away!

Chapter Fourteen

The early morning storm didn't bode well for a happy ending to the day. Dark clouds, heavy with rain, hung over the small town of Verner's Crossing, New York, hurling jagged bolts of lightning over the picturesque village and its surrounding wooded terrain.

Victoria watched from the window of the room on the third floor of the motor inn where she and Brody had spent the night. Gusts of wind bent the tree limbs with their thick coating of green leaves to the north and scattered small items down the streets and across the lawns.

After a particularly brilliant display of lightning, large drops of rain began splashing against the glass, and Victoria turned away in a sigh. In less than three hours the hearing for custody of Brody's daughters would convene at the courthouse facing the town square.

She felt sick to her stomach, and found her purse and the roll of antacid tablets she carried in it. It was just nervous indigestion, but she didn't want Brody to know. He had all the worries he could handle today without her getting sick and burdening him with even more.

While he finished shaving in the bathroom, she started dressing. She'd given a lot of thought to what she would wear for this occasion, and had finally selected a knee-length white silk pleated skirt, with a navy blue-and-white-silk crepe de chine T-shirt and a long navy cardigan jacket. It was expensive and elegant. Too elegant for a town this size, she discovered after she got here, but it was the only thing suitable that she had with her.

She was anxious to look just right for Brody. She hadn't met his children or their grandfather yet, and she wanted him to be proud to introduce her to them. When she and Brody had arrived in town yesterday afternoon, he'd called Ken Verner and asked to see his daughters. When he'd mentioned that he'd recently married and had his wife with him, all hell broke loose. From clear across the room Victoria had heard Mr. Verner yelling over the line.

That's when her stomach had started acting up. Brody had finally threatened to call his attorney, and the old man had reluctantly given in, but Victoria had convinced Brody to go without her. He was still a stranger to his girls. They needed that time with him alone before they were asked to accept an inexperienced, too young stepmother, and she needed the time to calm her jumpy nerves.

Apparently neither mission was accomplished. Brody came back after a couple of hours dejected by the kids' continued rejection of him, and her stomach was still queasy.

After having put on the peach-and-ivory, floral print bra and panty she'd bought to wear on her honeymoon she'd just reached for the matching slip when Brody came out of the bathroom wearing only a towel wrapped around his slim hips and tucked at the waist. Her gaze was drawn to him as eagerly as it had been the first time she'd seen him in the nude, and she felt the familiar tumult at her core. He didn't even have to touch her to turn her on.

When her glance reached his face, she saw that he was watching her with matching heat. He put his arms around her bare waist and nibbled tenderly on her equally bare shoulder. "Don't look at me like that," he said with a groan, "or I'm going to ravish you right here and now, and we'll never make it to the courthouse."

He nibbled on her other shoulder. "I'm constantly amazed at how quickly you can make me want you. It's more than a little scary. While I was shaving, I'd have sworn that nothing could take my mind off that custody hearing, but now I want you so bad all I can think of is tumbling you."

Victoria reached between them to unfasten his towel, and they fell together on the bed, wrapped in each other's arms. Their loving was quick and unrestrained—both of them were too aroused to hold back—and when it was finished, Victoria's stomach was calm and Brody was smiling happily again for the first time since his latest confrontation with his children and their grandfather.

That state of euphoria lasted until they and Brody's attorney were ushered into the small courtroom and seated across the aisle from Ken, Adriana, Patty and Ken's attorney. The hearing was closed to the public, so only those involved were in attendance.

Victoria's first glimpse of Brody's daughters was a shock. Although she'd known their ages, she'd pictured them as little girls. They weren't. Adriana was a beautiful young woman, willowy and blond, whose long curly hair swished around her shoulders. She wore a mauve mid-thigh length dress that showed off her long slender legs.

Patty was shorter and she bore a startling resemblance to her father. She had Brody's dark brown hair, and a softer, somewhat blurred version of his facial features. In another three or four years she'd be as beautiful as Adriana, although the two girls looked nothing alike.

Victoria wondered if Adriana looked like her mother, and that thought disturbed her. She didn't want Brody's wife to have been beautiful and sexy and desirable. She'd preferred to think of Gloria as rather plain and ordinary.

Talk about childish! She was probably going to be hard-pressed to prove to Brody that she was more mature than Adriana.

Patty wore her shoulder-length hair straight with bangs, and was dressed in a pink-flowered print dress.

Vicky was aware that the girls were also scrutinizing her, and her nerves tightened even more. In an effort to look older, she'd braided her hair in a French braid, but she wasn't sure it added either age or wisdom to her appearance. What did they think of their new stepmother? According to Brody, the only thing they'd been willing to talk to him about yesterday was their opposition to being taken away from Verner's Crossing and their grandfather.

It seemed to Victoria that Adriana looked grimly disapproving, although Patty seemed more curious than judgmental. One thing was certain, Mr. Verner looked positively apoplectic.

Maybe marrying Brody before the hearing wasn't such a good idea after all. Maybe she was more of a liability to him than an asset in his effort to regain his children. Her stomach muscles clenched, and she reached for her antacid pills.

A second surprise shook her when everyone in the room rose as the bailiff announced the arrival of the judge. It was a woman! The Honorable Lesley Young. Victoria had just assumed it would be a man. So much for her standing with the National Organization For Women. It had just slipped several notches.

Her Honor was probably in her early fifties with an attractive streak of white in her otherwise dark hair. It was impossible to tell how she was dressed under her judicial robe, but her eyeglasses had a jaunty tilt, which gave Victoria hope that she wasn't quite as prim and unbending as she appeared.

After they were all sworn in, the judge called on Brody's attorney, Farley Davidson. Farley was a handsome man in his late forties, impeccably dressed and with a commanding presence.

He stood and addressed the court. "Your Honor, my client, Brody Monroe, is seeking custody of his two daughters, Adriana and Patricia Monroe, who for the past eight years have been living with their maternal grandparents, Kenneth and Laura Verner."

He briefly related the reason why Brody had given up custody of his children, and his spotless record since his release from prison. "We will show that now Mr. Monroe is well able to provide a home for his daughters and the care and responsibilities of a father," he concluded, "and we ask that his daughters be returned to him and allowed to live with him and his wife, Victoria, in New Orleans."

Farley sat down, and the judge called on Mr. Zimmerman, Ken's attorney. He was a grandfatherly-looking man with receding gray hair and a portly build.

"Your Honor, Brody Monroe is a convicted felon," he began, and Victoria felt a cold touch of foreboding. This was going to get nasty. "He insisted on driving while intoxicated and lost control of his car, killing his wife and severely injuring two other people. He spent three years in prison and has been free for five years. In all that time he has never tried to see or communicate with his two children who have been in the legal custody of their maternal grandparents.

"Mr. Verner has been a father in every sense of the word to these girls for eight years, half of Adriana's lifetime, and only slightly less than two-thirds of Patricia's. They've lived all their lives in Verner's Crossing. Their friends are here, they are well established in their schools, and they both want to stay here and live with their grandfather.

"We submit, Your Honor, that it would not be in their best interest to wrench them away from all that is familiar to send them to live with a father they don't remember, a stepmother they've never met and in a new and frightening environment."

Victoria clutched at Brody's hand under the table. It was so unfair that he would have to go through this ordeal for something over which he'd had no control.

Mr. Zimmerman sat down, and Brody was called.

Victoria squeezed his hand before releasing it, and he smiled appreciatively at her as he stood and walked to the witness stand. There was no trace of the stereotypical ex-convict about him. He was dressed in a dark blue suit, white shirt and blue-and-gray-paisley tie, and he carried himself with an air of authority, head up, shoulders back, his stride firm.

The judge reminded him that he was under oath, and Farley began his questioning. "Brody, tell the court what happened the night of that tragic accident when your wife was killed."

Brody related the story very much as he had told it to Vicky, but when he told of changing places in the car with Gloria so she could drive, Ken shouted that he was lying.

The judge rapped her gavel. "Mr. Verner, I have to ask you not to interrupt—"

"He killed my daughter," Ken said, only slightly less loudly, "and then he took the coward's way out and blamed it on her because she was dead and couldn't defend herself."

Ken's attorney tried to quiet him as the judge again admonished, "You'll have a chance to present your side, but I will not allow you to disrupt these proceedings."

Ken slumped in his chair, and Victoria noticed that Adriana and Patty looked startled and frightened.

The judge turned to Brody. "You may continue, Mr. Monroe."

Brody finished his story, and Farley nodded. "It is your contention, then, that it was not you but your wife who was driving the car when the accident occurred?"

"It's not only my contention, it's my sworn statement," Brody said. "I was not driving that car, but there was no way I could prove it. I was found guilty and served my full sentence with time off for good behavior. While I was in prison I volunteered to work with alcoholic prisoners under the A.A. program, and I've continued that counseling at the government installation where I work."

"Why didn't you file for custody of your children as soon as you were released, instead of signing an agreement extending the Verners' custody indefinitely?"

Again Brody told of Ken's threats, and his own inability to care for the girls because he'd lost everything in trying to defend himself, and he explained how he'd had to start all over again. "I wanted my little girls more than I've ever wanted anything," he concluded, "but Ken was right, I had no way to take care of them at that time. I pleaded for visitation rights, but he refused and again threatened to take it to court if I didn't sign."

This time Ken jumped to his feet. "Damn right I did," he shouted. "So would any loving grandfather. I wasn't going to let that drunken bum drag those helpless babies around the country with nothing to eat and nowhere to sleep."

In the turmoil that followed, Victoria sprang out of her chair. Farley caught her before she'd taken more than two steps. "Vicky," he barked under his breath. "Don't make things worse. Sit down and let me handle this."

She did, and watched the other lawyer wrestle with Ken while the judge pounded on her desk with the gavel. "Mr. Verner! *Mr. Verner!* If you don't sit down and be quiet I'll have no choice but to have you removed!"

Ken sat down, and Judge Young looked at the attorney. "Counselor, I'm going to call a twenty-minute recess, and you would do well to advise your client of the consequences if he doesn't control himself."

In the hall outside the courtroom Brody and Farley discussed his testimony, and after a few minutes Victoria excused herself and went to the rest room. As she opened the door between the small lounge and the toilet stalls she heard someone crying. It was coming from one of the stalls, and she hesitated but then decided it was none of her business and entered another stall.

The weeping continued, and when she came out she knocked on the door. "Excuse me, but are you all right?"

Inside there was a gasp, then a sniffle and another sob.

Victoria didn't know whether to leave or try again.

A wail from the other side decided her. "Would you like me to get a matron or a policewoman?"

"No!" It was a moan of fear, but Victoria was sure it didn't come from a grown woman. It sounded more like a schoolgirl.

Oh my God. Could it be one of Brody's daughters?

She had to find out, even at the risk of violating somebody's privacy.

"Patty, is that you?"

There was a pause. "Yes. Who are you?"

"I'm Victoria. Please come out so we can talk."

"I don't want to talk to you." The child's tone was sulky, but more bewildered than angry.

Victoria well remembered those confused emotions from her own teenage years. "All right, you don't have to, but please come out anyway."

Again there was a pause, but then she heard the bolt slide back and the door opened.

Patricia Monroe's pretty face was red and wet with tears, and she looked thoroughly miserable.

Victoria's heart melted, and instinctively she put her arms around the child. To her surprise, Patty leaned into the embrace and started to sob again. For a minute Victoria just held her, then, with an arm still around her waist, she led her into the lounge area and they sat down on the couch.

Again Patty surprised Vicky by curling against her and burying her face in Victoria's shoulder. She seemed to need a woman's comfort. Victoria stroked the girl's hair back from her face. "It's a real bummer, isn't it?" Victoria murmured.

"Yeah." Patty agreed on a hiccup. "I wish Grandpa wouldn't yell all the time. He didn't used to."

"Your grandpa's hurting, honey." Victoria kept her voice soft and low. "He's grieving for your grandma. It's a terrible thing to lose someone you love."

Patty sniffled. "I know. I miss her, too."

"Of course you do. This is a difficult time for everyone, so maybe you can understand that your daddy's hurting, too. He's been grieving for eight years over losing you and Adriana."

Patty shook her head vigorously against Victoria's shoulder. "No he hasn't. He didn't want us. Grandpa and Adriana said so. He never wrote to us, or came to see us. He just forgot all about us." Again she was shaken by sobs.

Victoria could have cried, too. "Oh, Patty, that's not true. Haven't you been listening to what he's been saying?"

Patty sat up and reached in her pocket for a handkerchief. "Sure I have, but how do I know he's not lying? He says he wasn't driving the car when my mother was killed, but the jury found him guilty."

Victoria wished she were a lot more knowledgeable about counseling. She was terrified of saying the wrong thing and making the situation worse. This was Brody's field. If only the girls would give him a chance....

Unfortunately they hadn't so far, but now she had the opportunity to make his youngest daughter understand.

"Your dad had no way to prove that he and your mother had changed places in the car," Vicky explained, "but a lot of people saw him drive away from the party. It was your dad's word against the evidence, and the jury found the evidence more convincing."

Patty wiped her eyes and blew her nose. "Do you believe him?" she asked timidly.

"Yes, I do," Victoria answered without hesitation.

"Why?"

"Because he's a kind, gentle and honorable man, and I love him very much. Sometimes, Patty, you have to take a person's word that something is true, and that doesn't mean that your grandparents were lying, either. They honestly believe that your dad was responsible for your mother's death, but Brody's your father. Don't you think you owe it to him to at least listen to his side of the story?"

Before she could answer, the door swung open and Adriana Monroe walked in. She didn't look toward the couch, but headed for the door to the bathroom. "Patty," she called, "what's taking you so long? For heaven's sake, hurry up. They're calling us back into the courtroom."

"I'm over here," Patty said, and Adriana turned.

Her brown eyes widened when she saw Victoria sitting next to her sister. "What are you doing with *her?*" she asked her sister.

Victoria forced herself to be calm. "Hello, Adriana," she said cordially. "Patty was upset, but she's all right now."

"What did you do to upset her?" Adriana snapped. "I'll tell Grandpa's lawyer—"

"She didn't do anything," Patty interrupted. "She was just trying to help."

The last thing Victoria wanted was a quarrel between the three of them. It was time for her to get out of there.

She stood and looked at Adriana. "This is extremely difficult for Patty, so let's not upset her more by taking potshots at each other."

She turned to Patty, who was now standing beside her. "You'd better wash your face and comb your hair, and, honey, think about what I've said. Both your father and your grandpa love you very much."

Brody was waiting for her outside the courtroom. "What took you so long?" he asked anxiously. "Are you all right? They're ready to start again."

"I'm fine," she assured him. "Patty was in there, and she and I had a long talk."

Brody's anxious look made her hasten to add, "It's all right. She's a sweet girl. I'll tell you about it later."

Court resumed, and again Brody took the stand. Farley asked that the court reporter read the last question asked before the disruption and Brody's reply.

"So under the terms of the agreement which you signed under duress, you were prohibited from having any contact with your children?" the lawyer asked Brody.

"Yes."

"Have you paid the Verners child support during these past five years?"

"I tried. After I got a job I sent a check to them every month, but they always tore it up and sent it back. After the fourth or fifth time they did that, I opened trust fund accounts at my bank for each girl and deposited the money in those instead. I appointed the bank as trustee for the accounts, and they will go to each girl when she turns twenty-one. I couldn't withdraw the money even if I wanted to, once it is deposited."

Ken looked surprised and annoyed as Farley introduced the account books showing regular deposits and a hefty balance into evidence. Victoria hadn't known about them, either, and she felt a glow of pride at his thoughtfulness and the financial sacrifice it must have been.

"Now, Brody," Farley said when that was completed, "it's been five years since you were released from prison, and you've been amazingly successful in picking up the pieces and making a new life for yourself. Why haven't you petitioned to get your daughters back before this?"

Brody looked shaken. Both he and Victoria knew that his answer to this question was vital. Farley had warned them that he'd ask it because if he didn't the other side would, so it didn't come as a surprise.

"I wanted to," he said slowly. "For the first couple of years that was all I could think of, but it was more complicated than I'd expected. As a convicted felon I was pretty much an outcast. Since I'd worked for the government before and had an excellent record I didn't have much trouble being hired again in a different area, but my credit rating was zero. No one wants to take a chance on an ex-con so I had to pay cash for everything."

He cleared his throat and sipped water from a glass beside him. "It took three years of living in a one-room rundown apartment before I was able to save enough money for a down payment on a house and find someone willing to finance a mortgage for me, and then only at an exorbitant rate of interest. I bought the furnishings piece by piece as I could afford them. I'd learned woodworking in prison so I made most of my tables, and I bought my car at far below blue book price from a man who had run up a lot of gambling debts and needed money fast.

"I was sure the courts wouldn't take my girls away from the upper middle-class home they were used to and give them to me until I could support them properly, and, to tell the truth, I couldn't face the thought of going to court again when the chances were that I'd lose. Not only would it have been unpleasant for me, but it would have stirred up the old scandal and made things difficult for Adriana and Patty."

He turned in his seat and faced the judge. "Your Honor, I want it understood that I've always known that Ken and Laura were doing a good job of raising their granddaughters. As I explained before, I've had a private investigator check on them four times a year and report to me. The girls have been happy and well adjusted, and I've been hesitant to disrupt their lives after all this time. It wasn't because I didn't love them or want them with me. They were very young when they were taken away from me, and now I'm a stranger to them—"

He swallowed and looked away. Victoria knew he was having trouble controlling his voice, and hoped the judge could also see how difficult this was for him.

After a moment he brought his gaze back to the arbiter's, and he was once more in control. "But now the serenity of their lives has been disrupted through no fault of mine," he continued. "Their grandmother is dead, and their grandfather is a man in his seventies. His intentions are good, but he's too old to cope with two teenage girls by myself. They need their father, and I . . . I need them."

His voice was thick with emotion, and again he looked away, then shifted in his chair to once more face the courtroom. He glanced at Victoria, and she mouthed the words, "I love you." For a moment, the torment in his eyes was replaced by an equal, unspoken love until Farley resumed his questioning.

"I understand you've recently married again. Is your wife agreeable to taking on a ready-made family?"

"Yes, she is," he answered, still holding her gaze. "She knew when she married me that I was going to sue for custody of my children, and she's been very supportive."

Farley nodded. "Thank you. I have no more questions, but I'm sure Mr. Zimmerman will want to cross-examine."

Mr. Zimmerman most certainly did. He started off by questioning Brody's version of the accident. Farley objected, and Judge Young sustained the objection.

"Mr. Zimmerman," she said, "Mr. Monroe's guilt or innocence of that charge is not an issue here. It was decided by another court at another time and he's served the term of his sentence. Our concern is whether or not he is now fit and able to care for his minor children. Please confine your questions to this end."

He did, but he framed them in such a way as to make it difficult for Brody to answer without incriminating himself or seeming to be admitting to guilt and abandonment. Several times Farley objected, and usually his objections were sustained, but it was a grueling ordeal for Brody.

Finally Zimmerman came to the subject of Victoria, and her stomach objected. She took a deep breath and hoped it would calm down as she heard the lawyer say, "About your recent marriage, Mr. Monroe. It was rather sudden, wasn't it?"

Brody glared at him. "Not really. We'd known each other for several months. We were in love and saw no reason to wait."

"Still, it was quite a coincidence that you two 'fell in love' only after you decided to file for custody of your children," he said with a sneer. "Having a wife gave you a distinct advantage in the eyes of the law."

Brody's face flushed with rage as he opened his mouth, but Farley beat him to it. "Your Honor, I object."

Before the judge could rule, Brody interrupted. "Please, Your Honor, I'd like to answer that question."

Both Victoria and Farley stared at him as Judge Young, also taken aback, gave her permission.

Brody looked straight at the attorney. "Mr. Zimmerman, if I had intended to marry just for the purpose of getting my children back, I could have done that years ago."

His tone was firm, but he'd managed to keep the anger at bay. "Actually, I had no intention of ever marrying again. That's one of the reasons I'd hesitated to take my daughters away from their grandparents where they had a more normal family life with two 'parents' than I could give them alone. Then I met Vicky."

He shifted his gaze to her, and his voice became lower, huskier. "I think I fell in love with her the first time we went out together. She walked into my life and brought me peace and happiness for the first time since my first wife died so tragically. Victoria is warm, sweet and loving, and she's made me whole again. I love her more than I ever thought possible. I wasn't thinking of advantages or disadvantages when I married her. I just knew that life without her would be intolerable."

Chapter Fifteen

The quiet in the courtroom was palpable as Brody lowered his head. Tears of joy at the beauty of his words trickled down Victoria's cheeks, and Mr. Zimmerman cleared his throat and looked self-conscious and somewhat flabbergasted. The judge shuffled through papers on her desk, and even Ken looked pensive.

Patricia cried again, softly, and Adriana tried to comfort her until Zimmerman finally broke the silence. "Your tribute to your wife is very moving, Mr. Monroe, but you must admit that she does not fit the usual idea of a stepmother. How old is she?"

Victoria cringed, but Brody didn't hesitate to answer. "Vicky is twenty-four."

"And how old are your daughters?"

"Adriana is sixteen and Patricia is thirteen."

"So Victoria is only eight years older than your daughter."

Brody nodded. "That's right." Obviously he wasn't going to volunteer any information on this subject, and neither was he going to be put on the defensive.

And Zimmerman wasn't going to be put off. "Don't you think it's a little unrealistic to expect Mrs. Monroe to be a mother to teenagers so close to her own age?"

"I don't expect Vicky to be a mother to my daughters," Brody said firmly. "They had a mother who loved and nurtured them until she died. After that they had a grandmother who filled that role admirably. I hope Vicky and the girls will be close friends, but, I'm capable, willing, and entitled by the law of nature to be the parent to my children."

He looked directly at the girls. "You're my flesh and blood, and I intend to be there for you from now on whether I have legal custody or not. I won't be shut out of your lives any longer."

A flash of exasperation twisted Zimmerman's features. "Mr. Monroe, please confine your comments to answering my questions," he snapped. "Are you and Mrs. Monroe planning to have children together?"

That question jolted Victoria to attention with a sharp cry of protest which was drowned out by the noise Farley made jumping to his feet.

"Objection," he shouted. "That question is clearly inadmissible. Mr. Monroe doesn't have to testify about what may happen at some time in the distant future."

Oh, dear Lord, Victoria prayed silently. Don't make Brody have to admit under oath that he doesn't want more children!

"Sustained," came the judge's reply. "Mr. Zimmerman, you know better than that."

The attorney threw up his hands. "I have no further questions," he said, and returned to his seat.

Victoria felt faint with relief as Brody was dismissed.

"Do you have any other witnesses, Mr. Davidson?"

"No, Your Honor, we rest our case."

Judge Young then called on Mr. Zimmerman, and he put Ken on the stand. Kenneth Verner was an imposing-looking man—big, burly and powerfully built. Victoria could see why people were easily intimidated by him. He reminded her of an older version of the good old boys who had harassed her at work. Loud, a little uncouth and capable of doing anything to get his own way.

"All right, Ken," Zimmerman said in a folksy tone. "Now you can tell us your side of this story. Why do you feel you can take better care of Mr. Monroe's daughters than he can?"

"Hell, I've been doing it for most of their lives." He swaggered even when he was sitting down. "Brody Monroe's no good. Never has been and never will be. He—"

Farley and Victoria jumped to their feet at the same time. "Objection!" Farley shouted, as Brody pulled Vicky back down to her chair.

"Take it easy, sweetheart," he murmured as the two lawyers, the judge and Ken got into a noisy argument at the front of the courtroom. "Ken's his own worst enemy. He loses credibility every time he loses his temper. Just sit back and let Farley handle it."

Victoria was steaming. "But he said—"

"I know what he said, but it's not important, unless..."

"Unless what?"

"I don't know," Brody admitted. "Ken's a manipulator. He must know that this type of behavior will only work against him. I can't decide whether he's staging it with some ulterior motive in mind, or if his control and ability to reason have really degenerated this much in the past eight years."

Order was quickly restored, and the judge turned to Ken who was still on the witness stand. "Mr. Verner, I'm not going to warn you again. I will not tolerate these disruptions."

Ken slumped in the chair and rubbed his hand over his face. "I apologize, Your Honor." His booming voice was subdued. "It's just that... well, I'm still trying to pull myself together after my wife's sudden death, and now this man, who has shown no interest in his daughters for years, is trying to take them away from me, too."

He looked up at Judge Young with a soulful expression. "They're all I've got left, Your Honor. Brody Monroe has already deprived me of my only child when he insisted on driving while drunk. My grandchildren are my whole life." His voice broke, and he looked down again.

Brody clenched his fists and muttered an oath under his breath. "So that's his game," he whispered to Victoria. "He's going to play on the judge's sympathy and try to get an emotional ruling rather than a strictly legal one."

"Ken, did you threaten to fight for custody if Mr. Monroe tried to take his children away from you and your wife after he got out of prison?" Mr. Zimmerman asked.

"Yes, I did," Ken answered in a deferential tone. "But it wasn't a threat. It was a statement of fact. Like he admitted to the court earlier, he had nothing. He couldn't have even fed them decently, whereas Laura and I could give them everything they needed and then some."

"And did you refuse to allow him to visit or communicate with his children?"

"No, sir, I did not. He didn't ask for visitation rights."

"That's a lie!" Brody was on his feet and shouting before either Farley or Victoria knew what he was going to do. "I begged you to let me see them. I was even reduced to having to spend a day in the park where they were playing just to get a glimpse of them before I left the area to seek work.''

Again the judge's gavel banged. "Mr. Monroe. I'll not tolerate interruptions from you, either. Now sit down."

Brody apologized and dropped back in his chair as Mr. Zimmerman continued. "How's your health, Ken?"

Ken's chest expanded. "Never been better. I just had a complete checkup and the doc says I'm in great shape."

The attorney offered the doctor's report in evidence, then turned Ken over to Farley for cross-examination.

Farley questioned Ken from every angle about his assertion that Brody had never asked for visitation rights, trying to trip him up and show he was lying, but he steadfastly maintained that Brody had never asked to visit his children. Finally Farley gave up and court was recessed for lunch.

Brody, Victoria and Farley drove back to the motel and had lunch at the coffee shop while they discussed the case. "I'm almost certain that Zimmerman will put Adriana and Patricia on the stand this afternoon," Farley warned them. "If they say they don't want to live with you, I'm not going to badger them."

"Of course you won't," Brody snapped. "I wouldn't allow it, but they believe what Ken and Laura have been telling them about me. If they're asked, they'll say they want to stay with their grandpa, so you'd better be prepared for it."

Victoria covered Brody's hand with her own. "I talked to Patty in the rest room this morning. She was awfully upset."

Victoria went on to give him an account of her conversation with his youngest daughter. "I don't think she's nearly as certain as you seem to think that you're the cruel and uncaring father she's been told you are."

She looked at Farley. "Just be careful with her. She's emotionally fragile."

At two o'clock when court reconvened, Mr. Zimmerman called Patricia to the stand. "Patty, you understand what this hearing is about, don't you?" His tone was calm and friendly.

She looked pale and nervous, and her voice was barely above a whisper. "Yes. It's about whether Adriana and I will stay with Grandpa or go to live with Mr. Monroe."

"Mr. Monroe is your father. You do know that?"

She nodded. "Yes."

"Have you been happy living with your grandparents?"

Farley stood. "Your Honor—"

"I agree, Mr. Davidson," she interrupted. "Mr. Zimmerman, no one is disputing the fact that the girls have been well taken care of by their grandparents."

He frowned. "Yes, Your Honor. Patty, you're old enough to know what you want to do. If you were given a choice would you rather live with your father and Victoria in New Orleans, or stay here with your grandfather?"

She fidgeted but didn't answer, and after a moment the attorney asked the question again. "I...I..." She lowered her head and said something so softly that those sitting at the tables couldn't hear her.

This time the judge spoke to her. "Patricia, we can't hear you. Please look up at Mr. Zimmerman and speak louder."

She raised her head and swallowed. "I want to stay with my grandpa," she said, then in a surprise move she turned to look directly at Brody. "Why don't you love us anymore?" Her voice shook, and tears streamed down her face. "I remember when you used to read me bedtime stories and carry me around on your shoulders, but then you went away and never came back."

A sob shook her, and Brody slid back his chair and was across the room before anybody could stop him. Patty saw him coming and was just stepping out of the witness box when he got to her. Victoria couldn't tell which one reached out first, but at long last he had his daughter in his arms and Victoria didn't need to be close by to know they were both crying.

Ken, Zimmerman and the judge were all shouting at each other. The judge banged her gavel, but no one paid any attention. Victoria sobbed happily, and Farley had a big grin.

It wasn't over yet, but there was no doubt that Brody had one of his daughters back.

The rest didn't take long. When the chaos was finally under control, Adriana took the stand and said she didn't want to live with her father, she wanted to stay with her grandfather. Victoria wasn't surprised. Adriana had been older than Patty, and better able to understand what was happening during that terrible time when her mother was killed and her father was sent to prison. She'd been more deeply hurt by the scandal and the gossip, and could neither love nor forgive as easily as her sister.

After the attorneys had made their closing statements, the judge declared a short recess and told Adriana she'd like to talk to her privately in chambers.

For twenty minutes the tension built as Brody paced up and down the hall in one direction, and Ken paced in the other. The tension in the air was thick and nerve-racking. Farley and Victoria talked while Mr. Zimmerman seemed to be reassuring an anxious Patty. Victoria ached to go to the girl, talk to her and try to ease her distress, but she knew Ken wouldn't allow it and she didn't want to make things worse for the child.

She also had trouble keeping her mind on what Farley was saying as she watched Brody in his lonely vigil. She'd have paced right alongside him if she'd thought it would help him bear the suspense, but she sensed that he needed to be alone.

It would crush him if the judge refused to let him have custody of his daughters. Surely she wouldn't rule against him. Hadn't he suffered enough? Still, Ken Verner was a powerful force in this town, and he usually got what he wanted.

She was brought up short by Farley's question. "Vicky, have you heard anything I've said?"

He seemed more concerned than annoyed.

"I'm sorry, Farley, I guess I've been mentally pacing up and down with Brody. This has been a dreadful ordeal for him."

"Yes, it has," Farley agreed, "but what are your immediate plans for the girls if Brody is given custody? Will you take them back to New Orleans right away?"

"That depends on them," Victoria answered. "If they want time to get their things together and say goodbye to all their friends, Brody won't object. That can be a heartbreaking experience, especially when they're being taken away from the grandfather who raised them and the town that's always been their home.

"Brody understands what they'll be going through, and he wants to make it as easy for them as possible. We're planning to leave tomorrow. There's no way he and Ken can coexist in this town, but if we win this suit it may be a week or more before the girls come to us."

"That's a wise decision," Farley said just before they were called back into the courtroom.

When they were all seated, the door at the back of the room opened, and Judge Young and a somewhat somber Adriana entered from the judge's chamber. Adriana walked over to the table with Ken and Patty and sat down, while the judge took her seat at the bench.

Victoria could feel the tension radiating from Brody as the judge started to speak.

"I understand how difficult this day has been for all of you so I'll get right to the point. Mr. Monroe, I'm awarding custody of your two daughters to you, but with two provisions."

The tension in Brody seemed to release all at once, like a tightly wound spring that breaks loose from its moorings. With a glad cry Victoria threw her arms around him and he hugged her so hard that for a moment she couldn't breathe.

"Just a minute, please," the judge said, raising her voice. "I'm not finished."

Brody kissed Victoria on the cheek and released her as they sat back in their chairs.

The judge again looked at Brody. "You've paid the debt society imposed on you for the crime of which you were convicted, and since then your life has been exemplary. As the natural father of these children you are entitled to have custody of them, but Mr. and Mrs. Verner have been the only parents they've known for much of their lives. Mr. Verner has a right to consideration of that fact. Therefore I'm awarding him reasonable visitation which will be worked out with your attorneys at a later date."

Brody nodded his agreement. "Mr. Verner will always be welcome to visit his granddaughters, both at my house and at his. I have no intention of refusing him contact with them."

"Good," she said, and glanced at a paper in front of her. "Now, I have another matter that needs to be addressed. I don't mean to place restrictions on your freedom to raise your daughters as you see fit, but you must understand that my primary concern is for these girls."

Brody stiffened, and Vicky's stomach lurched. Oh, God, now what?

"Patricia seems to have accepted you back in her life with few problems, but the same is not true of Adriana. This is a situation that would be painful at any time, and at sixteen it's especially difficult to deal with. She's a bright, but troubled, young lady, and I want you to see to it that she receives counseling, both alone and as a family with you and Mrs. Monroe if that is deemed advisable. Is this also acceptable to you?"

Again Brody relaxed and looked relieved. "Yes, Your Honor. I'll do anything necessary to help Adriana to forgive me for what she perceives as the wrongs I've done her."

He looked at his daughter. "Believe me, honey, I've always loved you, and if I've failed you it was never intentional."

Adriana blinked and looked away, but not before Victoria detected tears in her big brown eyes.

Then the hearing was ended, and Brody walked over to the other table. Patty met him partway, and they hugged. Victoria hung back so she didn't hear what they were saying, but then he straightened and turned to Adriana.

He didn't touch her, but put out his hand in a conciliatory gesture. "It was because I wanted to spare you all this upheaval that I left you with your grandparents as long as I did," he said softly, "but you and Patty are my daughters, and I want you with me. If you're not ready to accept me as your father I hope we can at least be friends."

Her troubled expression betrayed her conflicting emotions, but after a moment's hesitation she slowly reached out and put her hand in his. They shook solemnly and then he leaned over and kissed her on the cheek. "I'll give you all the time you want to get your things together and say your goodbyes," he assured her, "but I'd be honored if you and Patty would have dinner with Victoria and me tonight."

Victoria was quite sure that nobody could resist Brody at his charming best, and she was right. Adriana's glance met hers for a brief moment, and Victoria smiled encouragingly before the girl shifted her attention back to her father.

"Thank you. That would be nice," she said graciously. "What time will you pick us up?"

The evening went surprisingly well. Brody and Patty positively beamed, and Adriana was distant but polite. Victoria joined in when the conversation was directed toward her, but mostly she was content to sit back and let Brody get reacquainted with his girls.

Adriana warmed up as the meal progressed, and by the time they all said good-night at the Verners' front door, she shyly called Brody "Dad" for the first time. Both Brody and Victoria hugged and kissed Patty, but Adriana offered only her hand.

It was going to take a while for her to let her father back into her life, even though she'd be living in his house.

Brody had let the girls pick the restaurant where they ate, and they'd chosen one that served Mexican food, hot and heavy. About halfway through the meal Victoria's stomach began acting up again, and by the time they got back to their hotel she barely made it to their room before she was violently sick.

She locked herself in the bathroom and lost everything in her stomach while Brody banged on the door demanding to know if she needed a doctor. She told him no, but by the time she finally got the nausea under control and her face washed he looked sicker than she did.

He was talking on the telephone and writing something down when she came back into the room. "Yes, I have it," he said into the mouthpiece. "Thank you, I will."

He hung up the phone and engulfed Victoria in his embrace. "Sweetheart, I called the desk and got the name of a doctor who's on call...."

He sounded thoroughly shaken, and her empty stomach clenched. Damn, why did this have to happen tonight when he'd been happier than she'd ever seen him before?

"Brody, I don't need a doctor," she interrupted. "It was just indigestion."

His arms tightened around her. "That wasn't indigestion and you know it. Now lie down while I get him over here."

She wasn't going to let him call a doctor to come to the hotel just to tell him what she would have to tell him herself before much longer anyway. But the very thought of doing that made the bile rise in her throat again.

She snuggled against him. Maybe she could take his mind off her stomach and focus it on another part of her anatomy. "Darling, I'm all right. Really I am. It was just that spicy Mexican food. I feel much better now."

She caressed his back while trailing kisses along his jaw.

Brody caught his breath but held her away from him. "Oh, no, you're not going to distract me. We're going to find out what's the matter with you."

He reached for the phone, but she put her hand over his before he could pick it up. "No! Please! It's nothing. Really. I have antacid pills in my purse. I'll take a couple and go to bed, and by tomorrow the problem will be gone."

At least it will until the next time it happens.

He looked at her warily. "You carry those pills around with you?"

She fell into the trap. "Yes, see, I have them right here." She got her purse off the dresser and produced the half-eaten roll of mints.

Brody's face turned grim. "So you've had these attacks before."

His hands closed around her upper arms as he stared into her eyes. His own were filled with fear. "For God's sake, Vicky, if you know what's wrong with you, tell me!"

She was caught. She hadn't intended to spring this on him until he'd had time to adjust to getting his daughters back, but now it couldn't be put off. She couldn't let him think she was seriously ill.

She took a deep breath and closed her eyes so she wouldn't see his expression when he grasped what she was going to say.

"I'm pregnant."

Chapter Sixteen

The words seemed to hang there suspended in the air until Brody's fingers dug into her arms.

"No!" It was a primal scream of denial. "That's not possible. We used double protection." He shook her lightly. "Open your eyes and look at me, Vicky."

She did, and saw the struggle between disbelief and dawning truth that ravaged his white face. "We didn't that first weekend," she said in a raspy whisper that struggled past her dry throat. "I guess we weren't as careful as we thought."

For a little while he just stood there staring past her at some private hell that no one but he could see. Then he loosened his hold on her and dropped his arms to his sides.

"Are you sure?" His voice was hollow. "It's awfully soon to tell."

"Yes, I'm sure. Last week when my period was ten days overdue, I took a home pregnancy test. It was positive, but

I was skeptical, too, so I went to the doctor. His test was also positive. He says I'm approximately six weeks along."

Brody dropped down on the side of the bed as though his legs wouldn't hold him any longer, but then he surprised Victoria by reaching for her hands and pulling her down on his lap. With a cry of relief she wrapped her arms around his neck and cradled his head between her breasts. Apparently he wasn't going to blame her, or send her away. At least not tonight.

"Why didn't you tell me?" he asked. "Are you all right?"

"I'm fine. Strong and healthy, and I would have told you, but later. You've been under such a lot of stress, and this evening you were so happy...." Her voice broke. "Oh, Brody, I'm sorry. I'd never have done this to you deliberately."

His arms tightened around her. "I think you've got that backward. I believe *I* did it to *you*, and I don't know why I'm so surprised. You get me so worked up it's no wonder you're pregnant."

She laid her cheek against the top of his head and sighed. He was taking this much better than she'd expected. Was it safe to hope...?

"What are you going to do about the baby, Vicky?" His tone was carefully neutral.

She tensed as her fledgling hopes fluttered and died. "What do you want me to do?" she asked carefully.

He raised his head and looked at her, his brown eyes filled with torment. "That's your decision. Do you want it?"

Yes, it was her decision, but she was presented with impossible choices. She could stay married to Brody, or she could have the baby, but she couldn't do both. Is that what he was telling her?

She tried to swallow, but her mouth was so dry she couldn't. "I... Yes, I do. I want your baby almost as much as I want you."

With a groan he again buried his face between her breasts, and they sat there locked in each other's arms, but dealing separately with their pain.

Finally he released her, then stood up and ran his hand through his hair. "Since I got out of prison there have been times when the walls seem to close in on me, and I have to get out in the open, walk and be alone to think. I feel that way now. Will you be all right if I leave you for a little while?"

So he wasn't going to let her help him through this. But then, how could he? If he couldn't accept the fact of the baby, and she couldn't come to terms with the finality of abortion, then there was no way they could help each other.

"I'll be fine, Brody," she said numbly. "You don't have to worry about me."

He turned and stared at her. "The hell I don't! You've just told me that you're carrying my child, and I'm behaving like a bloody bastard—"

"No!" Victoria jumped up, but the sudden movement made her light-headed and she swayed before she quickly sat back down.

Brody must have noticed because he again reached for the phone. "I'm going to get that doctor over here," he muttered.

"No, please don't." She stood up slowly this time and there was no dizziness. "Really, there's nothing wrong with me except that I'm tired. You go ahead and take your walk, and I'll go to bed."

She could tell from his expression that he was going to refuse, and she put her hand on his arm. "Please, Brody.

I...I'd like some time alone, too. I really would prefer that you give me a little space.''

A few minutes later Victoria was undressed and safely tucked into bed, and Brody walked through the hotel lobby and out into the fresh air. It was still hot although the sun was down and it would be getting dark soon.

For a while he was able to block out his stunning shock and just walk. The familiarity of the area brought back so many memories, some of which he'd buried deep in his subconscious.

When he passed the school, he heard again the glad whoops of freedom as he and the other students had flocked out of the building at the end of the day. As he neared the movie theater he smelled the aroma of hot buttered popcorn that always used to permeate the lobby, and a little farther on he was surprised to see that the rundown bar where his dad hung out had been torn down. There was nothing on the site but a gaping hole between the two buildings on either side.

As he continued south down Main Street, the buildings became shabbier and the streets dirtier until he turned a corner and walked a block to stand in front of the dilapidated old two-story house that used to be known as Jenny Monroe's Boardinghouse. The weathered sign was long gone, but he didn't have to go inside to see the big rooms with high ceilings and threadbare rugs. Nor did he have to close his eyes to see his mother in faded jeans and a shirt standing at the stove cooking interminable meals for the never-ending procession of down-on-their-luck boarders.

Jeez, Mom, you deserved so much better!

Although he hadn't intended to, a force inside him stronger than he was, guided his steps away from his childhood haunts and headed him north to the elite part of town where the Verner mansion, as those who lived in his seedier neighborhood called it, sat on a hill like a queen surveying her domain. Brody's daughters had resided there for the past eight years, but that's not where he was going.

He was going home to the place where he'd lived so long ago with Gloria and their little girls.

It was a four-bedroom, split-level house just two blocks from Gloria's parents. The Verners had given them the lot and loaned them the money to build on it, in effect buying the right to meddle in their daughter's and son-in-law's lives and violate their privacy.

It was nearly twilight when he reached it, and lights shone from inside the house. The red tile roof still looked like new, but the siding was different. The shrubs and flowers were not familiar but the elm trees he'd selected and planted had grown and thrived.

Brody suddenly realized that he was exhausted, both physically and emotionally. A glance across the street told him that no one was home at the Hewitt's house. At least it had been the Hewitt's house when he lived there, and he walked over to the bank of flowering shrubbery where he could sit without being seen.

Wearily he lowered himself onto the thick green grass and drew up his knees so he could fold his arms to rest on top of them. It was totally dark now, and he could see into his former living room through the large picture window. It was covered with sheer curtains, but the drapes were opened.

As he watched, he wasn't seeing the present but the past. Gloria sitting in the old-fashioned rocker with baby Patty at her breast. Adriana looking like a tiny princess in her new clothes as she prepared to start her first day at kindergarten. Himself, dirty and sweating as he wrestled the too-big roots of a tree into a too-little hole between his house and their neighbors' driveway.

He wasn't aware when the tears started, but they were running down his cheeks unchecked when a massive sob shook him. My God, he'd lost so much. He couldn't lose Victoria and her baby, too. But how could he justify bringing another child into his cursed, bedeviled life?

On the other hand, did he really have a choice? The only way he could protect the child from the grimness of his past would be to divorce Victoria and disappear from her life. He couldn't do that.

And besides, who was he kidding? That baby was as much a part of him as it was of her, and it was already too late to deny its effect on him.

In the short space of a couple of hours it had wrapped its minuscule, nonexistent fist around his heart and taken its place, along with its mother, as a vital life-sustaining necessity that he couldn't survive without.

Another sob was torn from him, and then another, and there was no hope of controlling them any longer. Brody buried his face in his crossed arms and released the storm of tears.

He wept for his dead wife, for the years of his daughters' lives that were irretrievably lost to him and for the innocent baby who would inherit the legacy of its father—an ex-convict.

Victoria had been sleeping, but restlessly, when she heard the key turning in the lock. Brody was back. It was dark. She reached over and turned on the bedside lamp as he came in.

"Shut the light off, honey," he said, but not before she'd seen his ravaged face and red-rimmed eyes.

She switched off the lamp, but threw back the sheet that covered her and sat up. "Brody, darling, are you all right? What time is it?"

"I'm okay," he said hastily. "Don't get up. It's a little after ten o'clock. I'm going to take a quick shower, and then I'll join you."

He went into the bathroom and closed the door. She lay back down and curled up in a ball the way she used to when she was a child and knew she'd done something she was going to be punished for. But this time she hadn't done anything wrong. Would Brody punish her?

That was a stupid thought and an insult to her gentle, loving husband. He was castigating himself, not her, and that hurt her even more. Why should conceiving a baby together in a frenzied but beautiful act of love be cause for retribution?

It was only a few minutes before Brody crawled into bed beside her, his nude body still damp and warm from the shower. He took her in his arms and kissed her gently, then cradled her against him.

Was he trying to soften the blow of what he had to say?

For a moment he just held her and let his hands move caressingly over her back and buttocks through the sheer cotton of her nightgown.

When he finally spoke, his voice was low. "I'm sorry I was gone so long. I didn't intend to be, but I had a lot of things to sort out in my mind and come to terms with."

She held her breath, not wanting to hear what he was going to tell her, but knowing she had to. "What did you decide?"

"I decided that I was the luckiest man on earth, and it was damn well time I admitted it before I lost you and that son or daughter of mine that you're carrying."

Victoria's eyes flew open, and she raised her head and pushed herself back to look at him. "You mean you want the baby?"

The only illumination in the room was lights from outside, but it was enough to see that he was smiling. "Of course I want it. I've always wanted children with you. Every time we've made love I've wished we could forget the protection and make a baby together."

He cuddled her against him again and settled her head on his shoulder. "I know you won't believe me, but my first instantaneous reaction when you said you were pregnant was pure joy, only it was immediately crushed by the weight of guilt for subjecting another child to my past mistakes."

She was having trouble assimilating everything he was saying. It wasn't at all what she'd expected, and she was afraid to believe he really meant it. "Brody," she said timidly, "are you telling me the truth, or are you just saying these things because I got pregnant by mistake and you're trying to make the best of it? Please don't lie to me."

"Oh, sweetheart." It was a moan of pain. "I don't blame you for being suspicious. I've hated lying to you about my feelings, but I truly thought I had to. This time I swear to God I'm telling the truth. I love you almost to the point of obsession, and I can't begin to tell you how proud I am that you're carrying my child."

His arms tightened around her as her doubts finally slipped away. "This baby is a very special gift, Vicky," he continued. "It was conceived against almost impossible odds, and I have to accept that as a sign that it was meant to be. I clung so stubbornly to the notion that because of my prison record my life was over. I was convinced that I could no longer care about anyone or anything because if I did it would be taken away from me again."

He lowered his head and kissed her on the temple. "Then, out of nowhere, you came into my life and showed me that I could not only care, but I could love even more deeply than before. I've never been an especially religious person, but I'll always believe that you and our child were sent to me as a sign that now I can get on with my life again.''

The tears that had been pressing against her eyes as he spoke spilled over and ran down her cheeks and onto his shoulder. Brody was the only man she'd ever known who could speak with such beauty and feeling that he made her cry with elation.

''If that's true then I'm overjoyed to be the one selected for that mission,'' she said tearfully, and kissed his damp skin. ''I love you so much, and I don't expect that our lives will be all sunshine and flower gardens.''

''You can say that again,'' he said, but she heard the teasing in his voice. ''If we have a daughter who's as beautiful and sexy as her mother I'll have to spend my old age beating off pimply-faced adolescent boys with a stick.''

Victoria chuckled. ''Sweetheart, I hate to tell you this, but that time is coming sooner than you think. Have you really looked at Adriana? She's not your little girl anymore, she's a lovely young lady, and Patty's not far behind.''

Brody groaned. ''Oh, no. Maybe we can arrange for this one to be a boy. At least he won't be subjected to sexual harassment in the workplace like his mother has been.''

Victoria bit him gently on the neck. ''Don't be too sure. We women are getting more aggressive all the time. In twenty years, if he looks like his daddy he'll be begging me to deal with the women who are harassing him. After all, why should men have all the fun?''

''And will you?'' he asked as he moved his hand to her breast. ''Deal with the women, I mean?''

''Yeah, I will,'' she said soberly, ''because even though I can joke about it now, harassment by either sex is not funny. I hope that in twenty years time it will no longer be a problem, but meanwhile I intend to teach my stepdaughters that they don't have to put up with it. That there are laws to protect them, but they'll have to be prepared to fight for their rights.''

"You do that, Tiger," he murmured. "Meanwhile, would you consider it harassment if I kissed you?"

"Not at all," she said with a distinct purr. "I'd consider it heaven."

* * * * *

THE DONOVAN LEGACY

from Nora Roberts

Meet the Donovans—Morgana, Sebastian and Anastasia. They're an unusual threesome. Triple your fun with double cousins, the only children of triplet sisters and triplet brothers. Each one is unique. Each one is...special.

In September you will be *Captivated* by Morgana Donovan. In Special Edition #768, horror-film writer Nash Kirkland doesn't know what to do when he meets an actual witch!

Be *Entranced* in October by Sebastian Donovan in Special Edition #774. Private investigator Mary Ellen Sutherland doesn't believe in psychic phenomena. But she discovers Sebastian has strange powers...over her.

In November's Special Edition #780, you'll be *Charmed* by Anastasia Donovan, along with Boone Sawyer and his little girl. Anastasia was a healer, but for her it was Boone's touch that cast a spell.

Enjoy the magic of Nora Roberts. Don't miss *Captivated, Entranced* or *Charmed*. Only from Silhouette Special Edition....

SENR-1

**It's Opening Night in October—
and you're invited!
Take a look at romance with a
brand-new twist, as the stars
of tomorrow make their
debut today!
It's LOVE:
an age-old story—
now, with
*WORLD PREMIERE
APPEARANCES* by:**

Patricia Thayer—Silhouette Romance #895
JUST MAGGIE—Meet the Texas rancher who wins this pretty
teacher's heart...and lose your own heart, too!

Anne Marie Winston—Silhouette Desire #742
BEST KEPT SECRETS—Join old lovers reunited and see what
secret wonders have been hiding...beneath the flames!

Sierra Rydell—Silhouette Special Edition #772
ON MIDDLE GROUND—Drift toward Twilight, Alaska, with this
widowed mother and collide—heart first—into body heat
enough to melt the frozen tundra!

Kate Carlton—Silhouette Intimate Moments #454
KIDNAPPED!—Dare to look on as a timid wallflower blossoms and falls in fearless love—with her gruff, mysterious
kidnapper!

**Don't miss the classics of tomorrow—
premiering today—only from**

VOWS
A series celebrating marriage
by Sherryl Woods

To Love, Honor and Cherish—these were the words that three generations of Halloran men promised their women they'd live by. But these vows made in love are each challenged by the tests of time....

In October—Jason Halloran meets his match in *Love #769;*

In November—Kevin Halloran rediscovers love—with his wife—in *Honor #775;*

In December—Brandon Halloran rekindles an old flame in *Cherish #781.*

These three stirring tales are coming down the aisle toward you—only from Silhouette Special Edition!

SESW-1

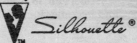

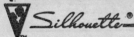